BAD DEEDS

DAVID J. GATWARD

WEIRDSTONE PUBLISHING

Bad Deeds
by
David J. Gatward

Copyright © 2025 by David J. Gatward
All rights reserved.

No part of this book may be reproduced in any form or by any electronic or mechanical means, including information storage and retrieval systems, without written permission from the author, except for the use of brief quotations in a book review.

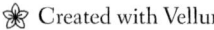 Created with Vellum

Grimm: nickname for a dour and forbidding individual, from Old High German grim [meaning] 'stern', 'severe'. From a Germanic personal name, Grima, [meaning] 'mask'.
(*www.ancestry.co.uk*)

HARRY GRIMM

To Kim and Josh ...
wishing you the best life together.
Forever.

ONE

Barnaby Shaw was sitting on a wooden stool in front of a tray of freshly baked butterfly cakes and already felt like throwing up. He'd been a baker since leaving school at eighteen, with three A-levels, and no idea what to do with them. The A-levels themselves hadn't been all that relevant to the career he'd eventually chosen, or indeed any career, really, what with them comprising Art, Geography, and Animal Husbandry.

Geography he'd taken because he actually liked the subject. Plus, it had involved a good number of field trips, one of which had been residential. That had meant time away from home—always a bonus—late-night sneaky beers behind the teachers' backs, and a moonlit fumble or two with a girl he'd really fancied.

Art was something he'd always had a natural talent for, and of the three, had turned out to be by far the most relevant, especially when he considered the number of cake-decorating competitions he'd won over the years. It had also given his brain time to relax, a place to escape to; even now, all these years later, all he really wanted to do some days was head to the river with a small pad of paper and the brushes he'd owned for years, and paint.

As for Animal Husbandry? Well, he'd done that because his best mate, Craig Fothergill, had opted to do it. His father had tried to persuade him that his A-levels should have sat together better, that there was some defining link between them, a direct path to a good career, but Barnaby hadn't listened. His father had blamed Craig, simply because he thought Craig didn't have enough drive to do something more with his life than his own father had. That wasn't true. It had never been like that at all.

Barnaby and Craig had been thick as thieves their whole lives. Craig even worked part-time for him now, keeping both the bakery and the café spotless, as well as using the van his parents gave him for his twenty-first birthday to deliver orders to shops and pubs and cafés up and down the dale. Barnaby's dad simply regarded that as proof that Craig was someone without vision, if all he wanted to do with his life was clean and drive a van. Barnaby, however, respected Craig's courage to try things out, to use his van to set himself up as an odd-job man, doing anything from doing people's shopping to repairing garden fences. He could turn his hand to pretty much anything, could Craig, and his keenness to give anything a good go had seen him well.

In the end, having decided university wasn't for him, Barnaby managed to use the grades he got for his A-Levels, which were very much below what his parents had expected, to land himself an apprenticeship at a local bakery. Whether he'd been right or not was neither here nor there, not now, because somehow, he'd managed to set up a nice little business for himself in Swaledale.

Yes, the early mornings were a drag, and yes, the nitty-gritty of running a business was perhaps not his strength, but he could bake! Not only did he have a successful little bakery in Reeth, but he also supplied pubs and shops and tea rooms all over the Dales and even had his very own, and very popular, little teashop in Muker. Life, in so many ways, was good. And yet, here he was, staring at the fruits of his labour, physically shaking.

Of the thirteen butterfly cakes he had baked, five were already gone, but this alone was not explanation enough for his current need to empty his stomach of its contents. They were good cakes, too, he noted, just this side of warm, to let you know they were fresh, but not so much so that the buttercream filling melted. It was that hint of warmth that gave each cake that mouth-watering aroma of freshly baked deliciousness. Despite that, though, Barnaby didn't want to eat anymore. Probably wouldn't want to eat another butterfly cake for the rest of his life.

'Do it.'

The voice was muffled, eerily deep, and came from a laptop on the other side of the tray of cakes.

Barnaby shook his head.

'I ... I can't ...'

The laptop screen showed a figure in silhouette. Barnaby had no idea who it was, or how they knew what they knew, and right then he'd never been so scared in his whole life.

'Do it.'

Reaching for another cake, he tried to keep his hand steady, but the rest of his body was shaking now as well, and every organ inside him felt like it was cramping, twisting, being crushed by the god-awful pressure he was now under.

Barnaby opened his mouth, closed his eyes, pushed the cake in, retched, spat it out again.

'Do it.'

Fear, desperation, rage, all mixed together, and Barnaby felt like he was burning up. Tears streamed down his face as he picked up the half-chewed mess, forced it back into his mouth, and swallowed.

'Who are you?'

No response.

Barnaby briefly wondered what would really happen if he just slammed the laptop shut and forgot about it all. But he'd been warned, hadn't he? About ignoring, blocking, going to the police.

'You've six cakes left.'

Barnaby's stomach was churning.

'I'm sorry.'

'Asking for forgiveness doesn't rid you of the punishment. Eat.'

'It's too much.'

'Eat!'

Barnaby stared at the laptop screen, wished he could reach inside it, grab whoever the hell it was on the other side, and throttle them. He'd want to know who it was first, though, to shine a light on that face hidden in darkness, and stare into their eyes as he squeezed.

Instead, he reached for the eighth cake. Once this was over, he'd never eat another.

The buttercream icing was cloying now, a thick, sweet glue which wanted nothing to do with being swallowed. The cake was no longer soft and moist, but tough and dry. Every chew was torture, every swallow, agony.

Which, Barnaby guessed, was the point.

From the silhouette on the laptop screen came only the silence of someone watching, waiting, knowing that in that moment, all the power was with them alone.

Five left, thought Barnaby, knowing though, that eating them was only part of the punishment. How the hell had his decisions come to this? How the hell was this in any way fair? Not that fairness had anything to do with it, and he knew that. Sometimes, life just turned around and bit you on the arse. And sometimes, secrets were uncovered.

The ninth cake Barnaby managed to chase quickly with the tenth, but one caught up with the other halfway down his throat, and the ball immediately refused to go either up or down. He grabbed at his chest, as though pulling at his T-shirt would somehow force the mass of cake to shift.

'Water ...'

Barnaby pushed away from the cakes, the laptop, stood up, stared around the small, industrial kitchen he called his second home. He stumbled across to the sink, slammed the water on full, thrust his face under the bright coldness which spewed from it, gulping the water down.

The mass shifted, and he returned to his stool.

The tray was littered with the ten empty paper cases of the butterfly cakes Barnaby had managed to consume. Three remained, and they seemed to grow in size as he stared at them, the smell of them becoming stronger and stronger, forcing its way inside his nose, teasing his brain with nausea-inducing sweetness. How would he ever bake anything again after this, never mind butterfly cakes?

'Nearly done. Then your lesson will be learned, won't it?'

Barnaby reached for the eleventh cake.

'If I ever find out who you are ...'

He slipped the cake into his mouth, narrowed his eyes at the black figure on the screen, chewed, swallowed, felt ashamed of the tears scorching his skin.

'You won't. No chance of that. Too careful, you see, been doing this a long time. Someone has to.'

The twelfth cake was in Barnaby's hand. It seemed so heavy, so dense. And yet it was soon in his mouth, then at last on its way to join the others.

Cake thirteen, the final morsel in this murderous baker's dozen, now sat alone on the tray. Scattered around it, like the discarded rags of the condemned, lay the papery clothes of its cousins.

Barnaby, swallowing hard, reached for the cake, peeled off the wrapper, held it up in front of the laptop.

'That's it, now. Just this last one.'

Barnaby hesitated for a moment, just staring through the cake and into the laptop screen behind it. Then, with a deep breath in and out, he opened his mouth and this time bit into the cake. He chewed, took another bite, chewed again, and with each bite, kept his wet, unblinking eyes fixed on the hidden figure staring back.

'There,' he said at last.

'Show me.'

'What? Haven't you been counting? I've eaten them all!'

'I said show me.'

Barnaby lifted the empty baking tray to the screen.

'See? Gone! I did it, you bastard! I fu—'

The screen went blank.

Barnaby hurled the tray at the wall and roared. That

done, and with sweat now starting to bead on his brow, he pulled his phone from his pocket and dialled 999. As he waited for his call to be answered, his body convulsed so violently that he toppled from his stool to the floor. Then the contents of his stomach thundered back up his throat, and Barnaby vomited blood.

TWO

As cafés went, Harry regarded the one he was currently sitting in as somewhat upmarket. But not in a good way. There was no doubt that the place was clean, the food tasty, but it wasn't comfortable. Harry was happier in the kind of place that had white walls, wipe-clean seats, and a simple menu that focused mainly on an all-day breakfast and bottomless mugs of strong tea. Not so here.

Instead, the walls were decorated with flowery wallpaper seemingly held in place by numerous black and white historic photographs, the chairs were fragile affairs of carved wood and gaudy cushions, and the food provided contained far too many mentions of the word 'artisan.' To add to the horror, the ceiling was bedecked in false wooden beams, and various shelves groaned under the weight of a collection of decorative teapots.

Mind you, thought Harry, *the food did smell good, so that was something.* Not that he was there to eat, which was a good job, really, as he'd rather lost his appetite.

The first sign that things were not quite as they seemed

was the lack of staff. The café had only been open a few minutes, but from the moment Harry had walked into the place, all he'd witnessed of their existence was the sound of rapidly closing doors. There was no one to attend to him, to show him to a table, ask if he'd like water while he perused the menu. And no sound at all came from the kitchen. This was a café bereft, for now, of life. *And with good reason,* Harry thought, taking in the huge shadow now blocking the door.

In Harry's experience, bodyguards came in two sizes: the first size were vast, hulking beasts, who no doubt spent most of their free time in the gym, lifting very heavy things a very short distance. They were imposing, portable blockades which, when used correctly, were certainly effective in keeping people away from whatever it was they were employed to protect. Some no doubt had a little boxing experience, maybe even a martial arts belt or two, but that was it; size was their weapon, and they used it well. They also all seemed to shop at Bodyguards-R-Us and could usually be found wearing a dark suit, sunglasses, and an earpiece. Nine times out of ten, the look was finished off with a buzzcut, and when the whole shebang was combined, there was never any doubt what the monstrous goons did for a living.

The other size was the polar opposite of the first: average height, average build, the kind of person you'd pass in a street without noticing. These were more often than not ex-forces, and not exclusively special forces or male either, just individuals who could read a situation, react accordingly, protect their charge and, if required, mete out a swift and brutal level of violence to whoever dared to get in their way. They dressed normally, blended in, shunned suits and shades and flexing their pecs to impress.

Back in the Paras, Harry had wondered if such a career might suit him at some point, but life had had other plans. His criminal father, murdering his and Ben's mother, had been one. The wounds he sported on his face from an IED another. He'd have been considerably wealthier, for sure, but happier? That much he doubted, because somehow the traumas of his past had gifted him a new life in the Dales, and with it a happiness the likes of which he'd never thought possible. Now, however, he was having considerable trouble holding back the burning rage bubbling inside his gut at where he was, and why.

Harry checked his watch. He'd been in the café for twenty minutes, the victim of a power play he'd fully expected, prepared himself for, but was no less impressed by.

His phone rang.

'Anything?' said the familiar voice on the other end of the call.

'Nothing,' Harry replied, and heard his old friend and one-time mentor, retired DCI Peter Jameson, sigh.

'How's the cafe; is there cake?'

'I'm not here for cake.'

'Neither am I, but, you know, I'm just saying, if there is any, within arm's reach, perhaps, then ...'

Harry did not reply.

'How long do you think he'll be?'

'How long's a piece of string?'

'That all depends on what you're using it for.'

The goon at the door glanced over his breeze-block shoulder to glare at Harry from behind his sunglasses.

'Why's he looking at you like that?'

Harry growled at that.

'I told you to stay in the car. I gave you a very clear

instruction to stay exactly where you were, and under no circumstances to—'

'I got a cramp,' Jameson said. 'Needed to stretch my legs. Just so happened to have a little pair of binoculars in my pocket as well. Haven't the faintest idea how they ended up there.'

'I'm sure you haven't.'

The goon turned back to stare out of the doorway he was happily blocking. The street outside was quiet, a perfect storm of early morning and midweek combining to give the market town of Kendal a breather from human traffic.

'A car's approaching,' Jameson said. 'And by car, I mean the kind that probably costs as much as a house.'

'About bloody time,' grumbled Harry.

'Shall I leave you to it, then?'

'For now, yes. Just get yourself back to the car and stay there.'

'What if something happens, and you suddenly need me? How will I know? You won't have time to call, will you?'

'Oh, you'll know,' said Harry, as he stared past the colossus in the door at the large car now pulling up outside. The thought of Jameson huffing and puffing to his rescue made him smile. Not that anyone would've noticed, though, as his ruined face turned the expression into something capable of curdling milk.

'Not sure I like the sound of that,' said Jameson.

Harry hung up.

The car came to a stop. The front passenger door opened, and a man emerged who was somehow even larger than the one standing between Harry and the outside world.

How he even got in there in the first place was baffling to Harry, as the man opened the rear passenger door with the kind of respect usually reserved for royalty. At the same time, on the other side of the car, the other passenger door opened. Another figure slipped out, then walked around to stand and wait at the rear of the car, as Harry narrowed his eyes to try and pierce the gloom inside the vehicle.

This second figure drew Harry's eye more than either of the other two, matching as he did, all the characteristics of the second type of bodyguard. Casually dressed in black denim trousers, a dark green T-shirt, and a tan-coloured fleece jacket, he was relaxed enough to let Harry know that if anything started, he'd be the one finishing it. Ex-military for sure, Harry surmised. In his left hand, he was carrying a small, black, hardshell case.

At long last, the darkness swilling around inside the car parted just enough to release a stooped figure who required a helping hand to stand in the soft afternoon light. The old man, who was dressed in a long, dark red, heavy wool jacket, despite the comparative warmth of the day, was then led to the front door of the café. The goon blocking it swung out of the way as though attached to the wall by hinges.

Harry stayed in his seat as the old man approached, his arm firmly clasped in the rough hands of the ex-military bodyguard. At the table, the old man waited for a chair to be pulled out for him. Then he lifted his face, and with a wolf's grin, stared at Harry with familiar eyes.

'Hello, nephew,' he said, and sat down.

THREE

Harry stared at the uncle he'd never met and said nothing. He was not here for pleasantries.

The man in the tan fleece, who was now standing a step behind Harry's uncle, remained impassive, relaxed, the black case on the floor beside him. The goon at the door had turned around now, his back to the world outside.

'Tea?'

'I think the kitchen staff took a break,' Harry said.

The old man waved a crooked hand dismissively at their surroundings.

'Not from here,' he said.

The man in the fleece lifted the black case and placed it on a table to Harry's left. He then proceeded to open it. Inside, in protective foam cut to fit the case's contents, Harry watched him remove a number of metal containers, two delicate cups with matching saucers, and the daintiest teapot Harry had ever seen. He placed a cup and saucer in front of both Harry and his uncle, then proceeded to make them a pot of tea, first spooning loose leaf tea from one of the metal containers into the teapot, before pouring steaming hot water on top of them from another.

'Milk or lemon?' Harry's uncle asked. 'Earl Grey, you see; it's the only tea I drink.'

'Milk,' said Harry.

From another container, a dash of milk was poured into his teacup. A few quiet minutes later, the rich, fragrant liquid from the teapot was added, and a slice of lemon was placed in the teacup in front of Harry's uncle.

Harry's uncle raised his cup.

'Here's to family,' he said, and took a sip, steam curling around his face like the ghost of a beard.

Harry, lifting his own cup to his mouth as delicately as he could, worried that he could crush the thing with his hands and probably not even notice. He took a sip, gave a nod of appreciation, then placed the cup back on the saucer.

'I'm going to stick my neck out,' he said, 'and guess that you didn't invite me here to talk about old times. Because there aren't any, well, certainly none that we share.'

Harry's uncle took another sip of his tea.

'These are a family heirloom,' he said. 'The cups and saucers. Belonged to my grandmother, as far as I'm aware. Do you like them?'

Harry glanced disinterestedly at the crockery.

'If you're leaving them to me in your will, that's very kind, but I'll have to decline.'

'Whenever she wanted to have a serious discussion, out the cups would come,' Harry's uncle continued, ignoring what he had just said. 'My mother continued with the tradition, and I have done the same.' He lifted the cup he was holding a little higher, as though inspecting it for damage. 'Think of the stories they would be able to tell us!'

Harry reached for his own cup once again, this time clasping it around the rim, rather than holding it by its fragile handle. He drained the cup in one gulp, then returned it to the saucer.

'Thanks for the tea,' he said. 'Now, how's about you get to the point and tell me why it is you wanted to meet? If it's to share memories about your brother, my so-called father, then if it's all the same with you, I'd rather not.'

Harry's uncle took another sip and stared at him through the steam just long enough for it to feel awkward, before setting the cup back on its saucer.

'He was not a good man,' he said.

'He was a bastard,' replied Harry. 'And now he's a dead one. But isn't it a little bit pot and kettle, you passing judgment? My understanding is that you're no saint yourself.'

Harry thought back to the letter he'd received from Andrew Guy, which had led him to where he was sitting right then. Despite everything that had happened, Harry had felt sorry for Andrew. He was a man defined by his grief; and Harry was relieved he'd been able to stop him taking his own life, even if he'd spend the rest of that life in prison. The letter Andrew had sent him led Harry to do his own bit of research on his uncle. He knew exactly what kind of man he was sharing space with.

'We all have done things of which we are not proud,' Harry's uncle said. 'Have we not, Harry?'

'I'm not here to talk about me. My business is my own.'

'But I'm very much here to talk about you,' his uncle replied. 'In place of my brother, there is no one else left. No one that I trust, anyway.'

That was an odd thing to say, thought Harry.

'Left? How do you mean? And for what, exactly? What are you getting at?'

'I was robbed of the chance to bring him round to my way of thinking.'

Despite the precarious nature of where he was now, what he was doing, and who he was sitting with, Harry laughed. The sound was rough and throaty and stumbled around the café as though intent on smashing up a few of those god-awful teapots on display.

'That's what this is, is it, then? You're thinking to try and turn me to your way of thinking, too? Give up my life of catching people like my father, like you, and putting them away, and instead, become just such a person myself?' Harry laughed again, couldn't help himself; the notion was so ridiculous it seemed the only natural response. 'Well, one thing's for sure,' he said, 'you're a lot funnier than my father ever was.'

'You misunderstand.'

'Do I now?'

'You hear, but you do not listen.'

Harry shook his head, rolled his eyes.

'A philosophy lesson now, is that it? What's next? You going to tell me the facts of life, explain to me all about the birds and the bees, because my own father wasn't around to do so?'

'Now, Harry ...'

'And there's another thing; you know my name, but I still have no idea what yours is, and I'm not about to sit here and call you Mr Grimm, now, am I?'

'My name is not important.'

'And neither is whatever it is that you want to say, because if it was, you'd have either got to the point already, or put a bullet in my head, right? You've done neither. So, if it's all the same with you ...'

Harry stood up, thrusting his chair away with the back of his knees. The abruptness of his movement caused a chain reaction he'd expected, though perhaps not on the scale it revealed itself.

The man standing behind Harry's uncle was suddenly at the old man's side, a pistol in his right hand, while behind him, the ape at the door was already running. As the man with the pistol lifted the weapon to point the barrel at Harry, instinct took over. Harry closed the distance, not with his body, but his chair, swinging it around from behind to smash into the man's hand. The chair connected hard, and the man roared in pain as flesh split and bones broke. The pistol spun out of his fingers and across the café floor clattering as it darted between the legs of tables and chairs and into the shadows.

Then Harry was into him with his left elbow, connecting it hard with the side of his head, to send him face-first into the table. He gave him no time to recover, instead grabbing and hurling him to the rapidly approaching bodyguard from the door. The men crashed into each other in a tangle of limbs, pain and swearing. Harry wasn't about to wait around to see if any other concealed weapons were about to make an entrance. He bolted for the door, his eyes now on the vehicle outside, ready for whoever was driving it to join in the fun.

'Enough!'

The bark of his uncle's voice was loud and desperate enough to have Harry, to his own surprise, pause.

'Please, Harry,' the old man continued, and Harry, despite the whine of adrenaline in his ears, heard a note of genuine desperation in the spittle-laced voice. 'I've travelled a long way to meet you. A very long way.'

Harry felt the air from outside breathe on his face through the now-open door, knew that out there Jameson was waiting for him, and probably watching.

His phone rang.

Harry took his phone from his pocket, lifted it to his ear.

'Just thought you should know that I've dealt with the driver,' Jameson said. 'He'll be alright. I think ... Anyway, how's everything in there? Looks to me like it's getting a bit unpleasant.'

Harry turned slowly, deliberately, to face his uncle and the two other men.

'I'm dealing with it,' he said.

'Grace will be very unhappy indeed if I have to take you back to her with a hole or two in you.'

Harry's uncle was on his feet. The two bodyguards were on either side of him, glaring. Both were bleeding, the gorilla from a broken nose courtesy of the collision, the smaller one from his ruined hand, which he was holding clamped beneath the armpit of his other arm.

'Go,' Harry's uncle commanded, not to Harry, but to the bodyguards. They hesitated. 'He's bested you once,' the old man continued, an edge to his voice sharp enough to cut through steel. 'Don't make me ask him to do worse.'

Another odd thing to say, Harry thought.

The two men glanced at each other, then walked towards Harry, grazing past his shoulders as they headed outside.

Harry's uncle beckoned him to join him once again at the table. On his way over, Harry spotted the pistol he'd knocked from the bodyguard's hand and retrieved it.

'I'll keep this,' he said, checking first it was safe, then

stowing it in his jacket. 'Wouldn't want it getting into the wrong hands, now, would we?' He then picked up his chair from the floor and sat down once more, his uncle joining him as he did so. 'Now, how's about you get to the point, then, and avoid any more unfortunate misunderstandings?'

'My apologies,' said his uncle.

'You need them on a tighter leash.'

'Right now, I find myself thinking that what I need is you.'

'I'm not for hire.'

'Pity.'

Harry took in a deep breath, exhaled, then leaned forward on the table between them, hands clasped.

'So, Uncle,' Harry said, making no effort to disguise his disdain for the word as he said it, 'what is it, exactly, that you want to talk about?'

As the old man spoke, Harry listened. And when he finally understood, he knew there was no refusing.

FOUR

Detective Inspector Ethan Morgan was staring at the screen on his phone, his own face staring right back at him in real time. He'd driven over from the small flat he was currently renting in the pretty and historic market town of Richmond, then parked up in Hawes marketplace, arriving just early enough to make sure that he had everything sorted for the day ahead. Of course, he knew that everything already was, but time spent on a final check of the important things was never time wasted, was it? Which was why, right then, he was using a tiny pair of scissors to snip away at a few stray whiskers threatening to make his beard look straggly and unkempt.

Yes, the important things, Ethan thought, and that didn't just mean the big stuff, either. He knew as well as anyone it was vital to read up on current investigations, work on his skills, make sure he was up to date on current practice in the Force, all with the aim of ensuring he was the best damned detective inspector he could be. What Ethan thought made him stand out, though, was the emphasis he put on the little things; the colour of the socks he was going to wear, the shine on his shoes, and especially so, the neatness of his spectacular beard. They said clothes make the man, and he couldn't agree more. It wasn't just about show and flash, though. There was more to it. For Ethan, the details, the fact that he bothered, didn't just make him feel confident, it helped him project that to the outside world, even when he wasn't feeling it. There was a strength to that, he thought, and some days it felt like a very welcome shield.

Ethan had started to grow his beard following a breakup a good few years ago, when he was on the other side of thirty. It had begun as a bit of rebellion, because his girlfriend at the time, Pamela, had hated beards and all who sported them. Disliking things, Ethan recalled, had been a hobby of hers, or so it had seemed.

She'd instantly dislike anyone who shortened her name to Pam and would rage against the merest suggestion of Pammy, thought seafood was disgusting, classed any film Ethan wanted to watch as beneath her, found his parents embarrassing, her own parents nauseating, and would shudder at the sound of polystyrene being squeaked.

How they'd ended up together at all baffled Ethan, but back then, he had been besotted enough to look past all of their differences to try and cling onto something that he'd known, deep down, was clearly never going to go anywhere. And in the end, it hadn't, for which he was eternally grateful. As for what she had seen in him, well, that remained a mystery.

A couple of months after they'd gone their separate ways, he'd bumped into her in town, having popped into a newsagent on the way to the pub. He'd fancied treating himself to a small pack of cigars, because the smell reminded him of his grandad. Pam had complained about those, too, despite being a smoker herself. He didn't smoke them at all now, but it had been fun at the time.

Queueing up to pay for the cigars, Ethan had then seen Pamela saunter into the small shop and had accidentally caught her eye. To his surprise, she hadn't recognised him, and instead of the expected sneer, she'd sent him a dazzling smile, her eyes widening a little. Despite himself, Ethan had smiled back and wondered at the time if this was a way for them to patch things up, get back together maybe. Then, in had walked someone else and blown that all to shit; another man, wearing another beard, and she'd thrown her arms around him in excitement.

Leaving the shop, Ethan had once again caught Pamela's eye. Before he could stop himself, the words, 'Hi, Pammy,' had slipped into the moment between them, sailing happily on a barbed note of contempt in his voice. Pamela's face had frozen in confusion as she'd stared back. Then the smile she had been wearing for her new beau had morphed into a sneer especially for Ethan, and she pinned it to her face with the daggers she stared at him as he'd walked past.

'Funny,' he'd said, looking at the new man in her life, then at Pamela, 'I thought you didn't like beards.' And that had been that.

The beard, from that day forth, had never been shaved off. It was a part of him now, something he didn't so much grow as wear. Ethan knew he over-thought its importance, but it had become almost like an old friend; dependable, trustworthy, something he knew would never let him down, something he could hide behind. And right now, as he was still finding his way around the final week of his second month with the new team he'd been placed with, the hiding was most important of all. It was also rather good at keeping his face warm; and for that he was already grateful, what with Autumn just starting to turn the leaves and chill the air,.

Ethan spotted another whisker. It hadn't been there before, had it? Must've just sprung out when he wasn't looking, just to annoy him.

'Right, then, you b—'

A knock at his window startled Ethan so much he stabbed himself in the nose with his little scissors.

'Bloody hell!'

On the other side of the window, a face was grinning back at him. A hand appeared next to it and gave a wiggly-fingered wave.

'How do, Ethan?' came the muffled voice through the glass. 'Pruning the facial topiary, are you?'

Ethan rubbed his nose, checked there was no blood, gave a nod and an awkward smile to the face of Detective Sergeant Dinsdale.

'Be out in a sec,' he mouthed.

His door opened.

'I was going to head straight into the office,' said Matt, 'but thought I'd nip up to the Penny Garth Café, if you fancy coming?'

Ethan's shoulders sagged a little.

'You do know that not every morning has to begin with a bacon butty, don't you?'

Matt's face turned serious. He leaned in close.

'Don't you go listening to rumours like that, you never know where they might lead.'

'A healthy diet, you mean.'

'Bacon's healthy.'

Ethan couldn't think of anything to say to that.

Matt stepped back.

'Come on, then, get yourself shifting. Thinking about it, I might just go for egg this morning. Have to see how the mood takes me, though.'

Ethan climbed out of his vehicle, shut the door. A bright sun was low in the sky, throwing a golden hue across the fell tops like scattered grain.

'I'll probably forgo a butty today, if that's okay,' Ethan said, locking his car to then walk up through Hawes with Matt.

Matt stopped, looked Ethan up and down.

'You need some meat on you, lad,' he said, giving one of his arms a pinch, before continuing on his way.

'I've always been this size. I'm athletic,' replied Ethan, back in step with the DS.

Matt laughed.

'You'd get knocked over by a cow's fart if you stood close enough.'

Arriving at the café, and a little unsure how to take Matt's comment, Ethan followed the DS inside. The place was quiet, with only a couple of customers sitting at tables happily scoffing particularly large breakfasts. The air was rich with the comforting aroma of simple food cooked well. Ethan's stomach rumbled.

'That looks good, doesn't it?' Matt said, nodding at the occupied tables and the customers tucking into their food. 'Grab yourself a seat.'

'No butty for me, though, remember?' reminded Ethan, as Matt walked over to the counter.

Pulling out a chair from under a table, Ethan sat down, caught a nod of hello from one of the other customers, then stared out of the window. A tractor rolled down the road from up beyond the primary school, towing behind it a huge trailer showing a green crown of grass poking out above its sides.

'Final silage cut of the year, that,' explained Matt, sitting down opposite Ethan and placing two large mugs of tea on the table. 'Can't beat the smell of freshly cut grass, like.' He lifted his mug, took a sip, pointed at Ethan's face. 'It's very impressive, you know, that beard of yours. I tried growing one once myself, but it came to nowt. Joan didn't like it either; told me it was like waking up every morning to find me lying in a hedge.'

Ethan tried to imagine Matt's jovial face with a beard.

'Pity,' he smiled. 'I reckon it would suit you.'

'Oh, it suited me alright,' Matt winked back. 'Gave me that rugged, mountain man look.'

A few minutes later, a young man from the kitchen appeared at the table, placed two plates down in front of Matt and Ethan, then left.

Ethan stared at the plates, then at Matt, then at the plates again.

'I said I didn't want anything to eat.'

'Did you?'

'Yes. I said I didn't want a butty.'

'Well, if I'm not mistaken, that's not a butty, now, is it?'

'It's a breakfast, Matt,' said Ethan. 'A full English.'

'Exactly! Now, get it down your neck. It'll do you good, I promise. Set you up for the day good and proper, like.'

Ethan took in a slow, deep breath, exhaled, and grabbed the knife and fork, which had been set down with the plate.

'There's no way I'll finish all this,' he said. 'I mean, just look at it. How is it possible to have that much food on one plate?'

'Rubbish,' said Matt, and pierced the skin of a meaty sausage. 'You'll be fine.'

A while later, when the breakfast was finished, and in a far shorter period of time than Ethan had expected, he drained the last of his tea and groaned. The plate in front of him was clean, an inescapable fact, and one he found hard to take in. His stomach felt not so much full as stretched.

'Now that's a proper way to start the day, isn't it?' said Matt, and patted his own stomach lovingly.

'I won't need to eat for a week,' Ethan replied, already sensing indigestion taking a grip.

Matt stood up.

'Best get to the office. Jadyn's been on duty and will be keen to head off home.'

To Ethan's surprise, Jadyn then walked in the door of the café, as though the mere mention of his name had summoned him.

'Thought you'd be here,' he said. 'Quicker to pop in and grab you than give you a call.'

Ethan saw a frown grow on Matt's forehead.

'Something's up?' Matt said. 'What's happened?'

'Accident,' Jadyn replied. 'Up on Long Road, over in Swaledale. Emergency services are already on their way. I'm heading over there now. Could do with an extra pair of hands.'

Ethan expected Matt to step in and volunteer, but instead, the detective sergeant said, 'Ethan, that'll be you. I'll go set myself up in the office, keep things ticking over with the rest of the team. Jim's on duty today, so I'll hand over to him once he's in, and follow on over.'

'Come on, then,' said Jadyn, looking now at Ethan. 'Best we get shifting. All we know so far is that there's two vehicles involved, a Land Rover, and a tractor with a trailer. A couple on their holidays witnessed the whole thing. They were following the tractor up High Lane from Swaledale. They called it in.'

Outside the Penny Garth, Ethan jogged around to the passenger side of Jadyn's vehicle and jumped in.

Jadyn thumped down into the driver's seat, and they both clipped in their seatbelts.

'Beard's looking sharp,' Jadyn said, then he started the engine, hit the blues and twos, and with the sirens and lights blaring, they were off.

FIVE

Hawes tried to cling to the back of Jadyn's vehicle as they headed through the town, and Ethan watched shops and houses and people shrinking behind them in the wing mirror. Jadyn took a left at the doctors' surgery, aiming them for the back road from Hardraw through to Askrigg.

'Isn't this route slower?' Ethan asked, as Jadyn slowed for the bridge spanning the River Ure.

He was getting to know the area a little at a time but was a long way off from the knowledge a local would have. He'd come here from Darlington, having transferred to the area when he'd been promoted to detective inspector considerably closer to home, in Swansea. The move itself hadn't been necessary, but it had come up, and he'd fancied a change, a reason to get away for a while from the hold that his home still had on him. It would force a little growth, he thought, help him learn new skills, and perhaps more about himself. The move had been a wrench, though, as he was now a long drive from home, but at least here he was among the hills and the fields. Sometimes, when the morning was rich with the iron tang of a cold breeze, he would close his eyes and sense the place of his birth, and whisper to it that he would return soon. He may have ended up working in Swansea, but home was the Black Mountains, and a move to the Dales was perhaps not that much of a move after all.

In the fields, which were crumbling slowly into the river, their edges folding over the peat-brown water, sheep grazed, unbothered by the car's speed and sirens. In another, cattle cared much the same, though one, Ethan noticed, stared at them over a tall gate, a warden keeping watch.

'Depends who's driving,' Jadyn replied, dropping a gear to send them up a hill fast enough to push Ethan back in his seat. 'Also, this route doesn't usually get as busy. The main road is wider, but that can't half get clogged up with caravans and bikers.'

At the top of the hill, Jadyn turned right. Had he gone left, he'd have had them along to Hardraw, a place Ethan had as yet not visited. He was keen, though, mainly because of the mention of the Green Dragon Inn, and the waterfall which sat behind it cut into the rock. He'd brought his camera gear with him to this new, temporary position in Wensleydale, thinking it was a hobby he should try to get back into. Trouble was, work had taken up so much of his time, he'd not even opened the bag to check through the lenses.

Hardraw, though, would be a good place to start, he thought, and made a mental note to get himself there when he was next off duty.

The road was indeed narrower than the route Ethan was used to taking out of Hawes, and for some reason, it felt older. It seemed to him as though they were zipping along a fine thread, a silvery grey line held in place by drystone walls, along which generations had travelled this ancient land.

A tractor rolled past, Jadyn raising a hand at the driver.

'Who was that?' Ethan asked.

'No idea,' Jadyn replied. 'Doesn't hurt to be friendly though, does it? That's how things work up here. It's the biggest difference I've noticed since moving from Bradford.'

'How do you mean?'

Jadyn was quiet for a moment, thoughtful.

'Can't remember where I heard it,' he eventually said, 'but there's this phrase, or saying, right? Scratch one, they all bleed.'

Ethan didn't like the sound of that at all.

'And how is that a good thing? Thought you said it was about being friendly?'

'What I think it means is that everyone's connected, if that makes sense? It can feel a little claustrophobic, true, especially when you find out that someone in Leyburn knows something about you that you probably didn't even know yourself, or had forgotten, that kind of thing. Everyone here looks after everyone else. The Dales, they're just like one huge village. And I like that.'

Ethan wasn't so sure and kept quiet.

Arriving in Askrigg, Jadyn slowed down just enough, and soon they were out the other side and climbing.

'You met the district surgeon yet?' Jadyn asked.

'Not sure,' Ethan replied.

Jadyn laughed.

'Well, you can't have done, because you'd know; Margaret's not someone you easily forget.' He pointed a finger at a house on their left as they whizzed by, climbing out of

Askrigg. 'She lives there. Bought a new Range Rover a while back now. Drives the thing more like a ship navigating the sea than a vehicle on a road. Her daughter's the pathologist.'

Jadyn took a right, and the road steepened and narrowed to a single lane. Neither of them spoke, and Ethan was glad about that. For one, his mind was on what they would find at the end of the journey, the severity of the accident, who was involved, how it had happened. Also, though, he was just enjoying the journey, and the countryside was reminding him of home.

A stab of homesickness clutched at Ethan's heart, and he almost gasped as the car rumbled over a cattle grid, the drystone walls which had herded them onwards fell away, and open moorland welcomed them.

'You okay?'

Jadyn's question caught Ethan off guard.

'What? Yes, I'm fine,' he said, forcing a smile, and the memories of his childhood in the Welsh Mountains, back down where he kept them, safe and secure.

'I thought you'd seen something I hadn't, and we were about to hit a random suicidal sheep.'

'Just enjoying the scenery,' Ethan smiled.

'It is beautiful, isn't it?' Jadyn agreed. 'I'm living over in Reeth, can't seem to persuade myself to leave, either. Just something about the place.'

'Where would you move if you had to?' Ethan asked. 'Closer to Jen?'

'Depends on what Steve had to say about that,' Jadyn said with a laugh. 'We've touched on the idea of moving in together. But, yeah, there's always Steve to consider. I'm sure I can persuade him, though.'

Ethan was confused. He had no idea at all who Steve was.

'And Steve is?' he asked, as innocently as he could, wondering if he was an older brother, or perhaps a friend being overly protective.

Another cattle grid rattled the car, and soon they were heading down into Swaledale, open moorland continuing on either side.

'Massive,' answered Jadyn. 'Thinks he owns the place. Especially the sofa.'

Ethan was no clearer as to Steve's identity and decided that asking further questions wouldn't necessarily help.

'So, what do we know about the accident?' he asked, realising they'd not talked about it yet.

'Not much more than I told you and Matt in the café,' Jadyn replied. 'Land Rover and a tractor with a trailer. Collision happened on a sharp bend.'

'How many people involved?'

'As far as I know, two. Might have to deal with sheep gathering around for a nosy. Could be dogs as well, as most farmers round here seem to be attached at the hip to at least one.'

'Like Jim and Fly,' Ethan said. 'Actually, on that, what's with DCI Grimm and Smudge?'

'Harry, you mean?'

'Yes.'

'Takes a while to get used to everyone using first names, I know, but it'll come. Anyway, Harry and Smudge ... Yeah, you'd not expect him to own a dog, would you? Smudge won him over, though. He rescued her from a puppy farm. Reckon that dog's done him the world of good.'

'In what way?'

'Well, I know he's not exactly cuddly, but he's definitely softened since he moved up here.'

Ethan couldn't quite get his head around what Jadyn had just said. He'd worked with some gruff senior officers in his time, but Grimm was on another level. Just a look from the man was enough to stop him dead. The injuries to his face only added to things, and not in a good way. He wondered if they were still painful; they certainly looked it.

'Softened? Seriously?'

'Oh, he's positively a teddy bear now compared to when he arrived, believe you me,' said Jadyn, then pointed at something through the window. 'Air Ambulance.'

Ethan looked to where Jadyn was pointing and saw the helicopter sitting just ahead on a patch of heather.

'That's not a good sign, is it?'

'Doesn't always get sent out,' Jadyn explained, 'but sometimes it's just a whole lot quicker.'

Rounding a corner, Jadyn braked hard as half a dozen sheep blocked the way.

'What did I say?' He sighed. 'We'll leave them for now, though, get ourselves down to the accident.'

The sheep, confronted with Jadyn's vehicle, stared at it for a moment, then turned around and started to walk back the way they'd come.

'Very obliging,' said Ethan.

'True, but considering the fact there's no walls and they could just run off across the heather, not that helpful.'

The sheep, as though having heard Jadyn, decided at last to skip off the road and allow them to pass. Then, as they rounded another corner, the accident came into view.

'Bloody hell,' said Jadyn, as they both stared out through the windscreen at the wreckage ahead.

'I second that,' agreed Ethan, spying just to the other side of the accident, a fire engine, and the paramedics' rapid response vehicle.

Jadyn shook his head.

'No, that's not what I mean, it's that ... The Land Rover ...'

Ethan narrowed his eyes at the mangled carcass of an old Land Rover. The bodywork was red, the wheels a milky white, and attached to the roof was a roof rack.

'What about it?'

'I recognise it,' said Jadyn.

'Really? How? This is Wensleydale, those old things are all over the place.'

'I know,' said Jadyn, 'but that one, I promise you, I know who it belongs to.'

'Who?'

'Mike, the mechanic.'

SIX

Jadyn was out of the vehicle, and Ethan quickly followed.

'There's one of those matrix signs in the back,' Jadyn said, pointing to the rear of his car. 'Not used it yet. Cones as well. And a few other more battered warning signs.'

'I'll get those set up,' said Ethan, opening the boot.

Jadyn took out his phone.

'I'm going to call Matt, get him to send Dave and Liz out as well; we'll be on with sorting through what's happened, so we need them to deal with traffic.'

'What about Jen?'

'Not on duty today. Don't want to be bothering her either.'

'Oh, is something up? She okay?'

Jadyn laughed.

'Oh, she's fine. She's just spending the day out shopping for new running gear, which'll mean half a dozen new pairs of trainers and no doubt some new technical clothes that save her a whole gram or two in weight when out doing an ultra.'

Ethan started to pull what he needed from the rear of the car.

'I'll put these a good way up the lane,' he said. 'Make sure people have plenty of warning.'

'Doubt we'll get much traffic, but we could do without things backing up,' said Jadyn. 'I know there's no walls here, but it's not exactly easy to turn around unless you're in a four-wheel drive. Last thing we need is some tourist in a fancy car bottoming out and getting stuck. Won't need to worry about the ambulance having to get through, though, as the air ambulance will be doing the taxi ride to the hospital.'

'What about the cattle grid?' Ethan asked.

'What about it?'

'Why don't I park the vehicle up there, blocking the way through for now, and then people can turn around before getting here, can't they?'

'That's a fair way back, but makes sense,' agreed Jadyn. 'Ground is a bit better there as well to have people swing round and head back. Bit of a detour for them, but better that than getting trapped here. And Dave and Liz will be on their way soon to take over.' He went to throw the keys over to Ethan, then stopped. 'Wait,' he said, 'you outrank me. I'll head up the road, you deal with accident.'

Ethan held up a hand to stop Jadyn, who was already making his way back to the car. He shook his head and tipped what he'd removed from the car back into the boot, slamming it shut.

'Rank's not an issue right now,' he said. 'You said you know the driver of that Land Rover, so get yourself down there. There's a good chance you know whoever else is involved as well. I'll be fine with this.'

'Sure?'

'Positive.'

Jadyn gave an appreciative nod, then turned towards the accident, phone to his ear.

Ethan jumped into the car and started the engine. With nowhere easy to turn round without risking getting stuck, he slipped it into reverse, turned to look over his shoulder, and started to head back up the way they had come. The lane was narrow, and as tempted as he was to speed up, he took it easy, aware of the escapee sheep as well as the possibility of someone coming the other way.

Though the lane was bordered by open moorland, still there was nowhere he could turn around easily, so onwards and upwards he drove, aiming for the cattle grid. Then, as he rounded a corner and saw his destination come into view, something bounded into the middle of the lane, forcing him to brake. Heart in his mouth, Ethan stared wide-eyed at what was now blocking his route: a roe deer, its small antlers signalling it was a buck. Then, as he was doing his best to take in what was happening, another young buck bounced out of the moors to stand beside its friend.

Well, Ethan thought, *this is certainly something I didn't come across in Darlington.*

Though the deer were only there for the briefest of moments, to Ethan, the seconds seemed to stretch, elongating time, almost as though, right then, it simply didn't exist. He wondered what they were thinking as they held him in their gaze, and then, as quickly as they had arrived, they were gone, leaping off the lane and then on across the moors. He watched them briefly, their brown coats shimmering in the light of the sun, then they were gone, the dale swallowing them whole.

Ethan noticed a patch of ground where he could turn

around, so he aimed for it, pulled off the road, and was then facing the right way. The rest of the journey was considerably easier, now that he wasn't having to stare over his shoulder.

At the cattle grid, Ethan drove over it to then manoeuvre himself into position. He was aware that he still needed to allow access through to the other side, so parked in front of the cattle grid but not so close as to block the way completely. That done, he took the signs out and wandered down the lane to give plenty of warning of what lay ahead. Then, it was back to the vehicle to wait for Dave and Liz, the two community support officers, to relieve him.

Leaning against the bonnet of the car, though, Ethan wasn't too worried about getting bored. With a view like the one before him, down into Wensleydale, and with the day bright and just warm enough to make it comfortable, he was happy to stay where he was for hours. Which was probably why, when, just fifteen minutes later, a police motorbike arrived, he felt a little disappointed that his time alone with the view was over.

The figure on the bike gave Ethan a wave, climbed off, and rested the machine on its kickstand. Then they walked towards him, easing off their helmet.

'Hi, Ethan,' Liz said.

'Wasn't expecting to see you so soon,' said Ethan. 'Jadyn's only just called Matt to have you over.'

'I think Matt must've second-guessed him, then,' Liz replied. 'He called me half an hour ago to get over here. He'd just got into the office. Dave's on his way as well. Might take him a bit longer, though, as he's over in Coverdale dealing with something. I was over in Widdale; farmer there had to deal with some idiots leaving a load of camping gear down by a river. Right mess it is: tents, sleeping bags, carrier bags of food spilling everywhere, burn marks from fires and barbeques.'

'That doesn't make sense,' said Ethan. 'I thought people who went camping did so because they liked the countryside. Why make a mess of it?'

'It's a very small minority,' Liz explained. 'And they're not out to enjoy the countryside, not these ones, anyway. More likely they've driven out here from a town somewhere to get drunk in a field. Or worse.'

'Drugs?'

'Not that I could see this time, but we've found evidence of it before. They know they can come out here and just party without anyone knowing; farmers can't keep an eye on every bit of their land, can they? Got plenty enough to be dealing with as it is, without having to keep an eye out for idiots. All they have to do is park up somewhere out of the way, then walk until they find somewhere nice and hidden, and that's them, isn't it?'

'What if a farmer or whoever finds them, though?'

Liz shrugged.

'Don't think they care. Safety in numbers and all that. Usually, it's just verbal abuse, but some have started to get a bit more physical. That's what I was talking to the farmer about earlier; he'd found them, ordered them off, and while most of them moved on, leaving their gear behind in the process, a couple of others came over to have a go. Could've been a lot worse than it was. He was fairly shaken up. He's worried they'll come back and cause more trouble, vandalise stuff, that kind of thing.'

'I didn't realise that kind of stuff goes on.'

'Wensleydale is a beautiful place,' said Liz, 'but bad stuff happens here as much as anywhere else. And we can't stop people bringing in their own version of stupid, can we? Just have to deal with it when it happens. Anyway, how's things here? How serious is it, the accident?'

'Wasn't there for long, as I came straight back up here, but it looked pretty bad. Air Ambulance was there.'

'Makes sense,' said Liz. 'Roads round here can be a nightmare for ambulances.'

'Jadyn recognised one of the vehicles as well,' said Ethan. 'Said it was Mike's.'

Ethan saw Liz's eyes widen.

'Mike? From the garage?'

Ethan shook his head.

'I don't know, he didn't say.'

'What about the vehicle? Did you see it?'

'It was a red Land Rover. Not a new one either.'

Liz, though, wasn't listening. She was on her phone.

SEVEN

Harry was driving past Hawes Cemetery when a call came in. He answered it on hands-free and was given no time to speak.

'Harry? It's Ben; where've you been? Grace said you'd left early for something but didn't know why. Where've you been? Where are you?'

The tone of Ben's voice was enough to let Harry know something was up.

'Just arriving in Hawes now,' he said, answering one question, ignoring the other two. He'd not told Grace where he was going, because to some degree it was police business. Well, it was, if you squinted at it enough anyway.

'There's been an accident.'

'What? Who? Where? What's happened?'

'It's Mike,' Ben said. 'Liz has just been on the phone to tell me. Over in Swaledale.'

'Did she say what happened?'

'She's not at the scene, just making sure traffic doesn't get in the way and complicate things. Jadyn's there, and Ethan. Dave's on his way as well, I think.'

'How's Mike?'

'She didn't say, because she'd only just found out herself when she arrived. All I know is that Mike wasn't at work when I arrived. No idea what he was doing over in Swaledale. I've checked the diary, phone messages, and there's no mention of any jobs over that way at all.'

'Well, I'm sure everything is in hand,' Harry said, as he slowed down over the bridge, beneath which Gayle Beck tumbled on cheerily, oblivious to the world around it. 'Appreciate you calling me to let me know, but—'

'No, it's not that,' Ben said, interrupting Harry.

'Then what is it?'

Ben was quiet for a few seconds.

'I ... Look, I just think it's a bit odd, that's all. Mike never goes off on his own from work like this, not without me knowing. Every job we're on with, it's in the diary. He's a stickler for things like that, runs this place like a military operation.'

Harry nearly laughed at that. He knew what Ben meant, that Mike ran a tight ship, everything organised, well planned. Trouble was, Harry knew from personal experience, that a military operation was often the opposite. Oh, it always started with the best intentions, to be a shining example of efficiency. More often than not, though, once things were in play, everything went to hell, and everyone was playing catch-up.

'There's only two of us working here,' Ben continued, 'so we need to make sure we both know where the other one is, or things can easily fall apart.'

'Maybe it was an emergency call out,' Harry suggested.

'Maybe he just forgot. It happens, Ben. I know Mike's organised, but even he's fallible.'

Harry knew that Ben held Mike in the highest regard. The man had been instrumental in helping him when he'd been released on probation, eventually taking him on full-time, training him up, really making him part of the business. In many ways, Mike had become the father figure that Ben had never had, and Harry would never be able to thank him enough for that.

'I know, I'm just ...'

Ben's voice faded to nothing.

'You're worried,' said Harry. 'Understandable that you would be. I'll keep you posted on what's what, how's that sound? Mike, I'm sure, would want you to know anyway. You're the closest thing he has to family, I think.'

'He's started dating someone, actually,' said Ben, and Harry heard a bit of a lift in his brother's voice.

'Maybe he was heading off to see her, then,' Harry suggested.

'It's not that. I know that for a fact,' replied Ben. 'For a start, she's from Kettlewell, so it's completely the wrong direction. Also, Mike wouldn't be mixing work with pleasure. He's not like that.'

Harry came to the end of the cobbles, indicated, then pulled over into a parking space close to the lane leading down to the Community Centre.

'Not suggesting that he is.'

Engine off, he climbed out of his vehicle, went to let Smudge out of the back, then remembered he'd left her with Grace. A sigh of disappointment escaped his lips, and he was tempted to give Grace a call to find out where she was and see if he could swing by and pick the hound up. Not that he'd openly admit it to anyone, but he really did miss that animal when she wasn't around.

'I'd best get on,' Ben said. 'With Mike not here, things could start to back up. Might have to make a few phone calls to juggle things.'

Harry was about to say goodbye, but knew he had to ask, even though he knew full well Ben wouldn't appreciate it.

'How are you doing, yourself?'

'I'm fine,' Ben replied. 'Really. You don't have to keep asking, though I know you always will. It should be the other way round, really, shouldn't it, considering what happened, what I did?'

And there it was, Harry noticed, the change in tone in Ben's voice that told him no, he wasn't doing as well as he wanted Harry and everyone else to believe. He understood why; having been blackmailed into kidnapping, then imprisoning his older brother in a disused mine, there was no way Ben could just shrug it off and move on. He was doing well, had in many ways been through worse, but Harry knew he was still trying to come to terms with it all. Liz had told him as much, and he'd observed it for himself.

'I do have to keep asking,' said Harry. 'I'm your brother.'

'I appreciate that, I really do, but please, you need to stop worrying. The more it's brought up, the worse it is. I'd rather just move on.'

'That's not how these things work, Ben. And you know full well that I know that better than anyone.'

'But this isn't anything like being blown up by an IED, is it?'

'Trauma's trauma, no matter how you dress it up.'

Ben fell silent.

'Well,' said Harry, realising he was going to get nowhere

with that line of questioning, 'if you do need anything, need to talk, whatever, just call me. Right?'

'I will, Harry, I promise. You'll keep me posted on Mike, yes?'

'Of course. Though Liz will probably do that for me. You and her good? Any thoughts on planning the wedding yet?'

That question managed to get a laugh from Ben.

'You do know how much weddings cost, don't you?'

'No,' said Harry. 'Not a clue.'

'Exactly.'

And with that, the conversation was over.

Vehicle locked, Harry started to walk down to the Community Centre when a voice called over to him. He stopped, turned, and saw a man he didn't recognise staring at him from only a few metres away. Despite the weather, he was wearing a long, dark brown jacket, the hem of which rested against his calves. Behind him was a sleek-looking black saloon. Harry couldn't tell the make, didn't really care, either.

'Do I know you?'

The man shook his head.

'I know you, though,' he said. 'How did the meeting go?'

'What meeting?'

The man laughed.

'He's a one, isn't he, my old man? Went ahead with the meeting despite my asking him not to.'

The face of Harry's uncle flashed in his mind.

'Your old man? You mean, he's your dad?'

Harry guessed the man in front of him to be around his own age, but it was hard to tell, what with his eyes hidden behind the darkest of sunglasses, and his face bearing a fashionable amount of stubble, flecked with a dusting of grey.

'Guess that makes us cousins, then, doesn't it?' the man said, and he closed the distance between them, just enough menace in each footstep to have Harry clench a fist.

Harry didn't move. He just waited for the man to approach.

'What do you want?' he asked, once the man had stopped in front of him just close enough to invade his personal space. 'Because if you're thinking this is going to be some happy family reunion, you couldn't be more wrong.'

'What did he say to you?'

'You don't know?'

Another laugh, though this one was quiet, subtle.

'Word to the wise,' the man said, leaning into Harry and dropping his voice. 'Ignore him. Whatever it is he's asked you to do, don't. That understood?'

Harry leaned in as well, until their heads were almost touching.

'Whatever the beef is between you and your lovely old pappy, that's between you and him, right? And whatever it is he spoke to me about, that's my business. So, why don't you slip back into that fancy pants motor you drove here in, and be on your way now?'

The man leaned away from Harry, puffed out his chest. Harry almost laughed at that, because intimidated he was not.

'He can't go through with it. I won't let him,' the man said. 'It's a family business.'

'Lovely talking to you,' said Harry, ignoring the man. 'I'll be getting on with my day now, though, if it's all the same to you, and doing my best to forget that this meeting even took place. Oh, look, there we are. I already have.'

Harry turned from the man and once again headed for

the Community Centre. As he passed the pet shop, and the unnecessarily terrifying mannequin the owner insisted on standing outside whenever they were open, he turned around to see the man, his supposed cousin, drive away. As he pushed through the community centre doors to find out more about Mike's accident, he had a horrible feeling he'd be seeing his cousin again.

EIGHT

The Land Rover was lying on its passenger side, the driver's side staring at the sky, the door missing completely. From the damage Jadyn could see, it looked very much like the vehicle had rolled before slamming into the tractor head on. How it had managed that on these roads was impossible to imagine, because such a thing would, for a start, take a hell of a lot of speed to achieve. And if there was one thing Jadyn knew about old Land Rovers, it was that speed was not the reason people had for owning one, with most having a zero to sixty time of never.

Not a single panel seemed to be undamaged. Wherever he looked, he saw metal that had taken a beating, scratched and cracked paint, smashed glass. The roof rack, though still discernible as such, was crushed beyond all repair, a tangle of metallic spaghetti. He saw large patches of dark sand on the road around the Land Rover, where spilled fuel had been dealt with to prevent a fire.

The tractor, from what Jadyn could see as he drew closer, seemed relatively undamaged. The Land Rover had managed to get itself jammed in between the front wheels, the front grill a royal mess thanks to the counterweight on the tractor. The impact had lifted the front of the considerably larger vehicle off the road a little bit, but other than that, it looked fine, the trailer still attached. For some reason, though, and despite the lack of damage elsewhere, Jadyn noticed that the windscreen was smashed. The tractor itself was parked at an odd angle, no doubt from where the driver had attempted to take some form of evasive manoeuvre as the Land Rover had come at him. Must have been terrifying.

A shout caught Jadyn's attention, and he looked up to see a firefighter waving him over. As he approached, the emergency services team came into view. In addition to the rest of the firefighter team, Jadyn spotted a man wrapped in a silvery foil emergency blanket sitting in the open door of the paramedics' vehicle. A border collie was lying at his feet. Away from this, three other paramedics were dealing with someone strapped to a stretcher. Even from where he was standing, Jadyn could see that the someone was Mike.

Helmet removed, the firefighter held out a hand.

'Catherine Hodgson,' she said.

Jadyn introduced himself.

'So, what've we got?' he asked.

'When we arrived, the driver of the tractor was walking around, clearly in shock, but otherwise fine,' Catherine explained. 'Easy to deal with, no real problems there. The other driver was still in the vehicle, and as you can see, it's not in the best of shape, is it?' She gestured over at the Land Rover, shaking her head. 'I saw that and was half convinced we were going to be dealing with a fatality. Amazingly, we're not, but getting him out of there wasn't easy. Land Rover bodies open like a tin can, and conveniently, the driver's door had been ripped off already. Trouble was, the steering column had him pinned, so we had to cut him out.'

'Was he conscious?'

'Barely. Had to stabilise him first, which wasn't easy; the way he was, we couldn't risk spinal movement. We managed to get him to communicate with us, but that quickly became him screaming out in pain. We don't use sedation as a regular course of action, but we had no choice. We needed him calm, and thankfully, the paramedics were able to sort that out. We were worried he'd start thrashing around, grabbing things, grabbing us. Couldn't risk it.'

Jadyn's eyes drifted to where Mike was being carried towards the Air Ambulance.

'He's lost a couple of fingers. They were probably ripped off when the vehicle rolled. Haven't found them yet. Good chance we won't, either, out here.'

'Why?'

'Crows, foxes, anything out here that's a bit hungry and fancies a nibble will come sniffing around. Unavoidable. He's lucky that's all he lost, though, really. There's so much bare metal inside those old Land Rovers. It's like being dropped into a food mixer if you're in one and it barrel rolls. Luckily, he was strapped in.'

'Luckily?'

'The vehicle is pre-nineteen seventy-two, so it isn't legally required to have seatbelts. Don't ask me why I know that because I don't know myself, I just seem to have a knack for remembering useless information. Thank God he thought it sensible to install one, otherwise we'd have been dealing with something else entirely, all of it in bits and pieces.'

Jadyn heard the helicopter thrum into life, and watched as Mike was lifted into the rear. The rotor blades were already spinning at an incredible rate and soon the sound of it was enough to drown out any possibility of further conversation. Then, with the two paramedics safely on board, the helicopter lifted off.

'He'll be in the hospital in Northallerton in minutes,' Catherine said, now that they could actually hear each other talk again. 'And there'll be a team prepped for his arrival.'

Jadyn kept his eye on the Air Ambulance for a moment longer, watching the aircraft speed away towards the horizon, then stared back at the wreckage of Mike's Land Rover.

'Did Mike say what happened?'

Catherine's eyes went wide.

'What, you know him? I didn't realise. I'm sorry.'

'He's the mechanic over in Hawes,' Jadyn explained. 'My boss's brother works with him.'

'Bloody hell. You forget how close to home this stuff can get sometimes, especially up here in the Dales. Does he have family?'

'Not that I know of.'

'Well, to answer your question, no, he didn't say anything about what happened. Mainly, I think, because he was in so much pain, and also because he was fading in and out of consciousness.'

'What about the driver of the tractor?'

'Probably best if you have a chat with him,' Catherine suggested. 'He had a few choice words to say about your friend, believe you me.'

That confused Jadyn.

'What? How do you mean?'

'Said he was going too fast, had obviously lost control. He tried to get out of the way—that's why the tractor's at that angle—but there was nothing he could do to avoid the collision. Mentioned something about a wheel coming off as well. And if you look, you'll see he's right about that.'

Jadyn glanced over at Mike's Land Rover and saw that the front wheel on the passenger side was gone.

'Ripped off in the accident?'

'We'll need the collision investigator to confirm what actually happened. She's already on her way. We've not had a chance to look around for the missing wheel, but it's conspicuous by its absence, that's for sure.'

'What? You mean it's not here? Where is it, then? Wheels don't just disappear.'

Catherine shook her head.

'Could be anywhere within half a kilometre of here, or further,' she said. 'Sounds mad, I know, but I've attended crashes where wheels ripped off in the accident haven't been found for days. With enough speed, a good sprinkling of luck, and a clear enough path, you'd be surprised just how far a wheel can get on its own. And you wouldn't want to get in the way of one either, that's for sure.'

Jadyn thanked Catherine for her time, then made his way over to the man sitting in the paramedics' vehicle. The dog saw him approaching, and to his surprise, started to growl.

Jadyn came to a dead stop.

'Don't you worry about Nap,' the man said. 'He's just a grumpy old sod, aren't you?'

The man leaned over and gave the dog's head a scratch.

'Nap?' said Jadyn. 'That's a new one on me.'

The man laughed.

'He's been a lazy bugger from the moment he was born. Only reason we kept him was because no bugger else would have him. Don't regret it, though. He's not got the get-up-

and-go of my other dogs, but he's loyal. Never leaves my side, do you, lad?'

Nap growled again, but the sound subsided with another scratch from his owner, and he wagged his tail lazily in response.

'I'm Constable Okri,' Jadyn said. 'Just wondered if you'd be okay to go through what happened?'

The man gave a nod, then with a groan, stood up and held out a hand. He was in his fifties, Jadyn guessed, tall, almost unnecessarily so, with broad shoulders and hands like shovels. He was wearing canvas overalls which had, at some point in their life, been blue. No more, though, Jadyn noticed, the colour hidden beneath stains of oil, muck, and goodness knew what else.

'Barraclough,' the man said. 'Andrew, though most folk call me Nevis.'

Jadyn was confused.

'You don't sound Scottish.'

'I'm not. Tall though, right?'

'Ah,' said Jadyn, understanding the nickname.

'Nevis stuck with me since I shot up in my teens.'

'How are you, after what happened?'

Andrew gave a shrug.

'I've been checked over. Everything seems to be working fine. A few aches and pains, but that's all. I've been advised to rest a while. That won't be happening though, will it? I've jobs to do. As my dad used to say, I'll rest when I'm dead.'

'Are you happy to go through what happened?' Jadyn asked. 'If you do need a bit more time, that's fine. I'll need your contact details anyway, so I can pop round and visit?'

Andrew waved away Jadyn's suggestion.

'Best to strike while the iron's hot, like. So, yes, I'm more than happy to go through what happened.' Andrew looked from Jadyn to the crash and then back to Jadyn again. 'By which I mean, I'm not far off thinking I'll be pressing charges against Mike. Idiot nearly killed me by driving so bloody fast his front wheel came off and smashed into my windscreen!'

'You know Mike?'

'Everyone knows Mike. This is the Dales; everyone knows everyone else, don't they? But driving like that? It's not on. And it's not like him, either, is it?'

Jadyn took out his notebook.

'Just tell me everything that happened,' he said.

'Oh, I will,' said Andrew.

NINE

Harry spent all of five minutes in the office before heading straight out again to get himself over to where the crash had happened. Jim had arrived a few minutes before him, and Matt had just finished going through a few things in the Action Book, and updating him on the accident, when Harry had walked in.

'No Smudge?' Jim asked, as his own dog, Fly, padded over to greet Harry.

'Sadly no,' said Harry, giving the dog's head a scratch. 'She's with Grace today.' He avoided having to explain why, by turning to Matt and saying, 'Ben's been on the phone; I've heard about the accident.'

'I'm actually heading there now,' said Matt. 'Jadyn and Ethan are already there, and Liz and Dave are heading over to provide support. I'll let you know how—'

Harry jumped in before Matt could finish what he was saying.

'I'm coming with you,' he said, and noted the confused look on Matt's face, the detective sergeant clearly wondering why there was a sense of urgency in his voice. 'I know Mike,' he explained. 'We all do. Seems a bit out of character for him to be in any kind of accident if you ask me, so I'd like to be clear about what's happened from the off.'

'Makes sense,' Matt agreed, then added, 'You had breakfast yet, or do we need to grab something first?'

Harry checked the time. He was hungry, but he was more concerned about the accident than anything. He'd not said that his concern was also because of what Ben had said, because he didn't think he needed to.

He narrowed his eyes knowingly at Matt.

'My guess, Detective Sergeant, is that you've already had a little detour to the Penny Garth and are just looking for an excuse to pop in again. Correct?'

Matt did his best to look innocent.

'Always makes me feel like I'm in trouble when you use my rank when speaking to me,' he said. 'Bit suspicious, aren't you?'

'Detective, remember?' smiled Harry, knowing that when he did so, the effect was that of someone grimacing in pain, then glanced at Jim. 'You're good for a day at the office?'

'Absolutely,' Jim replied, sending Fly over to the radiator to settle down on his bed.

'How's things on the farm?'

'Busy. I'm glad I'm around more to help out, that's for sure. Mum and Dad are relieved, not that they'd say as much.' He sighed. 'Can't be showing feelings now, can we?'

Though there was humour in that comment, Harry noticed a faint note of something else there, too.

'Your dad's a Dales' farmer,' said Matt. 'Not in their nature to be doing that, but I've no doubt he, and your mum for that matter, appreciates you dropping some of your time here to be on the farm more.'

'I know,' Jim shrugged. 'To be honest, I think it's just that sometimes having me around more reminds them both of what they lost, you know, when my brother ...'

Harry placed a hand on the PCSO's shoulder, gave it a squeeze.

'You're a good son to them, Jim,' he said. 'And don't you forget it.'

'He's right there,' Matt agreed. 'Don't read too much into it. I reckon you'd be more worried if your old dad started getting all emotional.'

'True,' nodded Jim.

Matt crossed to the office door.

'Away, then,' he said. 'Best we get there sharpish, like; Jadyn's running things, so anything might happen.'

Harry laughed and followed Matt out of the office.

'Jest all you want, but he's turned out to be a damned good police officer.'

'He has,' Matt agreed. 'Good job, too, really, considering ...'

'Considering what?'

Outside, Harry took in a great lungful of the sweet, Wensleydale air, fairly sure just doing so did him good.

Matt stopped, looked at Harry.

'He's not mentioned it, then? He said he would, having spoken to me first about it to see what I thought. Of course, I pulled his leg a bit, but it's about time, isn't it? Jen should think about it, too, really. Well, not the same thing, obviously, but you know what I mean.'

Harry, who had come to a stop, instead of just marching

on to leave Matt behind, just stared at Matt, one eyebrow raised.

'No, Matt,' he said, 'I don't know what you mean, because I've not got the faintest idea what you're talking about.'

'Of course you have!'

'How can I, if Jadyn hasn't spoken to me about whatever it is you're talking about?'

Matt opened his mouth, shut it again.

'Well?' said Harry, keen to get moving.

'He's going to apply to be a trainee detective constable.'

'That'll be a walk in the park,' said Harry, heading off again, with Matt skipping along to catch up. 'He doesn't need to talk to me about it at all. Surely you told him I'd say yes and support it?'

'I said exactly that, but he wants your approval.'

'He doesn't need it.'

'There's a difference, Harry, between want and need, isn't there? He knows he doesn't need it because he's done his probation time and then some, and he's got plenty of experience, all of it good, because it's with us, right? Anyway, he wants it, because he looks up to you; having you tell him that yes, you think he'll be a great detective. Well, that's what he's after.'

Harry was rather taken aback by that.

'Really?'

'Yes, really!' Matt replied. 'You really don't see it, do you, the way everyone looks up to you? I mean, you've got absolutely no idea what people think of you at all!'

They'd reached Matt's vehicle, and Harry was happy to go in that rather than his own.

'Can't say I've ever really thought about it,' he said. 'I'm not exactly easy to get on with, am I?'

Matt opened the driver's door.

'Get in,' he said, shaking his head.

With Matt offering no further response, Harry dumped himself in the passenger seat and clipped in.

'I'll tell him I think he'll be excellent,' he said, as Matt pulled them out of the marketplace to head over to Swaledale.

'No, you won't,' said Matt. 'If you start praising him, he'll be confused, think something's wrong. I'll give him a nudge. All you need to do is let him come and speak to you, then be your normal self.'

'And what's that supposed to mean?' Harry asked, indignation throwing extra grit into his gravelly voice.

Matt laughed.

'Knew I should've taken you to get a butty on the way,' he said, then took a left at the surgery, and followed the same route Jadyn had taken earlier.

TEN

Ethan was back at the crash site when Harry and Matt arrived. He was surprised to see the DCI, because this was nothing more than a road accident, and really, it didn't warrant his attendance. The team had it all in hand, and as a DI himself, he was plenty capable of overseeing everything. He tried not to take it personally, knowing that the way the team seemed to work was to have everyone involved in everything, even the PCSOs. Ethan didn't have a problem with that, it just took a bit of getting used to. Went against the way most teams operated, but then, perhaps, that was just the way it needed to be in the Dales. He wasn't sure yet whether he liked it or not, but he was happy to give it time.

'Here comes trouble,' said Jadyn, as Matt pulled in behind where Ethan had parked the car.

'Here to check up on us?' Ethan asked.

'Shouldn't think so. Probably more concerned about Mike being involved.'

That made sense, thought Ethan, and said, 'Fair enough, showing concern for a friend.'

Jadyn fell quiet for a moment, as they watched Matt and Harry climb out of their vehicle to walk over.

'No, it's not that,' he said. 'Well, it is, partly, because of course it is, but he'd learn more about Mike by calling the hospital or just turning up, which is more likely, if I'm honest.'

'What, then?'

Jadyn screwed up his face a little, scratched his nose.

'Not sure,' he said. 'But my guess is that Harry thinks this is a bit odd.'

Ethan couldn't see what Jadyn meant by that. Accidents happen all the time. Mike was still alive, so that was a win for sure.

'Odd? In what way?'

Jadyn didn't get a chance to answer as Harry came over, Matt just a step behind.

'Mike?' said Harry.

'Air Ambulance,' said Jadyn. 'He's alive. Had to be cut out. Lost a couple of fingers. He looked in a bad way, Harry.'

'Then he's in the best place, isn't he?' Harry replied, casting his eyes over the tableau of mangled vehicles. 'Do we know what happened? Where's the driver of the tractor?'

Jadyn took out his notebook, flipped it open.

'Picked up by his wife,' said Ethan, who had just returned from the cattle grid to meet Mrs Barraclough, a woman almost half the size of her husband, but who made up for that by having enough personality for her very own BBC documentary.

'Who was it?' Matt asked.

'Driver was Andrew Barraclough,' said Jadyn.

'What, Nevis? That's his tractor and trailer? Surprised he left it there.'

That got an odd look from Harry, Ethan noticed.

'You are?' the DCI asked. 'Why?'

'You've not met Nevis, then?'

'Should I have?'

'Well, you'd know if you had, so I'm guessing not. He's huge. Could probably pick the tractor up in one hand and carry it back home tucked under his arm.'

'Scottish?'

'Nevis is his nickname,' Jadyn explained. 'On account of him being about the size of a mountain.'

Ethan saw Harry's expression change into what he assumed was something akin to a smile, though it was hard to tell.

'Rather like that one,' Harry said. 'What did he say? Was there anything from Mike?'

'He was in and out of consciousness,' Jadyn said. 'Had to use sedation to get him out of his vehicle.'

'That's a no, then. And this Nevis?'

Ethan caught a glance from Jadyn. The constable had run through what Nevis had told him a few minutes ago, and he understood the worry he saw in his eyes.

'In short, he said he was coming up the lane when Mike's Land Rover swerved round the bend at high speed and out of control. He did his best to take evasive action, steering as best he could out of the way. However, he saw one of the Land Rover wheels snap off as it then flipped and barrel-rolled towards him. The wheel slammed into his tractor cab, and then the Land Rover smashed into him.'

'Did he see if there was a reason for Mike driving like that?' Mike asked. 'Sounds very out of character.'

'How do you mean?' Ethan asked.

'Wayward sheep, deer, anything like that jumping out on

you, and despite your best intentions, you're swerving out of the way and careering down a ravine or into a wall.'

'He didn't mention anything like that,' said Jadyn. 'He was adamant that Mike was going way too fast. He was angry. Confused by it, too, I think. He knows Mike; couldn't work out why he would be driving like that. Neither can I, if I'm honest. Not like him at all.'

'Hopefully, the collision investigator will be able to help with all that, then,' said Harry.

'Oh, I wouldn't be so sure,' came a woman's voice from somewhere in amongst the wreckage. 'This morning, she nearly left the house without her shoes on. Only realised when she got to the car and wondered why her feet were so cold. Can't see me taking up barefoot running any time soon.'

Ethan, along with the others, turned round to see someone staring at them from the other side of the tractor. She was wearing a dark navy jacket. Her dark hair, though pulled back in a ponytail, was free enough to have a fringe dance around her forehead like stick insects caught in a breeze.

'Caitlin Price,' said Harry.

The woman lifted a hand in a wave, then disappeared behind the tractor cab as she made her way around to see them.

Ethan had been told by Jadyn of her arrival but hadn't actually met her yet. Her opening gambit hadn't filled him with confidence.

Caitlin approached and held out a hand to Harry.

'If I'm right, the last time we met wasn't too far from here, was it?' she said, then turned around and pointed in no particular direction. 'Something about a motorbike, I think. There were soldiers as well. It was mostly Sowerby, the pathologist, I worked with of course, but it was your case, wasn't it?'

Harry gave a nod of acknowledgement, remembering the incident she was referring to.

'What do we know about this, then?' he asked.

Caitlin frowned.

'Well,' she said, 'I've only been on the scene for a few minutes, but I'm absolutely confident in telling you there's been a serious collision.'

'Which involved someone we all know very well,' Harry replied, and Ethan caught the snap of the whip in his tone.

'I know,' said Caitlin. 'I was in touch with the hospital on my way in; he's stable, in surgery already, but the general sense is positive.' She rested her eyes on the ruin of the Land Rover. 'He's very lucky, you know. They're not the safest vehicles on the road, are they? And certainly not so if you end up in a situation like this.'

Ethan was impressed by how Caitlin's thoroughness clearly went further than just checking over what had happened at a crash scene. He wondered though why she had contacted the hospital in the first place. He had worked with crash investigators before though knew little of their role.

'Is it common practice to do that, to call into the hospital, find out about who was involved?' he asked.

'Absolutely,' said Caitlin. 'Information regarding injuries sustained in a collision help me to identify the factors that contributed to the collision in the first place. I don't have access to individual medical records, because that's anonymised. Also, I don't need it. I've a liaison officer at the hospital who can provide me with details of people involved, help me with blood samples, collect medical opinions. I need to know all possible factors involved, and that can be anything from drugs or alcohol to road conditions, arguments in the vehicle with a passenger, music, animals, state of mind, environmental conditions.'

'Sounds like a lot.'

Caitlin nodded knowingly, then leaned in close to Ethan and said, 'That was rather convincing, wasn't it? Almost believed it myself. If I'm not careful, I'll start sounding like I know what I'm doing.'

'I know you'll be getting a report to me on all this, Caitlin,' said Harry, 'and I'd ask you to expedite that as, like I've just explained, the person in hospital is well known to us all. But what can you tell us now? Anything?'

'Probably not enough, not yet, anyway,' said Caitlin, and despite her joking about, Ethan sensed that she didn't just know what she was doing, she was good at it and loved it. 'It's hard to tell right now exactly what happened. I'll be here a good while. Need to take measurements of tyre marks on the road, damage to the surface, position of the vehicles, all kinds of stuff, really. Boot of my car is full of gear I need to remember how to use so that I can get on with it and get that report to you ASAP. There's a wheel missing from the Land Rover, too.' She pointed at the tractor cab. 'My guess is that it hit that there, then continued on its way in a misplaced bid for freedom. So, I need to find that as well, take photographs, have someone come out and collect both vehicles so I can get them back and have a proper look.'

Harry, Ethan noticed, stayed quiet, and that seemed like just enough to have Caitlin speak once again.

'At a glance, and considering the road, the position of the vehicles, the damage, it looks to me like your friend in the Land Rover lost control and, in the process, lost a wheel.

Beyond that, I can't say, not yet, but I promise I'll get something to you as soon as I can.'

'Best let you get on, then,' said Harry.

Caitlin turned away and walked over to her vehicle, which was almost hidden behind the great bulk of the tractor.

'So, what do you think?' Matt asked, and with Jadyn, Ethan stared at Harry, waiting for an answer.

'I think,' said Harry, 'that I need to visit the hospital.'

Then, without another word said, he marched back to the vehicle he had arrived in and dropped back into the passenger seat.

ELEVEN

As they were heading off, Harry turned to Matt and said, 'Thought you said Dave was on his way over to help out? He wasn't with Liz when we passed her at the cattle grid before the moors, so I expected to find him here.'

'So did I,' said Matt. 'He'll be with Liz now, for sure.'

Matt took out his phone.

'Quicker to just drive there,' said Harry. 'Signal's iffy up here as well. We'll be there in a couple of minutes.'

And he was right; two minutes later, they were slowing down to speak with Liz.

'No Dave,' said Harry to Matt, as Matt dropped his window.

Liz came over.

'How's things? Anything on Mike?'

'No more than what you know already,' said Matt. 'Collision investigator's arrived, and she's got folk coming out to collect the vehicles.'

'Road should be open soon, then,' Liz said. 'No rush,

though; there are worse places to spend my day than up here with this view.'

'Anything from Dave?' Harry asked.

Liz shook her head.

'I thought he'd be down at the crash site.'

'So did we,' said Harry. 'You mind calling him?'

Liz obliged.

'Nothing,' she said, as her call rang off.

Harry looked at Matt.

'When did you speak to him?'

'Same time I spoke to Liz. What's that, two hours ago now?'

'Give or take,' Liz nodded.

Harry asked, 'And where was he when you called?'

'Meeting with a local wildlife group,' said Matt. 'There's been reports of someone taking eggs from nests and boxes. Not just birds of prey, either, but anything they can get their hands on.'

'How do you mean, reports? Sightings? Rumour? What?'

'All three,' said Matt. 'Dave's looking into it. Knows a fair bit about all that, what with those cameras he has set up all over the place.'

Harry knew of Dave's hobby of keeping an eye on wildlife. He had cameras set up in Snaizeholme, watching red squirrels, and as far as Harry was aware, various others up and down the dale to watch the daily goings on at various badger sets and nesting areas. He even had some for his precious goats. He had once claimed that watching them gambol about was better than anything he could ever find on television to watch. Knowing the kind of stuff he'd flicked through himself of an evening, Harry wasn't entirely surprised.

'So, where is he now, then?' Harry asked, unable to disguise the concern in his voice. 'Someone like Dave doesn't just not turn up, does he? Neither does he disappear.'

'I'm sure there's nowt to worry about,' said Matt.

Harry gave a low growl in disagreement.

'I'll be the judge of that. Do you know who he was meeting with?'

'Of course.'

'Then give that information to Liz, here.' Harry then looked past Matt at Liz. 'Liz? Can you keep trying him, please? And get in touch with whoever he was meeting with to see if they know where he is. Wherever he is, I need to know.'

Matt did as Harry requested, and Liz got straight on with seeing what she could find out.

'I'll keep you posted,' she said. 'Give my love to Mike.'

Harry tapped the dashboard a little harder than he meant to.

'Come on, Matt,' he said. 'Shift it.'

Matt did as he was ordered, wheel spinning just enough for Harry to see dust clouds behind them in the wing mirror.

'Sorry,' said Matt, glancing in the mirror, 'but you did say shift it.'

'It's not me you should be apologising to,' Harry replied. 'It's Liz; she'll be spitting grit out of her teeth for hours after that.'

Once back down in Askrigg, Matt turned left and was soon speeding along just shy of the speed limit.

'Want blues and twos going?' he asked. 'Means I can push it a bit more with the speed.'

Harry was tempted but shook his head.

'This isn't an emergency. Us turning up five minutes

earlier than if we just stick to the speed limit isn't going to make any difference.'

'I know, but sometimes, it's tempting, isn't it?'

'It's always tempting,' agreed Harry. 'But you only need it to go wrong once ...'

'Speaking from experience?'

'Not my own, but an officer who was working under me. He decided that getting his Chinese takeaway home before it cooled down too much was an emergency. Had people pulling over as he came down the road, obviously thinking he was trying to get to a crime scene, not home to a movie and a feast of sweet and sour pork balls and special fried rice.'

'What happened? Nothing serious, I hope.'

'I found out,' said Harry.

'Ah. Definitely serious, then.'

'You could say that.'

Harry fell quiet. He had a lot on his mind. The day had started off weird, taken a detour through bizarre, stopped at deeply concerning, and was now zipping through very worrying indeed.

The meeting that morning with a man he now knew to be his uncle had been eventful, more so than he had expected. Not that he enjoyed things when they got physical, certainly not when weapons were drawn, but it had certainly given him a buzz. He yawned, wondering if that was because of the comedown after the dump of adrenaline he'd experienced at having a pistol aimed at his face.

'Yeah, I could do with a coffee as well,' said Matt, glancing at Harry. 'We can stop in Leyburn if you want? I'll be staying on this road 'til we get to Whipperdale Bank, then head down through there anyway.'

Harry checked his watch.

'No, just keep going,' he said, stifling another yawn. 'I'll be fine.'

Then his stomach rumbled, and he caught a knowing look out of the corner of Matt's eye.

'Okay,' he said, accepting momentary defeat, 'we can stop. I could do with a bite to eat.'

'I'll pop into Andy's Bakery, then,' said Matt, trying not to smile too much at the promise of food. 'What do you want?'

'Whatever's coming,' said Harry.

Matt continued on, and soon they had whizzed through Redmire, where Grace's dad, Arthur, lived. Harry and Grace had been around to his for dinner just a couple of nights ago. Harry had hoped to get a minute or two alone with the old man to have a chat about something, but that hadn't happened. He'd have to arrange to meet up for natter with him some other time, though he had no idea how he'd go about that without Grace getting suspicious.

Soon enough, Whipperdale Bank welcomed them, and Matt turned off the road they were on to head down into Leyburn. He parked up and was out of the vehicle without a word, giving Harry a minute or two alone.

He was still unsettled by what had happened that morning. What his uncle had told him, asked him to do, it seemed ridiculous, but what could he do about it? Jameson had tried to prise it out of him, but Harry had remained schtum. It was for him to deal with, and Jameson had been a great help already, having driven up from Somerset as backup. Not that Harry had asked him to, mind; he'd insisted. And he was staying in the area, too, having used the journey north as an excuse to have a holiday. He'd rented a little place somewhere in the dale, but kept the location to himself, and promised not to get in the way, or go accidentally on purpose getting involved with anything he shouldn't.

Then there was the supposed cousin who had been waiting for him in Hawes as a well-dressed, and menacing, surprise. Harry had taken an immediate dislike to the man, so at least his judgement of character was as finely tuned as ever. There was clearly more going on than Harry knew, and that made him nervous. Not much he could do about that right now, but still, he'd have to keep his eyes and ears open just in case things turned nasty. He had a horrible feeling that they could.

As for what had happened to Mike, well, perhaps there was something in what Ben had said. Especially now, having seen the crash site and hearing what Jadyn had learned from the other driver, Nevis, and the collision investigator. He hoped there was nothing more to it, that Mike had a good reason to be where he was at the time, that he'd simply forgotten to record it in the diary back at the garage. But that didn't explain the speed, the wheel coming off, the sheer luck that he'd survived such a horrific crash.

And now, to top it all off, he had a missing PCSO; just where the hell had Dave got to? His disappearance made no sense at all. Harry had to assume it was nothing to worry about, because worrying about something never made a damned bit of difference to the outcome, whatever it was. But Dave didn't go missing, did he? It just wasn't his way.

The driver's door was yanked open, and a hand was thrust into the car.

'Here you go,' said Matt, leaning over the driver's seat to present Harry with two white paper bags dotted with grease. 'Take these, will you, before I drop the coffees?'

Harry took the bags and Matt slipped himself down behind the wheel.

'What've we got?'

'Would you be surprised if I said pies?'

'No.'

'But what if I said two pies each?'

'I don't need two pies.'

'You don't think you need two pies; that's different.'

Harry decided to not argue with Matt's wisdom as the DS clipped in his belt and started the engine. Harry placed the coffees into a couple of spring-out cup holders in the dash.

'To the hospital, then,' Matt said, and with that, reached for one of the bags from Harry, pulled out a pie, took a bite large enough to demolish half of it, then eased away from where they had parked.

A few miles down the road, Harry found himself tucking into his second pie.

TWELVE

Arriving at the hospital in Northallerton, Harry and Matt were soon on their way through a maze of corridors to track down someone who knew something about Mike.

'I really don't like hospitals,' Matt muttered, as they doubled back, having taken a wrong turning after attempting to follow directions from a nurse.

'No one does,' said Harry, trying to work out where they'd gone wrong, while doing his best to stay out of the way of the patients, visitors, and staff bustling around the place. He felt like he was in a giant ants' nest, hurried along by the pressure of everyone else racing towards their own destinations.

'Joan spent a lot of time here,' Matt explained. 'You know, when she got ill. Terrifying time it was for us both, like. But that time together, it only made me love her even more. Impossible not to, really.'

Harry took a left.

'You're a lucky man, Matt,' he said.

Matt laughed, and the sound seemed to relish bouncing down the hallway. 'And she tells me that every day.'

'You need reminding?'

'Of course I don't!'

Harry stopped, checked a sign.

'This way.'

'Sure about that?'

'Not in the slightest.'

Harry crashed through double doors, spotted a reception desk, and jogged over.

'DCI Grimm,' he said, doing his best to sound friendly, calm, approachable, though he knew his face often gave the opposite impression.

The young man on reception stared up at him, his eyes clearly hardwired to a special part of his brain focused entirely on making him look utterly disinterested. It was a relief to Harry to have someone not look at him wide-eyed in horror.

'We're looking for someone who's been recently admitted. Car accident. Came in on the Air Ambulance.'

'Name?'

'I've already told you my name.'

The receptionist's eyes narrowed just enough to really focus his disinterest by adding in a good helping of disdain.

'Of the patient?'

Harry sucked in a sharp breath, exhaled slowly; the inflection he'd heard at the end of what the receptionist had just said had immediately got under his skin.

'Mike,' he said.

'Mike ...?'

Harry heard the pause, turned to Matt.

'What's Mike's surname?'

'No idea,' replied Matt.

'But you must know.'

'Why must I? I just know him as Mike. Everyone knows him as Mike. A lot of folk in the Dales are known only by whatever nickname they were given as a kid, so in many ways, he's lucky.'

Harry couldn't believe that neither of them knew Mike's full name.

'Look,' he said, forcing a smile, then taking out his police ID. 'This is me, right? I'm a detective chief inspector.'

The receptionist managed to eye the ID without moving his head. It gave Harry the unnerving impression he was being dealt with by a ventriloquist dummy which had somehow come to life.

'My guess, and hope, I might add, is that you've not been inundated with patients arriving by helicopter. So, if you could, would you please just help me out here?'

The receptionist turned his attention to a computer terminal at his side.

'We have one arrival as you have described,' he said.

'And?'

'In surgery currently. And you won't be able to visit him for a good while after that either, for obvious reasons.'

'Define a good while.'

'Hours.'

'Can you be more specific?'

The look Harry received in reply told him that the receptionist was very much considering a reply laced with sarcasm. Instead, all he got was a simple, 'I'm sorry, no.'

Harry sighed and turned away from the receptionist to pace for a moment around the waiting area.

'There's no point us both being tied up here,' Matt said. 'I'll wait, you head off.'

Harry shook his head, not to disagree with Matt, but in disappointment at himself.

'Could be the rest of the day,' he said, as a man walked past, heading towards the double doors that led back out into the corridor. 'I should've checked.'

Harry saw that the DS's attention was now drawn by the man about to leave through the doors. He was shuffling as he went, walking as though carrying a heavy pack on his back.

'John?'

The man stopped, turned around, and Matt raised a hand in a wave that didn't want to be noticed. The man was early sixties, Harry guessed, with the telltale signs of a bald patch catching the light. Dressed in various shades of brown and beige, his clothes were creased and looked almost as tired as his eyes.

'John!'

The man turned round, stared at Matt.

'Matt?'

He made no attempt to move away from the doors, instead holding the handle of one as though to let go would be to have him crash to the floor.

Matt walked over, and with little else to occupy him, Harry followed.

'What are you doing here, John? Everything okay?'

Harry watched as the man lifted tired eyes to Matt's face, glanced at him briefly, then shook his head.

'It's ... It's Barnaby ...'

The pain in the man's voice was so sharp it turned every word to splinters.

Matt looked at Harry.

'This is John,' he said. 'Used to belong to the Mountain Rescue. Barnaby's his son.' He turned his attention back to John. 'What's happened, John? Is he okay?'

Considering where they were standing, Harry had no doubt that John's answer to that question was a very emphatic no.

John shook his head, slowly, deliberately, as though the movement itself caused him pain. His hand dropped away from the door handle, then his knees gave way.

Harry lunged, not looking to grab onto anything in particular, but just to do something to stop John from slamming into the floor like wet cement. He caught him, one arm under an armpit, the other clamping around his chest. John's dead weight nearly took them both to the floor, but Harry managed to stay on his feet.

Another voice called out.

'John!'

Harry, straining a little under the weight, and with Matt now trying to help him carry the man to a nearby chair in the waiting area, looked over his shoulder to see a woman running towards them.

'John! What happened? Is he alright? Oh God, it's not a heart attack, is it? Please don't let it be a heart attack! I can't lose him, I just can't! Not with what's happened to Barnaby. John! Please, Love, don't ...'

Her voice broke, leaving her sentence unfinished, though Harry could easily guess where it had been about to go.

'I think he's okay,' he said, trying to reassure her. 'Just seems exhausted, that's all. Needs a sit down, have a rest.'

'Sweet tea,' said Matt. 'Penny, can you sort that?'

The woman's eyes flitted from her husband to Matt and then back to her husband again. Harry noticed that she didn't even flinch at his own face, which was saying something.

'Penny?'

She looked again at Matt, as he and Harry lowered John into a chair.

'Sweet tea,' he repeated, voice calm. 'It'll do him a world of good, I promise. I'm sure there's a machine somewhere close by.'

Penny didn't move.

'Are you sure he's okay?'

A shadow reached over the small gathering, and Harry looked up. With some relief, found himself under the gaze of a tall woman in a white lab coat.

'I'm doctor Ashworth,' she said. 'What happened?'

Matt quickly explained, as the doctor checked John over.

'Exhaustion, I think,' she said. 'Sweet tea sounds like a great idea.'

'But you're sure he's going to be okay?' Penny asked again.

John opened his eyes.

'I'm okay, Love,' he said. 'I'm ... I'm sorry about that. Didn't mean to give you a scare. It's just with, well, you know, Barnaby, and being here, the lack of sleep, the worry ...'

Penny dropped herself on top of John, throwing her arms around his neck, both weeping.

Harry managed to pull his arms out from between Penny and John. He leaned back in his chair.

With a nod to Matt, he said, 'Tell you what, why don't I go and get John here that tea?'

He didn't wait for an answer and was up on his feet and out through the door before anyone could stop him.

THIRTEEN

By the time Harry had returned with the tea, John and Penny were gone.

'Something I said?'

Matt's response was to reach out expectantly for the tea.

'You don't like sugar in yours, so I may as well have it,' he said.

Harry sat down.

'Probably best they get themselves home anyway,' he said, wishing he'd sorted himself a tea as well. 'Looked like they were going through a rough time of it.'

Matt blew on his tea then sipped it.

'Barnaby, their son, was rushed to hospital last week. Been in an induced coma ever since to allow his body to recover. He called emergency services himself. John and Penny only know any of what I'm telling you because the staff at the hospital told them; Barnaby was unconscious when the ambulance arrived. He hasn't been in any fit state to tell anyone what actually happened to him, or how.' He gave his chin a thoughtful scratch. 'Mind you, there's a why in there as well, isn't there?'

'Is there?' said Harry. 'About what?'

'Barnaby's a baker. Owns a bakery in Reeth, and a quaint little café in Muker. Can't believe I've never taken you there. I'll have to rectify that. Joan loves the place. Mary-Anne seems to always get a free biscuit as well, usually one with chocolate. You should see her face after—what a mess. Mind you, mine's often no better, especially if I've gone for an apple turnover.'

Harry leaned back in his chair.

'Still none the wiser, Matt.'

'What? Oh, right, yes ... Anyway, like I was saying, he was unconscious when the ambulance arrived. He'd been vomiting not just the contents of his stomach but a lot of blood. They stabilised him, rushed him straight here. From what we've been told, they managed to communicate with him enough while they did all that doctor stuff, you know, IV fluids, blood transfusions, oxygen. They mentioned an endoscopy as well. Right now, his body's shut down to try and heal itself.'

'So, what happened to him, then? What had him vomiting blood and passing out?'

Matt shook his head, not because he didn't know, Harry guessed, but because he did, and he was disturbed by it.

'Rat poison.'

'Maybe he'd been laying traps to keep rats out of his bakery?' suggested Harry. 'Seems the most obvious reason he'd be dealing with the stuff. If he was tired and wasn't handling it right, it's easy to see how an accident can happen. Easy to do.'

'That's what the parents were saying as well, but they don't think that makes sense.'

'Why?'

'Because Barnaby, being a baker, is somewhat fastidious when it comes to cleanliness. John was telling me how his kitchen is spotless, at work and at home. Also, he has nothing to do with pest control at all, won't go near anything like that. Instead, he employs a professional, someone who knows what they're doing.'

'Then perhaps whoever it was didn't know what they were doing,' said Harry. 'Maybe we should look into it?'

'Glad you said that,' agreed Matt. 'I've suggested the same. Penny gave me the contact details for the person Barnaby uses. I'll give them a call later. Can't help but think the hospital should've called us to let us know it had happened.'

'Really?' said Harry. 'Why?'

'Well, it's poisoning, isn't it? What if it was deliberate? What if it's criminal negligence?'

Harry said, 'Hospitals have no obligation at all to call the police. We may want them to, like you've said, and I understand all of that, but a hospital is all about prioritising patient care and medical treatment.'

'But what if they think it's a bit odd?'

'If they think there's something suspicious about what's happened, if what they've been told happened doesn't match up with what they're dealing with, then the police are called in. It just doesn't happen automatically. And to them, it's easy to see how this sounds like nothing more than an accident. Just because the parents think it's off, well, that's not really enough, is it? But, like I've said, I think we should have a nosy, if only to help his parents understand what really happened.'

Matt fell quiet.

'Imagine it,' he said eventually, 'your kid ending up in here because they've been poisoned.'

'Awful, for sure,' said Harry, 'but point one, my guess is Barnaby is somewhat older than what you and I would regard as a kid. And point two, saying *they've been poisoned* suggests that you think it's more than an accident. Don't be swayed just because you know them and have seen a friend upset.'

Matt pushed himself to his feet, strolled around the waiting area, before returning to stand in front of Harry.

'So, what are we going to do, then?' he asked. 'About waiting for Mike, I mean. You were going to head off, I think.'

'We hadn't exactly decided, but thinking about it, that's probably the best solution, isn't it? If you're still okay to stay?'

'You head off,' said Matt. 'I'll let you know as soon as I hear anything.'

Harry stood up and walked over to the doors.

'Wait,' he said. 'How am I actually doing this? We came in your vehicle. If I go, you're stranded.'

Matt rummaged around in his pockets, found his keys, threw them to Harry.

'Take it,' he said. 'I'll message you when I need picking up. Just don't send Liz, okay? I've been on the back of that motorbike of hers, and I know how terrifying it is. Never again.'

Harry laughed at that, the image of Matt hanging on for dear life as Liz raced them through the dale with a grin on her face, burst into life in full technicolour in his mind.

'Wish him all the best from the team,' he said, then

pushed through the doors, and made his way out of the hospital.

Out in the hospital car park, Harry was heading over to Matt's vehicle, when he heard someone call out. Turning, he saw a woman waving at him, had no idea who it was, thought to ignore them, then realised it was Penny Shaw. He walked over to just make sure that her husband hadn't had another episode and didn't require actual medical help.

'Everything okay?' Harry asked, coming up to Penny and John's car. It was a large, brown estate, and looked old, but was in seriously good condition. Harry had no idea what the make was, had never really been into vehicles, but from it already knew a little more about John; if this was his car, if he was the one who had either renovated it, or owned it from new and kept it in tiptop condition, then he, like his son, or so Matt had said, was also meticulous.

'There's no way Barnaby could've poisoned himself,' Penny said, grabbing Harry's arm and taking him away from the car and her husband. 'He's too careful to do something that silly, believe me.'

'Accidents can and do happen,' said Harry. 'Even to the best of us. I mean, you only have to look at me to know that, don't you? Not blaming your son, by the way, just trying to help you not find yourself disappearing down a rabbit hole.'

Penny stepped back and stared, as though noticing Harry's terrible scars for the first time. Perhaps she was, he wondered, thinking back to when they'd first met in the hospital.

'That wasn't an accident, was it?' she said.

Harry shook his head.

'No, but I was being very careful at the time, believe you me, and I still got blown up. I'm just saying that things like this happen, and it's best not to jump to conclusions. However, I've been speaking with Matt, and I believe he's going to look into how the poison is used around your son's business.'

'He is?' Penny said. 'We really appreciate it as well. I'm just saying, though, that Barnaby can't be at fault. It's impossible.'

Harry gave a reassuring nod.

'Let's see what Matt has to say when he's done a bit of digging, shall we? Now, best you get yourselves home, don't you think? You're exhausted. You need to rest if you're going to be any use at all to your son when he wakes up.'

As if on cue, Penny yawned.

'We only know he'd called the ambulance because he rang us straight after he'd spoken with the emergency services. He collapsed on the phone, trying to tell us what had happened. We raced round to the bakery, worried sick, obviously, only to see the ambulance pulling away. Craig was there, too, and he had no idea what was going on. But when does he ever? We chased off after the ambulance. That was at one in the morning, I think; bakers work silly hours really, don't they?'

'I'm sure,' said Harry. 'And who's Craig?'

Penny's shoulders dropped under the weight of a heavy sigh.

'Barnaby's best friend from childhood.' She crossed her fingers together. 'Been like that from the day they first met at primary school.'

'Why was he round at the bakery?'

'Works for Barnaby part-time. Cleaner, van driver, that kind of thing. He cleaned up the bakery. He's good at that. Not the most ambitious, but there we are.

Harry bit his tongue because it was obvious that Penny was upset and worried about her son. He was feeling for Craig, though, and personally, he didn't have much time for people who judged others on what they did or didn't do as a job or career. Most often, the person doing the judging had zero idea about the other's circumstances.

'And you said Barnaby called you at one in the morning?'

'Yes, and that's really rather early, even for him,' Penny continued. 'He's not normally in 'til around four. We'd spoken to him the night before as well. Seemed quiet. No idea why. Been visiting him every day since. It's exhausting, but what else can we do?'

'Did Craig know why?'

Penny waved a dismissive hand in the air.

'Craig doesn't know much at the best of times, really. Means well, though'

Harry bit his tongue once again, then said, 'Running a business isn't easy. Being a baker, all those early mornings must catch up with you, so maybe that's what happened to your son?'

'I suppose, but even so ...'

Penny said no more, then, with a glance over to where her husband was sitting behind the wheel of their car, thanked Harry for his help, and headed off.

Back in Matt's vehicle, Harry kicked the engine into life. He headed out of Northallerton and soon saw the Dales' fells far off but drawing closer. The time was only just gone three in the afternoon. *So far,* he thought, *the day has somehow managed to pack in enough goings on to keep me busy for at least a month.* The temptation to just go home was overwhelming. Then Grace rang, and made the decision for him.

FOURTEEN

'What do you mean, pregnant?'

Harry knew the question was as ridiculous as it sounded, but still, he asked it for want of anything else to say.

Grace, who was leaning against the dining table, arms folded, was doing her best to not smile. Harry noticed an oily metallic smell in the air but couldn't quite place it.

'Vet confirmed it for me. Thought that was for the best. You didn't need to rush back, she's absolutely fine. Though, while you're here, you can have a look at this. It was delivered about an hour ago.'

Grace handed Harry an envelope.

'Special delivery as well,' she said. 'Must be important, considering it looks like it's just a letter.'

Harry took the envelope, then lowered his eyes to Smudge. She was sitting at his feet and, he felt sure, was also smiling sheepishly. Not that dogs smiled, because of course that was ridiculous, he knew that. Even so, the way she was looking at him ...

'How did it happen?'

In response to the question, Smudge stared up at Harry and wagged the end of her tail.

'Don't you go looking at me like that.'

Smudge's tail-wagging grew stronger.

'She never leaves my side. And if she does, she's with you, right?' Harry paused as a name floated to the top of his mind. 'Fly! It'll be him, won't it? The randy little bugger! Bloody hell, Grace, we're going to be overrun by puppies with the appetite of a Labrador and the energy of a border collie! Well, I tell you now, Jim's going to have to take some of the pups, because he's just as much a part of this as we are!'

Grace shook her head.

'It's not Fly. Jim had him snipped early on because he didn't want a load of puppies randomly appearing at the farm thanks to a bit of how's-your-father with one of his dad's bitches.'

'Then, which dog is it, if it's not Fly? Smudge doesn't really spend time with any others, does she? Whoever the owner is, I'm going to be having words, that's for sure, because they can't just go letting their dog have its way with—'

'I already have,' said Grace, interrupting. 'Dad had Smudge a while back, didn't he? Took her out with a mate of his who had a young Labrador with him. I think one thing just led to another.'

'Arthur's responsible for this?' Harry couldn't believe what he was hearing. 'Thought he'd know better. And how do you mean, one thing led to another? I think that's a marked understatement, don't you?' Harry took out his phone, at the same time slipping into his pocket the envelope Grace had given him. 'Who's this mate of Arthur's, then? Where does he live? What's his number?'

Grace's composure finally broke, and she burst out laughing.

Harry stared at her, his phone clasped in his hand.

'What?'

Grace's laughter subsided just enough for her to speak.

'You should see yourself right now; you're reacting like Smudge is your teenage daughter, you're the protective father, and you're off to find the lad responsible, shotgun at the ready!'

'I don't have a shotgun.'

'You know what I mean.'

Harry waited a moment, thinking about what Grace was saying, then stuffed his phone back into his pocket.

Grace pushed herself up from the table, walked over to Harry, and cut off whatever it was he was about to say by landing a kiss on his lips.

'Even so, Grace ...'

Another kiss, only this one was firmer, and lasted a good while longer.

'Well, I suppose if you put it like that.'

'It'll be fine,' said Grace, and she dropped to the floor to give Smudge a scratch. 'Won't it, lass?'

Smudge slumped down onto her side, then rolled onto her back, tail wagging. Grace obliged with a tummy scratch, and one of the dog's back legs started to kick in response.

'How did you know?' Harry asked. 'And how did I miss all of this?'

'You've never owned a dog before, so it's hardly on you,' Grace said. 'There were a few signs, changes in behaviour, that kind of thing. She was getting a bit clingy, not to you because she always is, but to me, which wasn't really like her. She's lost her appetite a bit as well this last while, and the few times I've had her with me, she's not had the energy she usually does. Was happier to just stay in the Land Rover and sleep.'

'I just thought she was a bit under the weather,' said Harry, dropping to the floor to join in on giving Smudge some fuss, and feeling more than a little guilty about not spotting what had been going on.

'So did I, to be honest, but then she started nesting.'

Now that was a word Harry hadn't been expecting to hear.

'Nesting? How do you mean? She's a dog. Hardly going out and gathering sticks and moss and feathers, is she?'

Grace sent Harry just enough of a look to let him know he was being ridiculous.

'She's been dragging blankets and cushions into the corner of the room,' she said. 'That kind of thing. Digging, too, and that's what had me check. She was out the back with me as I was cleaning my guns, and next thing I know, she'd disappeared!'

'That explains the smell,' said Harry. 'Gun oil, right?'

Grace gave a nod and lifted her hands to wiggle her fingers.

'It's a smell that lingers,' she said. 'Reminds me of childhood, helping my dad out. Anyway, back to what I was saying ... So, Smudge has gone, and my first thought is that she's jumped over the wall, which is not like her at all, is it, but what else could it be? There's me running around yelling her name, whistling for her, when out of nowhere she appears behind me with a face covered in mud.'

Harry noticed then that Smudge's face still held the telltale signs of her burrowing escapade, with flecks of mud on her fur, and her whiskers a little matted.

'There's now a hole in the garden big enough for her and a litter of pups. Amazing, really. A proper little den. She must've been at it a few days. I've not filled it in yet, not had time, and I thought you might like to have a look yourself; it's quite impressive.'

Harry's leg started to cramp, so he pushed himself back up onto his feet and strolled around the room to stretch it out a bit.

'Pregnant.' He sighed, shaking his foot mid-stride. 'Puppies, then.'

'The dad's yellow, so it'll be fun to see what colours we end up with.'

'Fun? How is any of this going to be fun? And what do you mean about the colours?'

'You've a combination of dominant and recessive genes in both the mum and the dad, so there's every chance we'll have yellow, black, and chocolate puppies running about the place.'

'How many?'

'Anything from one to thirteen.'

'Thirteen? You can't be serious? How the hell are we going to deal with thirteen!'

Grace gave Harry a moment to calm down.

'Usually a litter is around seven, though, so you don't need to panic too much. Though you've probably just got that out of your system, haven't you? Selling them won't be difficult either; both she and the dad are good gun dogs, and there's always folk looking for one of those in the Dales. We might even make a few quid from it. Probably best to get her spayed once she's done, though, unless we want the same thing happening again.'

'Which we don't.'

Harry dropped himself onto the sofa, and Smudge came over to rest her head on his lap. He gave her nose a scratch and thought then, quite to his surprise, that puppies might be a bit of fun. Not that he was about to admit that out loud, though. Not yet, anyway.

'How long have we got, then?' he asked. 'Like you said, I've never owned a dog, so I've no idea about any of this.'

'Vet thinks about a month now,' Grace replied. 'Hard to say, though. We'll just have to keep an eye on her and have somewhere ready for when she decides it's time. The outbuilding should be okay for that. We just need to give it a good clean, get a load of blankets in, make sure it's all comfortable and dry for her and the wee ones when they turn up.'

Harry wasn't so sure.

'They won't be cold out there, then?'

Grace shook her head.

'It's sheltered, dry. Means it's all clean and contained as well, rather than in the house. And Smudge will like that independence and privacy, instead of having us walking past her every few minutes and disturbing things.'

'Well, just tell me what I need to do, and I'll do it,' said Harry, when his phone buzzed. He read the message. 'Matt,' he said, and pushed himself back up onto his feet. 'Needs picking up from the hospital.'

'How is Mike?'

Harry realised then he'd not mentioned anything about what he'd been involved with that day over in Swaledale. That Grace knew already said all that anyone needed to know about the people of the Dales.

'Lucky,' he said. 'His Land Rover is a mess. They had to cut him out. Collision investigator arrived just before I headed off with Matt. Won't hear from her for a day or two, though.'

'Bit odd, though, isn't it?' said Grace. 'Mike in a road accident?'

'That seems to be the general consensus, yes,' nodded Harry. 'But accidents happen to the best of us.'

'Ben will be worried.'

'He's enough on his plate now, keeping the garage going on his own. But yes, he will be, and he is. I'll give him a call once I know how Mike is.'

'You'd best head off, then.'

Harry walked to the front door. Smudge followed.

'No,' he said. 'You're not coming with me. Not in your condition.'

Smudge sat down and stared up at Harry.

Grace said, 'She's fine to come with you. Probably do her some good.'

Smudge, almost as though she knew what Grace had just said, wagged her tail.

Harry opened the door.

'Come on, then,' he said. 'We'll go pick up Matt.' And with that, they both tramped over to the car and headed back down the dale.

FIFTEEN

Come morning, the team had assembled at the office, and two things were on their minds. One was the accident involving Mike, the other was the whereabouts of Dave. Mike's accident was still regarded as just that, an accident, and though everyone thought it odd, there was nothing yet to suggest that anything untoward had happened. As for Dave's whereabouts, he was no longer missing, so that was something, but he was still to arrive at the office and was now running late. Harry wasn't happy.

As the team milled about the small room, chatting over mugs of tea, and enjoying a supply of biscuits Jim had brought in for everyone from his mum, Harry took Jen and Matt to one side.

'Any thoughts on what's going on with Dave?'

Matt glanced at Jen, then back at Harry.

'Not really, no,' he said. 'And right now, we know as much as you do yourself about yesterday.'

'Run it by me again,' said Harry, who had heard from Liz

on his way back to fetch Matt from Northallerton to tell him as much as she'd been able to find out.

'He had the meeting with the wildlife group, which went well. He was shown evidence of what's been going on, video mostly, but also physical, as he was able to check out some of the boxes raided by whoever it is taking the eggs. A couple of the boxes had been taken off the trees and just abandoned close by.'

'Doesn't explain why he disappeared.' Harry spotted Liz on the other side of the office, and was fairly sure she wasn't supposed to be on duty. He called her over. 'Two things,' he said. 'First, how was Dave when you spoke to him yesterday? Did he sound a bit off, not himself, maybe?'

Liz didn't say anything for a moment, but her frown was telling.

'Subdued,' she said. 'Dave's usually all, well, you know ...' She made a gesture with her hands that Harry didn't quite understand.

'Loud?' he suggested, giving it his best guess.

'Yes,' she said. 'But more than that, right? He's big, isn't he, in everything he does? But for some reason, he sounded, well, small, actually.'

'Small?'

'That's the only way I can explain it; small. He was quiet, subdued.'

'And he didn't tell you what he was doing?'

'Just said something had come up.'

'That's not very Dave.'

'No, you're right, it isn't.'

Harry glanced over at the door. Dave didn't walk through it.

'And neither is him being late. Matt, you mind giving him a call?'

Matt pulled out his phone and turned away to walk out of the office.

'This is turning into an odd week,' Harry muttered to himself.

'Er, Harry?'

Harry looked to see that Liz was staring at him.

'Yes?'

'You said there were two things?'

'I did?'

Liz gave a nod.

'And you only said one, which was Dave. So, what's the second?'

Then Harry remembered.

'You're not on duty today, are you?'

Liz's expression showed that she was trying to think of an explanation.

'Didn't think so,' continued Harry.

'It was just that, with what's happened to Mike, and how Ben is about it, I thought I'd be more use here.'

Harry smiled.

'I understand that,' he said. 'But we'll be fine, I'm sure.'

'I really don't mind staying.'

'I do, though. If we need you, we'll call you. After the meeting, you're heading home, understood?'

Liz went to protest, but gave up immediately.

'Good,' said Harry. 'Now, sit yourself down.' He then turned to the rest of the team and said, 'Right, then, let's get the day started, shall we?'

The team all gathered together, dragging chairs into a half circle. Jim was there, too, and Harry found himself staring at Fly somewhat suspiciously, even though he knew the dog wasn't guilty of anything at all. He'd left Smudge at home, as he'd felt that a wild morning of jumping and bouncing around with Fly probably wasn't for the best.

'We're still waiting for Dave,' said Harry, 'but he should be along soon enough. So, why don't we get cracking?' He looked over at Jen. 'Action Book?'

Jen shook her head.

'And what's that supposed to mean?'

'Nowt much in it to action,' Jen said. 'Been a quiet couple of weeks. There's nothing urgent.'

'Doesn't need to be urgent,' Harry said. 'Run through what's been going on, just so we're all aware.'

He was playing for time, really, because he wanted Dave in the office, too.

Jen grabbed the book, which, Harry noticed, was looking rather tired and forlorn.

'Starting with last week, Jadyn and Jim attended a disturbance at the Bolton Arms in Leyburn—'

The office door opened and in walked Dave, cutting off Jen before she had a chance to say anymore.

Harry looked over to see that Dave was somewhat dishevelled. He was in uniform, but it was badly creased, and his hair was all over the place. He'd not shaved, either. Something was very clearly wrong.

Everyone stared at the new arrival, mouths agape at the state of Dave.

'Sorry I'm late,' he said, then yawned dramatically. 'I've been ... I mean, I've not slept well.'

'Everything alright?' Harry asked.

Dave gave a weary nod and yawned again.

'Doesn't look it.'

'I'll explain later.'

'Yes, I think you will,' Harry agreed. While Dave settled himself into a chair, he motioned for Jen to continue with her read-through of the goings on as recorded in the Action Book.

'You were right,' he said, when she finished a few minutes later. 'It has been quiet, hasn't it? Best we run through where we are with the road collision, then.' He looked over to Jadyn and Ethan, who were sitting next to each other.

Jadyn stood up, and said to Ethan, 'I'll jot it all down, if you're happy to run through where we are with it all?'

Even though Ethan was the higher-ranking officer, Harry was impressed that he was humble enough to sit back and let others take the lead. He was already showing the kind of team-player characteristics that would allow him to do well here. As for his obsession with being so neat and tidy, well, that would be dealt with in time, he was sure.

Ethan stayed where he was and started by running through the details everyone already knew: who was involved, what had happened, and where.

'The collision investigator oversaw the collection of evidence from the site, and the removal of the vehicles involved.'

'Did she give you any idea of when she'll be getting back to us with anything?' Harry asked.

'As soon as she has anything, was all she really said,' Ethan replied. 'She did say that at first glance there didn't seem to be anything out of the ordinary about what had happened, just a usual case of taking a corner too fast, and then a culmination of factors all coming together.'

'Like a bloody great big tractor being in the way,' said Matt.

'There's a wheel still missing from where the collision happened,' continued Ethan. 'A search was carried out, but it seems to have just disappeared.'

'Which it obviously hasn't done,' said Harry.

Jadyn said, 'We're going to go for another look once we're done here. The fields round there belong to only a handful of farmers, so they might find it at some point.'

Harry read through what Jadyn had written so far.

'Wheels don't just come off,' he said.

'Old vehicle, though,' said Jim. 'Bearings can come loose, and you have to keep an eye on everything with an old Land Rover. But that's half the fun of owning one.'

'And half the reason I'm mentioning it,' said Harry. 'If there's one person in the dale who knows about bearings and keeping an eye on anything mechanical, it's Mike.'

'You're sounding awfully suspicious,' said Liz.

'Not suspicious, just ... Well, yes, I suppose so,' Harry conceded. 'I'm not saying anyone's at fault, though if it's proved that Mike was driving dangerously, then that's another matter, isn't it?'

'But that would mean he was putting his entire livelihood in jeopardy,' said Jim. 'Why would he do that? Do we know where he was going when it happened? I've spoken to Ben, and he doesn't seem to know.'

Harry looked at Matt.

'Well,' said Matt, 'and we are checking up on him, just so you're aware, but Mike is currently in a medically induced coma. Reason being it was a severe enough crash to have the doctors want to protect the brain from further damage and reduce swelling.'

There were a few audible gasps in the office.

Jim said, 'What, Mike's got brain damage?'

'As far as I'm aware, it's a preventative measure,' said Matt. 'If the brain swells, that'll reduce blood flow and oxygen, so it helps with that. Also helps by reducing stress and helping the brain to heal, because the brain's activity is reduced.'

Harry was impressed with Matt's answer and told him so.

'I asked a lot of questions,' Matt explained.

'Was anything found at the scene?' Harry asked, eyes back on Ethan.

'Like what?' Ethan replied.

'What was the surface of the road like? Was there loose gravel, water, oil, anything like that?'

Ethan checked his notebook.

'Mike's phone was found outside of his vehicle.'

'Got thrown out during the crash, then.'

'Seems that way,' said Ethan. 'Looked like it was fairly beaten up before the accident,' he added. 'Amazed it was still working.'

'How do you mean?'

'It was held together with duct tape,' said Jadyn.

'Duct tape? Why would Mike use duct tape?'

'Maybe it was all he had to hand,' Matt suggested.

'You said it was still working,' said Harry. 'How do you know?'

'It was on when it was found,' said Ethan.

'Why?' Harry asked. 'Only reason I can think of is for music or satnav. And considering both the vehicle and the driver, you wouldn't hear music no matter how loud it was, not in an old Land Rover, and Mike wouldn't need a satnav to be driving over into Swaledale, would he?'

'There's you being suspicious again,' said Jen.

Harry went to speak, but Jen hadn't finished.

'And before you say it, I'll say it for you,' she said. 'Detective, remember?'

'Exactly.'

'Wasn't either of those actually,' said Ethan.

Harry narrowed his eyes at the DI.

'Then what was it? What was on Mike's phone?'

'My guess is that it just turned itself on due to being thrown from the vehicle during the crash and the impact when it landed,' Ethan said.

'That's not answering my question.'

Ethan looked again at his notes.

'Can't remember which one it was, and I didn't jot it down, but it was one of those end-to-end encrypted chat apps.'

'You mean like Signal or Telegram?' said Liz.

'It wasn't WhatsApp, that much I do know,' said Ethan.

Harry wasn't sure he cared because right then, he couldn't see how such a detail was important.

'Everyone has those on their phones now, though, don't they?' he said.

'I don't,' said Matt.

'Well, you're not missing much,' said Jim.

Harry considered for a moment what they'd been talking about, then looked over at Dave.

'Well, as there's little if anything in the Action Book to be worrying ourselves over for now, let's all see if we can't find that missing wheel from Mike's vehicle,' he said. 'Matt, you'll keep in touch with the hospital anyway, so any news on Mike, tell me. Ethan, I want you leading this for now, so gather the troops and sort out the details of where you're going and what you're going to do. The collision investigator will want the wheel, I'm sure, even if it's just a box-ticking exercise.'

He went to dismiss everyone and take Dave through to the interview room, when he remembered something else.

'Oh, and another thing, well, two things, actually; anyone know of the bakery over in Reeth?'

Everyone nodded, though it was noticeable that Matt's was the most vigorous. *A regular customer, no doubt*, Harry thought.

'Well, the owner, Barnaby Shaw, somehow managed to land himself in hospital last week due to rat poison. Bumped into his parents during one of their visits when we turned up at the hospital to find out about Mike. That'll need looking into, mainly because his mum seems convinced there's no way her son would be careless enough to do something like that.'

'It's easy to do,' said Jim. 'Have to be so careful with that stuff. Terrifies me. We have rats at the farm and use poison in traps, as well as shooting, to control them. You're never rid of them fully, though.'

'What's the other thing?' Liz asked.

Harry shook his head.

'It's Smudge,' he said, and saw looks of shock and horror in the eyes of his team. 'She's okay,' he added quickly. 'There's nothing wrong. I thought Fly was to blame initially, but you'll be relieved to hear that he's in the clear.'

'Fly?' said Jim. 'What are you talking about?'

Harry smiled.

'She's pregnant,' he said.

SIXTEEN

With the team gone, and Liz now on her way home, Harry was now in the interview room with Dave. As the team had all left the office, they'd all of them shaken his hand and offered him their congratulations at the news regarding Smudge and the impending litter of what, in Harry's mind, was at least a thousand puppies. Well, he'd thought, at least they were pleased about the news, because he still wasn't so sure that he was.

'Tea?' Harry said, having given Dave a minute or two on his own while he made a pot. He'd brought it through with the few biscuits left from Jim's mum. He didn't wait for an answer, just poured two mugs and handed one to Dave. No one refused tea in the dale.

Harry grabbed a biscuit, took a bite, and sipped his tea. Dave did the same. For a moment or two, silence was the main contributor to the meeting, but Harry wasn't about to interrupt; Dave knew why they were sitting together, so it was down to him to speak first.

'Good news about Smudge,' he said. 'You thought yet about who you'll sell the puppies to?'

'Not given it any space in my mind at all,' Harry replied. 'Will cross that bridge as and when. Just making sure she's comfortable right now, really, eating well, drinking plenty of water. We're going to sort the outbuilding for her; Grace thinks that'll be fine, better than having them in the house.'

'You'll love it,' said Dave. 'When my goats have kids, it's the best time of the year.'

'I'll take your word for it.'

Harry remembered having to chase one of Dave's goats through Hawes after it escaped the day he and Grace moved in together. That had been fun ...

Dave took another sip, finished his biscuit.

'I know you're waiting for an explanation,' he said at last. 'I feel terrible about letting you down.'

'Dereliction of duty is a serious issue, Dave,' said Harry.

'But it wasn't that. Something happened, and I had to deal with it. I knew you had enough of the team to sort the accident out.'

'Irrelevant,' said Harry. 'Not for you to decide, either. You're a PCSO, Dave, you're not in charge.'

'Wasn't suggesting that I was.'

'Then you need to understand that if I'm told you're on your way, then I expect that's exactly what you're doing. You're not suddenly on with something else because it's more interesting or exciting, or whatever reason it is you're going to give me for why you didn't attend the crash.'

Dave's eyes dropped to the last remaining biscuits.

'Well? What is it that came up yesterday, Dave, that caused you not to do what you'd been ordered to do? And does it have anything to do with why, when you turned up today, you look like you've been dragged through a hedge backwards?'

Dave looked up again and Harry could see real pain in the man's eyes.

'Whatever it is, it can't be that bad, surely,' Harry said. 'And even if it is, better we both deal with it rather than you on your own, don't you think?'

'I think I know who's raiding the nests for eggs,' Dave said.

Harry heard the weight of the words in his voice, so much so that as he said them, Dave's head sunk lower and lower, as though at any point, voicing them would drag his head through the table to the floor.

'Really? Who?'

'There's no evidence, though. Well, there is, but not enough.'

Harry leaned back in his chair, his mug of tea now resting on his lap.

'Again, who, Dave? If you know who's doing it, then we need to do something about it, don't we?'

'It's not that easy.'

'That's where you're wrong.'

'I'm not.'

Harry was finding Dave's reluctance to come clean a little frustrating.

'You do know how this works, don't you?' he asked. 'People do bad stuff. Illegal stuff. Our job is to find out who they are, what they've done, and stop them doing it. Very simple.'

'I wish it was.'

Harry finished his tea.

'Dave ...'

'It's my goddaughter, she's the one doing it!'

The words blurted out were so at odds with what they had just been talking about that Harry was fairly sure he'd not heard him correctly.

He sat forward, rested his now-empty mug on the table.

'You recognise her, then, from the footage you've seen?'

'Recognise her? I know her!' Dave replied, voice louder now, and strained. 'But not from the footage, something else.'

'Well, that doesn't make much sense. I didn't even know you believed in God, never mind had a goddaughter.'

'I'm a fairly private man,' Dave said. 'I don't go to church much, but when I do, I like it, makes me feel peaceful. Can't say that I do believe in God, but neither can I say that I don't. It's an ongoing discussion between me and whatever IT is; maybe that's the best way to look at it?'

'Okay, I can see that,' said Harry, 'but what's any of that got to do with you having a goddaughter?'

'You know I worked offshore for years, right?'

'I do.'

'Well, it meant I'd end up being in the Dales for a few weeks at a time. Rotations changed. Sometimes it was two weeks on, two off, other times it was four, sometimes even six on, six off. That's a lot of time to be hanging around at home. So, I'd keep myself busy, volunteer for things.'

'And?'

'There was a scheme at a school over in Bedale where adults could go in and sort of act as a mentor to the kids there. I did it a few times, like. Really enjoyed it. I'd meet up for a couple of hours every week with whoever it was I was mentoring, keep in touch while I was away. It was all about being an additional role model, helping them to develop social and emotional skills, that kind of thing. One girl, though, she was a right one, I can tell you.'

'In what sense?'

'Maddie was wild,' said Dave. 'Problems at home, problems at school. Ran away a couple of times. Seemed to be constantly striving to get kicked out of school, even though she knew it was where she needed to be.'

'And she's your goddaughter? How's that work?'

Dave shook his head.

'No, but her daughter is. It's years since I've done the mentoring. Maddie's early thirties now, can't remember her age exactly. Married. She asked me to be a godparent. I wasn't sure, but I said yes in the end. Don't think the husband cared. I used to pop round a fair bit, saw her daughter grow up, leave primary school, move to secondary school. But you know how things are, you lose touch, don't you? Not seen her in a few years, now. Sad, really, isn't it?'

'You're sure it's her daughter?'

'Positive.'

'Why?'

Dave reached into his pocket and pulled something out, which he then placed on the table.

'That,' he said, 'is evidence enough.'

On the table was a gold chain with a locket attached. Harry reached over, picked it up, and opened the locket. A photo stared back at him, one he hadn't been expecting at all.

'Found that at the base of one of the trees where a nesting box had been raided,' said Dave.

Harry lifted the locket up so that he could stare at it and Dave's face at the same time.

'Handsome chap, weren't you?'

'That's Maddie and me, just after she completed her A-

Levels. She was so proud. Me and her mum, we took her out for pizza. Her mum died a couple of years after that photo was taken. Then she met Gary, who she married a little too quickly, really, but she seemed happy.'

Harry rested the locket back on the table.

'Am I right in thinking you were round at Maddie's yesterday, then?'

'Went round to speak to her, but her husband answered the door. Realised there were problems as soon as I saw him.'

'Why?'

'Middle of the afternoon and he answered the door with a can of beer in his hand, could barely stand up. Told me Maddie was at work, slammed the door in my face.'

'Doesn't explain why you turned up looking so rough today, though, does it, Dave?'

'Slept in my car. Wanted to keep an eye on the place. Not just to see if Maddie's daughter was around, what she was up to, but also because the whole thing worried me. Maddie's the closest thing I'll ever have to an actual daughter of my own. I didn't know what else to do.'

'There's talking to me, for a start, isn't there?' said Harry, resisting the urge to reach out and give Dave a slap. 'You can't just go off doing stuff like this. For a start, it's dangerous; you've no idea what this Gary is like, what's going on at home, anything!'

'I know ...'

'You need to give me a while to think about this, Dave,' Harry said. 'That okay with you? Well, actually, don't answer that; it has to be.'

Dave fell quiet.

'Dave?'

'Yes, you're right. I know you are. I'm sorry. I ...'

Harry stood up.

'I need you to head off and join the rest of the team,' Harry said. 'Whatever's going on with Maddie's daughter and her thieving eggs, you need to park that for the moment and focus. Understood?'

'Yes.'

Harry walked over to the door to the interview room and opened it.

'Get yourself gone, then,' he said. 'We'll chat about this later.'

Dave left the room. Harry closed the door behind him, sat back down in his chair and wondered where most of the morning had gone and what he was going to do with the little that was left.

There was plenty to be getting on with, he knew that, and it would easily take him into the afternoon, but where to turn his hand exactly, he wasn't sure. In an odd way, he felt almost surplus to the needs of the team, because they were working so well together now. And really, a road collision wasn't going to be all that taxing, was it?

Or was it? he thought. Because something had niggled him from what Ethan had said about Mike's phone, the app that had been open on the screen when it had been found.

The duct tape detail was weird, too, wasn't it? Why would anyone use duct tape to fix a phone? Well, at least it would distract him from the meeting in the café the previous morning. Or it would've done if, as he'd left the interview room, a certain man hadn't been standing in the entrance hall of the community centre waiting for him like a cat hunting a mouse.

SEVENTEEN

Caitlin Price, despite all that she did to try and pretend to be the exact opposite, was really rather good at her job. She knew it, too, which was why she always made out that she wasn't. Or maybe it was that her self-deprecation was a barrier to hide behind, a way to try and draw attention away from herself.

Probably a bit of both.

Throw in a childhood of never being good enough for one's parents, a private education at a boarding school, and ending up at university with no real idea of what she actually wanted to do, and Caitlin knew that the biggest fight she had most days was to accept that she had to be seen. She really didn't want to be.

All she actually wanted to do was stay at home, to shut the front door on the world, and disappear into a fantasy world of imaginary characters exploring wild worlds. Reading was her thing, for sure, and she positively devoured books, but what she never told anyone, not a soul, was that she was also a writer.

Caitlin's mind was a machine that simply refused to switch off. Sleep could be a problem because of it, which she combatted by reading until her eyes felt like they were going to fall out of her head, or by listening to audiobooks. If things got so bad that neither of those worked, she'd get up, regardless of the hour, make a mug of herbal tea, get out her laptop, and type.

How many books was it now? she wondered. She'd lost count, if that was possible. Not of the ones she'd finished, because she hadn't, not yet, but of all the ones she'd started and never completed.

The reasons for this were many and varied. Some she'd dropped because they were rubbish, especially her earlier works, books she'd started to pen in her teenage years, great sprawling romances across vast distances between the stars that had burned up in the atmosphere often mere moments after launch. So many scattered first and second chapters, so many characters waiting on a page, their lives barely started, their dreams mere ghosts.

Others she'd dropped due to distraction; doing her degree, falling in and out of love, starting work, getting a promotion, travelling the world, coming back to start a completely different career, which just so happened to be the one she was now in.

Some of those unfinished pieces had shown promise, she was sure of it. Characters who had lived and breathed when she'd thought about them, who had leapt off the page, begging her to forge a path ahead for them, through the dark mountains of the most terrible, terrifying tales they knew lay ahead, for was that not the reason for them to even be in the first place?

Now, though, there was, at last, one book she'd not given

up on. In fact, she believed in it so much, she'd even gone ahead and sent off the first three chapters to numerous literary agents in the hopes of something happening, something dreamlike and impossible, surely, because there was no way she was ever going to be published, was there? But she knew she still had to try, because if she didn't, then what was she, really?

Today, she was staring at the forlorn carcass of a smashed-up old Land Rover. She'd already had a look at the tractor it had crashed into and learned all that she could from that. Namely, that in such an impact, a tired old Land Rover would always come off worse. There was, of course, the smashed windscreen from the Land Rover wheel, but the wheel hadn't been found, though the police team she'd met had said they would be on with that today. She wasn't sure what she could learn from it if they did, but it seemed right and proper to have it found anyway. At least then, she would be able to say for sure that it didn't tell her anything.

She'd been up early, writing. Because of this, for the second time that day, Caitlin was nursing a herbal tea. Staring at the old vehicle, she found her mind drifting off into her work in progress. No agent had yet replied, but that wasn't about to stop her. This was the first time she'd realised that she wasn't simply penning or writing something. No. This time, she was crafting a story.

Crafting! Ha! Ridiculous, Caitlin thought as she sipped her tea. How could she ever think that? And what would her dad say? Not that it mattered, seeing as the old git was dead. And bless him if he wasn't still controlling her life, because wasn't he - and what had happened to him - the only reason she was standing where she was, doing the job she was now doing?

He'd love that, she thought, that even in death he had influenced the direction of her life. But what choice had she had? The investigation into the accident that had killed him had been a right proper balls-up from the off. She'd known that, everyone had, but no one had done anything about it. Though, she still didn't know why she had been so incensed by it all.

Maybe it had been for the sake of her long suffering mum that she'd gone back to college, aced the necessary qualifications, got a job in the relevant role, worked hard, and eventually, through being a royal pain in the arse as much as being so bloody good at the role, reopened her dad's case and proved what she'd always known; someone else had been responsible. Her work had led to a conviction and some faint praise in the press.

What had meant the most, however, was that her mum, on hearing what her daughter had achieved, had promptly had a heart attack and died. To this day, Caitlin found the whole thing rather funny, like Fate had played a dark prank, and she was the butt of the joke.

Despite everything she'd done to help, she had still been left on her own. There was no blame, no remorse really either, or sadness, but there was an emptiness, and it was that emptiness Caitlin filled, not with the work, but with the writing, building her own world the way she wanted it to be, because so much of her life had been lived in a world not of her creation or her choosing. What she was now, was fully in the moment, because she was no longer under the shadow of either parent. Which was why, as she was looking through the various items pulled from the Land Rover, all of them in neat little bags on a workbench in front of her, her eyes were drawn to the phone.

Each piece from the vehicle had accompanying notes, and as she flicked through to those on her iPad, her mind was immediately drawn to an anomaly, the phone. There was another, as well, something about that missing wheel wasn't right. That still needed a little more examination, if only to confirm what she was thinking, and it really did need confirming, too, because right now, her conclusions really didn't make any sense at all.

As to the phone, well, it had been switched on when it had been found on the road beside the Land Rover. There was nothing unusual in that of itself, because phones were often on in vehicles, whether they were supposed to be or not. That it had been showing an open chat on one of those apps she hated, well, that had confused her. At first, she'd thought that the accident had simply caused the app to open, but on further investigation, it was clear that was not the case. No. Because instead, the app had been open for some time, hadn't it? And on a video chat, of all things. But why?

Then there was the duct tape. The phone had been wrapped in it, carefully enough, too, to make sure that the screen was accessible. On removal of the tape, she'd discovered that her initial thought that it was there to fix it, to keep the phone together, was completely wrong. The phone was in good condition, and the tape was serving no purpose at all. Well, certainly not in keeping the phone in one piece.

Further investigation of the Land Rover, however, had discovered more of the duct tape, attached to a bent piece of metal bolted to the inside of the Land Rover just to the left of the driver. It hadn't taken much of a leap to realise that the phone had been attached to the piece of metal with the duct tape, and for a while Caitlin had found the primitive approach to fixing a phone into a vehicle laughable. She'd also found herself thinking how these little details would be great in a novel, because real life really was stranger than fiction.

Then she'd got to thinking about the whys, the reasons for it to be where it was, and having scratched out the use of satnav, she'd been left with a disturbing thought; the driver had had the app open on the phone, not just for texting, or for talking, but with his camera switched on so that whoever he had been speaking to could see him. That had led to one final, god-awful thought: someone, somewhere, had watched the whole accident unfold.

EIGHTEEN

The man was dressed in the same clothes as the day before, the only difference being that despite being inside, he was now smoking a cigar.

On seeing the man, Harry stayed where he was, standing outside the interview room, glaring down the corridor at the new arrival. He'd not liked him the first time they'd met, because really, what was there to like? Though they'd said little to each other at the time, the undeniable feeling he'd been left with was one of threat. That feeling only increased with this second appearance.

That wasn't to say that Harry felt in any danger. Quite the opposite. He'd been threatened so often that at one point, back in his life down south, not a day went by without someone trying to get in his face about something, telling him what they were going to do to him, how painful it would be. He'd heard it all, from blow torches to barbed wire, from hammers to being hung by his thumbs from a steel beam, and he was still here. Water off a duck's back, all of it. Harry knew that the people you really wanted to be afraid of weren't the ones who were threatening you. No. It was the ones who bypassed threats completely and just got on with it, nastily.

Harry walked up to the man, and without a word reached up for the cigar, snatched it from his mouth, pushed past him, through the double doors of the Community Centre, and into the outside air. He then dropped the cigar onto the tarmac beneath his feet and ground it into mush with the heel of his shoe.

He heard the door open behind him but didn't bother turning around.

'Have you any idea how much that cigar cost?'

Harry ignored the question.

'What do you want?'

'Just a chat. How about over lunch? It's nearly midday, isn't it? Surely somewhere in this backwards place serves something edible.'

Harry gave his blood a few seconds to boil at the slur against Hawes, then said, 'Come back tomorrow. I won't want to speak to you then either, and I definitely won't want to be sharing lunch, but it'll give you an excuse to get out and about a bit again, won't it? You obviously have little else to do if this is how you fill your time, harassing police officers.'

'Am I harassing you?'

'I don't know, are you?'

The man stepped closer.

'I heard about what you did. To Dad's bodyguards. They're not happy.'

'Give me a moment while I fetch a violin.'

'Do you often break the hands of those trying to protect others?'

'Not always, no,' said Harry, and held out his hand as

though offering a handshake. 'I'm happy to break yours for no reason at all, if you'll let me.'

The man grinned, slipped his hand into Harry's own.

'It would be my pleasure.'

Harry felt fingers clamp around his palm and squeeze.

'Work out, do you?'

The squeezing increased.

'A little. What gave it away?'

'Nothing,' Harry replied. 'Yet.'

'Yet?'

'Gym strength, it's all for show, isn't it? Makes you look good, makes you feel good, but there's no stamina to it. What do you bench? One-fifty?'

'Good guess. One seventy-five.'

'That's your one-rep max, then. Not bad.' Harry gave the man's hand a quick, sharp squeeze, heard a gasp. 'Your grip, it's impressive, I'll give it that, but how long can it last? That's what I want to know.' He gave another squeeze, this one harder, and knew from the look in the man's eye he'd sent a pulse of pain through his body. 'I doubt I could bench the same as you, not now, anyway. But ask yourself this ...' He held up his free hand, which, like the other, was a gnarled thing of scars from the IED, calloused from his life as a soldier, and rough from those days working undercover. His fingers were thick, like knotted rope. 'Does this look like the kind of hand that can't take a bit of pain?'

At that, Harry felt the man start to squeeze back, trying to crush his hand like a vice.

'I don't know what it is that you want,' he said. 'All I know is that what your father said to me, is between us, not between us and you. In fact, there was no mention of you. None. I didn't even know you existed until you turned up yesterday like that one relative no one wants at a wedding because most have forgotten you, and those that haven't probably hope you're dead. Maybe there's something in that for you, maybe not. Regardless, whatever your problem is, it's with your father, not me.'

Harry paused, thinking he'd finished what he had to say, then realised there was more, so just kept going, refusing to let the other man, still held in his grip, get a word in edgeways.

'Cousins we may be, family we are not. I have a job to do, other things considerably more important than standing here playing some piss poor version of peanuts. So, please, do me a kindness, and yourself a favour, tell me exactly what it is you want, or think you want anyway, and then go? Because I can't be doing with wondering if you're going to pop up round every damned drystone wall in the Dales looking like a reject from a low budget gangster movie.'

And with that, Harry gave one final, violent squeeze.

The man's eyes went wide, he let out the faintest of whelps, and Harry let go.

'Well?' Harry said.

The man lifted his hand and stared at it a moment as he tried to shake it free of pain.

'That's ... that's police brutality.'

'Not yet, it isn't, but you're getting very close to finding out what is.'

Harry was actually quite shocked by his own behaviour, but something deep-seated told him that this was the only way to deal with his cousin. Politeness wouldn't work, neither would the threat of arrest. Instead, it had to be strength, and a willingness to go just a little too far if required.

The man flexed his hand, then gingerly slipped it into a jacket pocket.

'He can't give it all away. He can't. It's mine. It was promised to me. I've worked for it.'

Harry said nothing, just waited for the man to continue, because it was very clear he had more to say.

'What, he thinks it will absolve him, is that it? It's dirty money, all of it. He's a bad man, Harry, like your dearly departed dad, only worse. Heaven won't let him in, no matter how many good deeds he thinks he can now achieve.'

Harry closed his eyes, leaned his head back, and for a moment simply enjoyed the brightness of the sky through his eyelids, and the gentle caress of the breeze on his skin. He hadn't asked for this, hadn't looked for it, and yet here it was, someone else's shitstorm for him to navigate.

Harry opened his eyes again and lowered his face to look at his cousin. Then he smiled.

'You really don't know anything at all, do you?' he said, and with that, turned on his heel and headed towards his Rav.

The man didn't follow, of that Harry was glad, but he sensed the daggers from his cousin's eyes stabbing him in the back. Then his phone buzzed, knocking what had just happened from his thoughts. He checked the screen and saw a simple, two-word message from Jadyn: 'Found it.'

As he then went to make a call himself, the phone buzzed again, this time with someone calling him on a number he didn't recognise.

'Grimm.'

'It's Caitlin Price.'

Harry took a moment to remember who that was, then said, 'Actually, I was going to call you. The phone …'

'What?'

'The phone, it's bothering me,' said Harry. 'Something's not right, I just don't know what.'

'I was calling you about the exact same thing. Got a minute?'

'I've as many as you need right now. The wheel's been found, by the way. Heard just as you called.'

Caitlin was quiet a moment, then said, 'You're not busy, then?'

'Why?'

'I'm coming over.'

Before Harry had a chance to reply, the line went dead.

NINETEEN

As soon as Caitlin had hung up, Harry had tried to call her back with no success. He'd tried a further three times, then given up, and called Jadyn.

'Where are you?'

'At the Dales Bike Centre,' said Jadyn. 'The owner of the field the wheel is in is meeting us here.'

'Why there? Why aren't you meeting where the wheel is?'

'He wouldn't tell us where it is. The location of the wheel, I mean. Said he didn't want a convoy of vehicles roving across his field and making a mess.'

'A convoy? Bit of an exaggeration.'

'Also, he said he had better things to do than spend the rest of the day pulling us out of the mud we are bound to get stuck in.'

Harry told Jadyn he'd be over as soon as Caitlin arrived, and that he should, as soon as he knew, send the location to him, but not to tell the owner of the field someone else would be joining them.

With Caitlin at least an hour away, Harry was stuck with little to do besides going back to the office and to try and look busy. The whole episode with his supposed cousin had left him on edge, so he knew that he couldn't just sit and do nothing. Flicking through the Action Book didn't help either. He found himself wishing that Smudge was there to keep him company, but he was happy that she was with Grace and being looked after properly.

Jumping on the office computer, Harry did a search for cafes in Muker and bakeries in Reeth. The list provided wasn't exactly extensive, so Harry quickly found the establishment he was looking for.. The website for the business provided a bit of history, so Harry read the biography of the owner, Barnaby Shaw. There was nothing in it about his parents, but just enough to say he'd been brought up in the Dales, had stumbled almost by accident into the world of baking, and that the rest was history. He'd won awards as well, and a good number of them judging by the list, none of which Harry had ever heard of.

What Harry wasn't getting a sense of was how Barnaby, who's face shone out at him proudly from the screen, could have made such a foolish error with rat poison. The website, what it said of the business, how it had grown, the awards and accolades and reviews, did not point to the kind of person who would get it so wrong with something so deadly. And that was another thing; did rat poison really affect a human so dramatically and so quickly?

Harry started to do a deep dive into poisons, during which Jadyn sent him the location of the field containing the wheel from Mike's Land Rover. He knew a little about poison, having come into contact with it during various cases, but researching it in any sort of detail he'd always left to others, and he was surprised by two things; one, that it was so readily available, and two, that the main customers seemed to be gardeners, judging by the websites he was trawling through.

It struck him as bizarre in the extreme that from the same website he could order garden furniture, a birdbath, vegetable seeds, an axe, and enough rat poison to rid half of London of the long-tailed menace. He also found a link to a poison garden up in Northumberland, which struck him as a very macabre tourist attraction, plenty of links to crimes involving poisoning, and even a clip from a government safety video from the seventies.

That film was called Apaches. It supposedly warned children of the dangers of playing in farmyards, with one of the characters in the film dying from drinking rat poison. Mind you, that hadn't been the worst death in the short film, not by a long shot. That trophy belonged to the poor sod who had drowned in a pool of slurry. The mention of the movie took Harry straight back to one of his first cases in the Dales; and to think he'd thought moving north was going to be dull.

Harry lost track of time as he clicked through link after link, trying to absorb as much as he could. And in the end, what he concluded was that modern rat poisons, though effective, didn't immediately lead to death if come into contact with accidentally. In fact, to do so at all was unlikely, with UK law now requiring the use of bait stations if poison was being laid. Harry simply couldn't work out how someone running a bakery, winning multiple awards, would then be so remiss in handling something that would not only put him in hospital, but also put his entire business at risk. It made no sense. Maybe tiredness had played a factor in what happened. After all, hadn't Barnaby's mum said her son had seemed quiet when they'd spoken to him the night before?

Harry shut down the computer. It had been interesting, for sure, reading up on Barnaby and then the various ways in which rat poison killed, but in the end, all he was seeing was a tragic accident.

He was about to give the hospital a call, not only to see how Mike was, but to check up on Barnaby Shaw, and then nip out to grab something to eat, since lunchtime had already flown past, when there was a knock at the office door.

Harry got up to answer it, only to have it open before he arrived.

'Caitlin,' he said, as the collision investigator stood in the doorway in front of him.

'Took me longer than expected,' Caitlin said. 'So, where are we going?'

Harry decided the best way to answer that was to take her there.

'Come on,' he said. 'We can talk about the phone on the way.'

TWENTY

Though Caitlin did her best to start a conversation, Harry kept quiet for the first ten minutes or so of the journey. Not because he was being rude, but more so to just go through everything he'd been reading up on, about Barnaby, and about rat poison. He was also somewhat taken up with eating a tasty pie from Cockett's, which he'd nipped out to purchase before taking himself and Caitlin over to the lost and now found Land Rover wheel. Caitlin herself had declined the offer of something from the bakery, because she'd already eaten on the way.

By the time Harry had finished the pie, and brushed a good sprinkling of pastry flakes off his trousers and his seat, they were only a minute out of Askrigg. Driving through the village reminded him of Gordy, of Anna, and the happy memories briefly mixed with sad ones, which suited the smile he wore as they drove past the church.

Caitlin, however, hadn't stopped talking. About what, Harry wasn't so sure, as he'd not been listening. It had started about the phone, but he'd not joined in, and since then, the topic had morphed into various other things. Now, as he tuned back in, she was talking about books, not a strong subject for him at all.

'... which I've just finished, and it was amazing. Best book I've read in years. Well, maybe. Anyway, like I said, fiction is what I read. I've tried self-help stuff, because I was advised to, but it didn't do anything for me. I guess I just like escaping into imaginary worlds. So, what's your favourite book, then?'

'Not really a reader,' Harry replied, now aiming them up into the fells, rumbling out of Askrigg, and past the house of one of his favourite humans, Margaret Shaw, the district surgeon. He'd not seen her in a while, nor her daughter, Rebecca, which was almost a good thing, really, considering the circumstances that usually conspired to have them bump into each other.

Harry realised Caitlin had, at last, gone quiet. He glanced over at her, saw her staring at him, a look of bafflement in her eyes.

'Something I said?'

'You don't read at all?'

'Oh, I read, sometimes,' said Harry, and remembered Gordy a good while ago now persuading him to give it a go, even buying him some books to start off on. 'But then I forget, and months go by, and when I pick the book up again, I've forgotten what was happening.'

'You should read more often, then,' Caitlin suggested, wagging a knowing finger at Harry. 'Just fifteen minutes a day.'

'I'm too busy most of the time.'

Harry felt the wide-eyed stare from Caitlin only grow at that statement.

'Too busy? Really.'

'Yes.'

'Do you watch television?'

'What's that got to do with anything?'

'I'm just asking; do you?'

'I guess.'

'What, an hour a night, maybe, more at the weekends?'

'Depends what's going on, I suppose.'

'Regardless,' said Caitlin, 'you've got enough time to sit and watch television, which is passive and requires nothing of you and, well, anyways, if you can do that, you can spare fifteen minutes for a book, can't you?'

'Lot of effort, though.'

'That's not a bad thing.'

'Never said it was.'

The conversation stalled. Harry drove them along the narrow lane, and soon the sound of a cattle grid thrumming the tyres presented them with open moorland.

'We're not far off where the collision was,' he said. 'You fancy another look while we're here?'

'What about the phone?'

'We can talk about that while we're having a nosy, can't we?'

Not for the first time, Harry was lost then to the beauty of the Dales. Here, up on the fell tops, the landscape presented a vista as bleak as it was beautiful. Slowing down automatically, just so he could enjoy it for a few seconds longer, he dropped his window into the door and took in a breath of the air. Sweet notes of honey mixed with deeper, earthier scents, as he drank in the pollen from the heather, which took as its dance partner the damp notes of peat from the moorland it called home. Beyond that, other scents came to him, of meadows and the beasts that occupied them, all curling in and out of everything from tractor diesel fumes to the musty perfume of small woodlands. God, it was heavenly.

'It's certainly beautiful up here,' Caitlin said, as Harry, approaching now where Mike had had the collision with the tractor, began to slow down.

'Never ceases to amaze me just how much,' Harry replied. 'Back in the Paras, I used to be outside an awful lot, spending my time tabbing across moorlands in the worst weather, but I never really appreciated it then. Had other things on my mind, I suppose, like getting some sleep, finding time to eat, staying warm, being the best soldier I could be. Now, though, I can't get enough of it. Have to pinch myself sometimes that I'm here at all. Lucky man, really, and I never thought I'd ever say that. Might even be the first time.'

Harry slowed to a stop, pulled off the road.

'How did you end up here?' Caitlin asked. 'That accent, it's not exactly Yorkshire, is it?'

'Neither's yours.'

'I don't really have one. Blame private education.'

'Well, that's something I can't do.'

Harry turned off the engine, climbed out. Caitlin did the same and came around to stand with him.

'You're very mysterious,' she said.

'Not really,' said Harry. 'Just not much to tell, really. Paras, police force, somehow ended all the way up here from Bristol. Best thing that ever happened to me.'

Caitlin began walking up and down the road, where Harry could still make out the scars of what had happened the day before. To most people, he knew that all they saw was scratches in the tarmac, gouges where metal had cut into it, stains on the road from spilled oil and fuel. To Caitlin, though, he guessed it was a whole lot more.

'Here's what I don't get,' Caitlin said, having made her way back up the road. 'Your friend in the Land Rover came from that way, yes?' She pointed up the road, back towards where they'd crossed the cattle grid. 'And the tractor is coming up from that way.' She turned on her heels and pointed in the other direction. 'There's nothing in the way to stop him seeing the tractor, is there? No trees, no walls in the way, no rise in the ground. He would've seen him because that tractor, well, it's huge, right? It was impossible for him to miss.'

'What's your point?'

'He didn't slow down, Harry. He just kept going at speed 'til he hit the corner. Why?'

'How do you know he didn't slow down?'

'Well, if he had done, then the collision wouldn't have been half as dramatic for a start, might not even have happened.'

'Can't say that for sure.'

'No, but we can both see that the odds weren't in his favour, right? If he'd slowed just a little, instead of the collision we're now dealing with, we could've instead been looking at maybe the Land Rover off one side of the road to avoid impact, perhaps, with the tractor ending up over there to get out of the way.' She pointed a finger past Harry at nothing in particular. 'Also, there's no evidence at all on the road surface that he even attempted to use the brakes. At the speed he would've been going to cause the damage he did, there would be tyre marks, long ones, too. I've seen plenty in my time doing this, and instinct alone would have you stamp on the brake pedal. Then you'd have screeching tyres, lines of rubber on the road surface, but like I said, there's nothing.'

Harry pointed at some black lines on the road.

'What are those, then?'

'They're the Land Rover trying to hold on to the road, the tyres trying to grip but failing. They stop just over here, which is where he slammed into the front of the tractor.'

'So, you're saying that he saw the tractor coming, made no attempt to slow down, purposefully fought the instinct to hammer his foot down on the brake pedal, hit the corner at speed, tried to hold it, and ultimately failed.'

She looked up at Harry.

'Exactly that.'

Harry asked, 'Did his brakes fail, then?'

Caitlin shook her head.

'Checked and double checked; nothing wrong with them.'

'What about the wheel, the one that went on a little jolly all of its own?'

Caitlin moved a few steps, then pointed at the road again.

'Came off here,' she said, and Harry saw that she was pointing at a great gouge in the metalled surface. 'That's where the axle hit.'

Harry walked over for a closer look himself.

'Going to be a good while before anyone comes up here to fix that. Wheels don't just come off though, do they?'

'No,' said Caitlin. 'And as you can see from the marks in the road, it had already made its break for freedom before the vehicles collided.'

'Well, that makes no sense, does it? Why would it come

off before the collision? Mike's a mechanic, his vehicle would be absolutely sound; that's what his reputation is built on.'

'Which is why I want to see the wheel,' said Caitlin.

TWENTY-ONE

Arriving at the location Jadyn had sent him, Harry found himself staring at a field, through which a rutted track had cut its way from the lane to a barn on the far side. Of the vehicles the team had used to travel over from Hawes, all but the police Land Rover were parked just inside the gate. *Sensible,* thought Harry, because not one of them would've made it across without getting stuck or bottoming out.

Harry rolled forward, slowing to a crawl, as the front wheels of his old Rav4 eased into the deep ruts.

'You'll never make it across that, surely,' said Caitlin.

'It'll be fun finding out though, won't it?' Harry grinned.

Relaxing his hands on the steering wheel, because the ruts would pretty much guide the wheels themselves, Harry allowed the vehicle to do what it had been designed to do. With an ease and confidence usually associated with a more specialist, and considerably more expensive, off-road vehicle, the Rav4 chugged on. The cabin rolled left and right, the suspension doing just enough to take the violence out of the ride, and soon enough, the journey was over, and Harry had slid them in beside the police Land Rover.

'I'm impressed,' said Caitlin, unclipping her seatbelt.

'Got this from Mike,' Harry said, doing the same and opening his door. 'Which is yet another reason why I'm baffled by the accident. Mike only deals in vehicles he thinks are roadworthy. And when you buy something from him, you know it's had a good going over.'

In front of them stood an old barn in the process of being converted into a house. Scaffold poles had been set up around the entire property, which gave Harry the impression that they weren't so much holding the building up, as preventing its escape. Neat stacks of bricks were rested beneath various sections, along with wood, piping, and lots of other stuff Harry had no idea about. Whoever owned the place, he was impressed they'd take on such a project. He could think of nothing worse. Yes, the result would be fantastic for sure, but the process of getting there? Awful.

Standing outside the Rav, Caitlin came to join Harry.

'Quite the project, isn't it? I'd love to do something like this one day. Imagine how great that would be, putting all your creativity into your dream home!'

Harry avoided commenting, thankful to see Matt, then the rest of the team, emerge from the front door.

'Now then, Boss,' Matt said, strolling over. 'Caitlin.'

'Where's the wheel, then?' Harry asked.

Matt pointed up behind the barn, across the fields.

'Couple of fields that way,' he said. 'We've not been up yet; thought it best to wait for you. And now that Caitlin's here, she can deal with it properly.'

'Where's the person who found it?'

'About that,' said Matt, with an air of mystery.

'About what? Where are they?'

'He's out the back, should be ready in a few minutes, give or take.'

Harry frowned, or tried to, which was never easy, seeing as his face was pretty much in a permanent frown anyway. To move it into any other kind of expression often felt like he was trying to force his muscles and skin to do things they simply couldn't do.

'And what's he doing that's so important he's not here now, taking us up to fetch the wheel?'

Matt didn't answer. Harry shifted his glare to Jadyn. Jadyn glanced at Matt, who shrugged.

'Maybe you should go look for yourself,' suggested Matt.

Harry decided to do exactly that, checked which was the least treacherous route around the house, and strode off. Everyone else followed.

Coming around to the rear of the house, Harry was presented with a sight he simply wasn't prepared for, and never could've been either, even if Matt had told him what he was about to see. As it unfolded before him, he found himself staring, like he was witnessing a car crash; he knew that he didn't want to see what was happening, but he also couldn't yank his attention away.

The man, who even at this distance looked well into his seventies, was standing nearly waist deep in a huge metal trough. As Harry drew closer, he could see that the trough was filled with water, on top of which was an awful lot of ice, glinting in the sun like jewels. The man was, thankfully, not naked, but the only garment he was wearing was a pair of running shorts from the eighties. Stood beside the trough was something Harry recognised from his distant past, back in the days when he used to take fitness a little more seriously; built from scaffold poles was a pull-up bar buried into the ground, and next to that, a set of rusting kettlebells.

With a great bellow that rolled off down the dale, the man dropped into the icy water, fully submerging himself. Then he exploded up out of it, climbed out of the tub, and proceeded to bash out a dozen pull-ups.

'Matt,' said Harry, calling the DS over, 'what, exactly, is going on?'

Jen stepped forward.

'That's Norman.'

'You know him?'

'Ish.'

Norman had dropped from the pull-up bar and was on with swinging a kettlebell the size of his head out in front of him.

'I'm going to need more than ish,' said Harry.

'I've bumped into him on a few runs, that's all,' said Jen. 'He's a bit of a recluse, looks after himself, lives on a vegan diet, I believe, and that's really all I know about him.'

Norman, finished with the kettlebell, plunged back into the trough of icy water.

'Any idea how long he's going to be?'

Matt checked his watch.

'I think he's nearly done. Said he'd be half an hour, and that's about now.'

Norman once again exploded out of the water. *A wiry Godzilla of sorts,* thought Harry, especially with that roar of his once again being sent off down the dale to terrify innocent animals in bushes and trees.

Harry watched as Norman climbed out of the trough and turned to face them. There wasn't an ounce of fat on him, and his face was half hidden behind an impressively long, snow-white beard tugged into a point with a silvery bead.

Norman walked straight up to Harry, eyes narrow.

'I'm not one for people,' he said.

'Well, they can be overrated, that's for sure,' said Harry.

'Don't mind the police, though. Used to be on the force myself a good few years ago now.'

Harry noticed that Norman's accent was more akin to his own than that of someone like Matt.

'Where were you based?'

'Wiltshire. Devizes, if you've ever heard of it. Most folk haven't. Shame, really, it's a nice little place. Don't miss it, though. Not been down that way in twenty years.'

Harry knew it well but decided to avoid a discussion about it.

'What brought you up here, then?'

'A need to escape. Sold up, buggered off, ended up here with a barn that I somehow managed to get planning permission for.'

'Looks quite a project.'

'Keeps me occupied.'

For a recluse, Norman's surprisingly talkative, thought Harry.

'So, this wheel, then,' he said, but Norman had, without a word, disappeared inside the house through a stable door.

'Does that a lot,' said Jen.

'More talkative than I expected, considering what you said, though,' said Harry.

'Oh, he's happy to talk. He just prefers his own company.'

'That's not quite true, though, is it?' said Matt.

At that, Harry noticed everyone in the team go just wide-eyed enough to wonder what the next surprise was going to be.

'Is this where I find out he has the mummified remains of his mother in a rocking chair upstairs? Because if it is ...'

Then, out through the stable door, walked the largest dog Harry had ever seen, its black hide shimmering in the sunlight like obsidian. Norman followed on behind, pulling the stable door to as he did. Harry half expected him to jump up onto the animal and ride it.

The dog strolled up to Harry, its head level with his chest.

'Say hello, Betsy,' said Norman, coming to stand beside the dog.

The dog raised its eyes to stare up at Harry, and for a moment, he felt sure she was about to attempt to swallow him whole. Then she sat down, lifted a front paw, and gently rested it against his torso.

'She's the only Great Dane in the dale,' said Norman. 'Looks like the kind of thing you'd expect to find guarding the gates of Hell, but she's gentle as a lamb.'

Harry gave Betsy's head a scratch.

'It was Betsy who found this wheel you're here for,' said Norman. Think she thought it was a dog toy. She got all excited and tried to drag it halfway down the field. Anyway, shall we get going?'

Norman didn't wait for an answer, and instead, just walked between Harry and the others, with Betsy falling in beside him.

TWENTY-TWO

'Sorry about the teeth marks,' said Norman. 'She really didn't want to let go of it; did you, Betsy?'

Harry's eyes fell on the dog's huge maul, and he almost felt sorry for the tyre.

'Where did you find it?' Caitlin asked.

Norman pointed further up the field.

'Can't work out how it managed to get even that far,' he said. 'The lane must be at least half a mile away.'

'You'd be surprised,' said Caitlin, dropping to her knees to examine the wheel more closely. 'With enough speed and a bit of luck, plus the fact it was heading downhill, getting to where it is, wasn't an issue.'

The wheel was facing skywards, and considering what had happened, it looked relatively undamaged. Something was off about it, though, and he couldn't quite work out what that was.

Caitlin stood up.

'We've not discussed the phone yet,' she said.

'Well, let's get the wheel out of the way first,' said Harry.

'Any thoughts? Anything from it that gives you an idea about what happened up on the lane?'

'Actually, yes,' said Caitlin, folding her arms. 'Don't suppose you can see anything unusual about it, though?'

Harry looked back at the wheel. What was it he was missing?

'It's staring me in the face, isn't it?'

Caitlin didn't respond, which was confirmation enough.

Harry looked at the rest of the team.

'Anyone?'

Dave raised a hand.

'Yes, Dave?'

'Where's the wheel hub?'

'What?'

'The wheel hub,' Dave repeated. 'Why's it not attached?'

Harry looked at the wheel, then at Caitlin, then finally back at Dave.

'Should it be? I mean, it's come off, hasn't it, so …'

'No, that's not what I mean,' continued Dave. 'That wheel would be bolted to the wheel hub, right? There are five wheel bolts holding it fast to the hub.'

Harry again glanced at the wheel.

'But there aren't any bolts,' he said. 'So, how can it be attached to the hub?'

'Wheel bolts don't just come off,' said Dave. 'They just don't.'

'Maybe they snapped,' suggested Jadyn.

Jim said, 'No chance, particularly not all five at the same time.'

'Maybe they sheared off in the accident,' suggested Harry.

Dave shook his head.

'None of what I'm seeing in front of us makes sense. If the wheel snapped off during the collision, then I'd expect to be looking at a rusting, knackered thing, not this, which looks almost new. Even then, I'd be surprised to find it just lying here, relatively undamaged, and with no bolts or anything else attached.'

'He's absolutely right,' Caitlin agreed. 'What else?'

Harry was fairly sure he saw Dave's chest swell a little at being asked to explain further. He was pleased; after what had happened over the last twenty-four hours, he needed a boost.

'I only know this because I used to own an old Land Rover. Used to tinker with it when I was home. An axle will really only snap under a few conditions. You've got fatigue, which'll happen due to age, wear and tear. You'll get cracks developing, that kind of thing. Overloading it can cause a break. If the vehicle's not looked after and maintained well, then that's an issue, and it can snap under impact as well. Even then, I'd expect something else to go first.'

'Like what?' asked Harry.

'Connection to the differential isn't as strong as an axle; I've snapped one myself.'

'Me, too,' said Jim.

'But not a wheel?' Harry asked.

Both Jim and Dave shook their heads.

'And the problem with everything Dave's just mentioned,' said Jim, 'is that any vehicle owned by Mike wouldn't have those problems, would it? He checks everything.'

An odd sound lit the air, and Harry saw then that Caitlin was clapping rather enthusiastically.

'That was fantastic!' she said. 'You'll put me out of a job!'

'They're right, then?' Harry asked.

'Completely,' replied Caitlin. 'For a start, there were no cracks in the axle, and it's intact anyway. Everything about that Land Rover speaks of a vehicle that was really well maintained; lots of new parts, that kind of thing.'

'So?' said Harry. 'What does all that tell us, then?'

'The missing wheel nuts,' said Jim.

'Exactly,' said Caitlin. She dropped to the ground by the wheel, and the team gathered round.

Norman stayed back a way, but Betsy was, for some reason, interested to see what was happening with her new toy, and stuck her head in next to Harry's.

'Here, you'll see that two of the holes where the wheel nuts would go through to secure it to the hub are deformed. My guess is that hitting that corner at speed caused them to snap.'

'Why do I get the feeling that you're saying more by saying less?' said Harry.

'Two holes,' said Caitlin. 'Two. Why are the other three absolutely fine? Why aren't they deformed as well? Why don't all the holes look like they've had the bolts wrenched in half by the accident, twisting the metal?'

Harry caught what Caitlin was saying.

'But that doesn't make sense! There's no way Mike would ... I mean ... he just wouldn't!'

'Wouldn't what?' Caitlin prompted.

Harry couldn't believe he was about to say what he was going to say, but he had no choice.

'There's no way Mike would attach a wheel to a vehicle with only two bolts. He just wouldn't. He's a mechanic. He's thorough. Everyone trusts him. And he's certainly not that forgetful. Even if he'd been distracted by something in the workshop, he'd have checked, I'm sure of it.'

A murmur of agreement rippled through the team.

'And yet, here we are,' said Caitlin. 'Remember, I've checked the rest of the vehicle. Like I've said, it's in really good condition. It's been looked after. But this right here doesn't tally with any of that, because the only way for this wheel to have come off—the only way—is for it to have been held on with two bolts, and for those two bolts to have been loose. Your friend hit the corner, and the wheel couldn't take it because it wasn't attached to the hub properly. Plus, there would've been a gap between it and the hub because the bolts weren't fully in. With all those forces in play—the speed of the vehicle, its weight, the corner—everything just gave way.'

Harry stared at the wheel, trying to reconcile the facts before him with what he knew of Mike.

Matt said, 'There's no way Mike would allow any vehicle of his to go out onto the road like that. He just wouldn't.'

Harry turned to look at Matt.

'I couldn't agree more,' he said. 'And yet, here we are.'

TWENTY-THREE

Having gathered back at Norman's house, and with little left of the afternoon, Harry decided that the best thing to do with what was left of it was to eat cake. Jadyn's mention of the Dales Bike Centre had got him thinking that taking the team back there would be no bad thing. It would be a decent way to round things off. Caitlin was happy to tag along, plus they also still hadn't discussed Mike's phone. So, with the wheel recovered and now in the back of the Rav, Harry led the way.

Pulling into the bike centre gave Harry a strange feeling, one he simply wasn't used to, that being the notion that going away on holiday wasn't just a nice thing to do, it was important. The buzz around the place was infectious, with people dropping off mountain bikes they'd hired to go exploring, then resting in the café to drink coffee, eat cake, and talk excitedly about how great a time they'd had. Not that Harry wanted to hire a bike and try and avoid killing himself on some mountain trail, but the idea of going away for a while with Grace again bubbled to the surface of his mind. Then he remembered something from a while ago now, that he'd asked Grace if she'd consider going on holiday with him. He couldn't remember exactly when that had been, but he could remember where she'd suggested, and that had been Tuscany. Harry remembered that he'd looked into it a bit, done some research, but then one thing had driven out another, and they'd not talked about it since. Well, maybe it was time to have a chat about it again, he thought.

With the evening surprisingly warm and giving everyone the impression that early autumn was the height of summer, Harry sat everyone outside around a large, wooden table. He then took everyone's order and headed inside. Caitlin followed.

'I'll give you a hand,' she said.

'No need,' said Harry.

'Also, the phone ...'

Standing at the counter, Harry grabbed a couple of trays, handed one to Caitlin, then told the young woman on the other side what everyone wanted to drink, before adding in a selection of delicious things from behind the glass.

'You always do this for your team?' Caitlin asked. 'If so, I'm changing jobs and moving.'

'We all look after each other, really,' Harry said. 'More family than team, I sometimes think. Took me a while to get used to working like this, but if you ask me, it's the best way, really.'

'That's nice.'

'It is.' Harry moved along to where he would collect the drinks and the various sweet delights he'd picked. 'So, this phone, then ...'

Caitlin leaned in a little, lowered her voice.

'When I called about the phone, you said you were about to call me to talk about it as well. Why?'

Harry gave his chin a scratch and placed the first of the drinks on his tray. Two small plates then arrived, loaded with large slabs of something very bad for whoever was going to eat it.

It took a moment or two for him to remember what it was that had bothered him about Mike's phone enough for him to want to call Caitlin. Plus, there had been the distraction of his supposed gangster cousin once again turning up uninvited. He was going to get very angry, indeed, if that kept happening.

'Two things,' Harry said eventually, as various other drinks were handed over, and yet more cake. 'One, the app that was open when the phone was found, and two, the duct tape.'

'Seems like we're thinking alike, then,' said Caitlin.

'How terrifying.'

Harry handed some of the drinks and cakes to Caitlin as another batch arrived.

'Start with the first thing, then,' Caitlin suggested. 'The app. What's bothering you about it?'

'Can't work out why it would be on,' Harry said. 'I guess it could've been booted up, or whatever the phrase is, for the app to load by accident, but I'm not convinced.'

'Why?'

'It's an encrypted chat thing or whatever, isn't it, right? So, why would that be the app the phone opens by accident?'

'If it's by accident, then couldn't just any app open, which would mean it's just a random event?'

Harry shook his head, unconvinced.

'Here's the thing,' he said. 'If you drop a pistol, right, it's not just going to go off, despite what the movies and television want you to think. There's a lot of moving parts in a weapon, and a jolt on the ground, well, that's not going to be enough to set everything in motion for it to go off.'

Harry could see that Caitlin was confused.

'What's that got to do with a phone?' she asked. 'I'm fairly sure it wasn't loaded or anything like that.'

'The difference is if the weapon is primed for firing. So, in the case of a pistol, that's with the safety off and the hammer back. You can also just pull the trigger if you want to go bang-bang-bang and pretend you're all gangster, but you've still got to pull the trigger to get the hammer to move.'

'You're losing me.'

Harry lifted his left hand and pointed his index finger at Caitlin like the barrel of a pistol, thumb flat against the top of his hand.

'Pretend for a moment that my hand is a pistol,' he said. 'My thumb there, that's the hammer. Now, for this pistol to fire, that hammer—my thumb—needs to be cocked first. Do you think that's easy to do by just, oh, I don't know, knocking it against the counter here, for example?'

Harry tapped his hand against the counter to demonstrate.

'No,' said Caitlin. 'You'd have to prise it up somehow, wouldn't you?'

'Exactly,' agreed Harry, and flexed his thumb back. 'There,' he said. 'Now it's cocked, yes? What happens, then, if I accidentally bang it against the same surface?'

As Caitlin watched, Harry knocked his hand once again against the counter, and this time his thumb snapped forward, back into his hand.

'Bang!'

Harry hadn't meant to say the word so loudly and was surprised by how much Caitlin jumped. He also got some rather dirty looks from the staff, and from some of the customers, too.

'Sorry about that,' he said. 'But you see my point, yes? For the pistol to go off, that hammer kind of needs to be in place already. I think it's the same with the app and the phone. If it appeared there by accident because of the collision, that's because it was already up on the phone, wasn't it?'

'It actually was,' said Caitlin. 'I'd have expected to see satnav or something, not that.'

'Moving onto the tape ...'

Harry paid for the drinks and the various cakes and picked up his tray. Caitlin did the same, then followed him across the café, back outside to the rest of the team.

Passing out the drinks, he said, 'Help yourselves to cake. No fighting, though. Share them if you have to, and I'm looking at you, Matt.'

'Bit unfair,' said Matt, but Harry saw the smile through which the words slipped out.

As the team all got on with their coffees and cakes, Harry took his own drink and stepped away just enough to continue his chat with Caitlin without interruption. It wasn't a secret by any means what they were talking about, but he just wanted to go through it all with as few people discussing it as possible.

'No one uses duct tape to repair a phone,' he said, sipping his coffee. 'That's what bothered me about that. Maybe it was all Mike had to hand, but I doubt it. Anyway, if you are using duct tape to repair a phone, my guess is that it's already somewhat beyond repair.'

'There was actually nothing wrong with the phone,' said Caitlin. 'I thought the same as you, that it was a bizarre choice. Finding that there was nothing wrong with the phone at all, well, that really was weird.'

'What was it on there for, then?' Harry asked.

'Inside the Land Rover, just to the left of the steering wheel, there was this piece of metal bolted in. It was bent in just such a way that, if you attached a phone to it, you could see the screen really easily. I think Mike used the tape to attach it to that; there was duct tape on the piece of metal as well.'

'That would make some sense if he'd been using his phone for directions, but he'd have no need, would he? Mike's local, knows the area inside out and back to front. Could probably drive every road blindfolded and never crash.'

Caitlin paused, took a mouthful of coffee, which was so hot she spat it back out again into her cup.

'Sorry about that.'

Harry said nothing.

'Anyway,' said Caitlin, 'the phone ... Well, for a start, the app? It had been open for some time, from well before the collision.'

'What? Why?'

'It was on video chat as well. Which means ...'

Caitlin paused, but Harry didn't have time for that.

'Which means what?' he said. 'What does it mean?'

Caitlin turned and faced Harry, staring him directly in the eye.

'It means that your friend had the app open for video chat while he was driving. Somewhere out there is the person who was on the other end of the chat, and they had a front-row seat to the collision that nearly killed him.'

TWENTY-FOUR

Grace woke with a gasp. She wasn't one for vivid dreams, but whatever had been going on in her subconscious had been enough to kick her awake. Her heart thumping, she sat in the darkness, hand on her chest, forcing herself to calm down. The night was cool, the air tainted a little by the smell of stone as the old house breathed.

She had no memory, as such, of what had woken her, just shadows of things, which, the more she tried to hold on to, to examine, the fainter they became. Then, finally, they were gone, but Grace knew she'd not be getting back to sleep for a while.

Best to get up and have a nice mug of tea, she thought. To do that without waking Harry, though, that was the problem. Except, as soon as that thought had entered her mind, she noticed something: Harry wasn't in bed.

Confused, and still a little disturbed by being woken so suddenly by something she doubted she would ever be able to remember, she slipped out of bed.

In the thin blade of silvery light cutting across the room from between the curtains, she managed to navigate around to the door to grab her dressing gown from where it was hanging on a hook. Where her slippers were, she hadn't the faintest idea, though she guessed the dogs would probably know, seeing as they were always ferreting them away somewhere. Her dog, Jess, was a fan of going to sleep with her nose stuck in one.

Guarded against the chill of the night if not the danger of stubbing her toes, Grace made her way from the bedroom to the stairs and slipped down them as quietly as she could. Not because she was afraid of waking someone, because she knew Harry was already awake, but more that it seemed wrong to disturb the night more than necessary. The darkness was a blanket, and the world felt comforted by it, so it was not her place to go stomping around.

Coming up to the door to the large room at the front of the house, she saw flickering light beneath it, tiny tongues of orange and yellow and red, all of them dancing with broken feathers of shadow. She eased the door open to cast her eyes across the dining table, past the kitchen area, and over to where she saw Harry sitting on the sofa in front of the lit stove, its door open to help it draw better.

Grace could see that Harry was busy with something, though what, she couldn't tell. He'd not noticed her opening the door, so whatever it was, he was fully absorbed by it. She thought for a moment that perhaps she should head back upstairs, leave him undisturbed, but as she was about to pull the door to and do exactly that, she heard the sound of dog claws tapping across the flagstone floor.

Harry looked up, distracted by the sound of Jess sauntering over to say hello to her owner, and caught Grace's eye.

For a moment, neither of them said a word, just stared and smiled. Grace broke the silence.

'Hi.'

She stepped into the room, leaning over to give Jess a scratch on her nose. The dog had one of her slippers in her mouth.

'Thought you might have those.' Grace smiled.

Jess rolled onto her back, offering Grace her tummy. Grace gave it a scratch and looked over to see that Harry had been reading something; it was the letter that she'd handed him when he'd come home all full of indignation about Smudge being pregnant. Then, almost as though he'd been caught red-handed doing something he shouldn't be, he tossed the letter and the envelope into the flames.

Harry said, 'Hope I didn't wake you.'

'Not at all,' said Grace. 'Bad dream, I think, not that I can remember it. Decided to come down to make myself a mug of tea, then realised you weren't in bed.'

'Lot on my mind, that's all.'

Grace moved across the room to the kitchen, filled the kettle, flicked it on.

'Like what?' she asked, as she found a couple of mugs and the teabags, then fetched milk from the fridge.

Harry yawned, though Grace thought that it looked a little forced.

'Oh, you know, work stuff.'

'Mike, you mean?'

'I can't go into it, obviously, but it's a strange one, for sure.'

'It is,' Grace agreed, now looking for some biscuits. 'Mike's not one for having prangs, is he? Used to do grasstrack racing, you know? He'd do up Minis in his garage, then take them out and race them, usually returning with a trophy or two. He can certainly drive.'

'I didn't know that,' said Harry, pushing himself up from the sofa to walk over to the kitchen.

Smudge, who Grace hadn't spotted because she'd been sitting between Harry and the fire and thus out of view, followed him over.

The kettle boiled. Grace filled the mugs with steaming water, offered Harry a biscuit, which he took readily.

'He'll be okay, though, won't he?' she asked.

'He's in an induced coma,' said Harry.

Grace didn't know what to say to that. Instead, she reached over and gave Harry's hands a squeeze. Then she sorted them both a mug of tea and led Harry and the dogs back to the sofa. She sat down, and Harry dropped down beside her.

'Was the letter from a secret admirer?' she asked, sipping her tea.

'What?'

'The letter. You just threw it onto the fire. It was the one I gave you, the one that came special delivery.'

'Oh, it's nothing,' said Harry, lifting his mug to his lips to blow the steam away and cool it a little before taking a sip.

'Didn't look like nothing. Looked important.'

'It wasn't.'

'But you were reading it in the middle of the night.'

Harry took another sip.

'I couldn't sleep, didn't want to put the TV on, and then I remembered it was still in my pocket, that's all.'

Grace leaned back into the sofa.

'You're being very mysterious.'

Harry looked down at her, and Grace saw a warmth in his eyes that made her breath hitch.

'I don't know how not to be. Comes with the job I think.'

'What was the letter about, then? Why send it special delivery if it's not important?'

Harry took a deep breath, held it, the released it slowly.

'It was from an old army mate, that's all,' he said.

'Really? Well, that doesn't sound unimportant at all.'

Harry took a sip from his mug, then held it with both hands, his forearms resting on his knees.

'Something about a reunion, that's all. Not my kind of thing. If I'd wanted to stay in touch, then there would be no need for a reunion, or that's how I see it, anyway.'

Grace wasn't so sure. About what, exactly, she didn't know, but something was off. Harry was stubborn, though, so getting to the bottom of things was hard at the best of times. As she wasn't really sure what she was trying to get to the bottom of, that made it especially hard to do.

'You can't just dismiss it like that,' she said. 'And why would you throw the letter in the fire? Not everything has to be so dramatically final.'

'Well, it's done now, isn't it?' said Harry. 'Reunions just aren't my kind of thing. Been to one before, and that didn't go too well to say the least. We all went through a lot together. Not sure I want to stand around going over it all again. Bad memories always get stirred up by the good, don't they? Not for me. Not now. Not when I'm as happy as I am right now.'

Grace watched as Harry did his best to smile at the same time as giving her knee a squeeze. The scars on his face did their best to resist him, but she saw it, and she knew it was genuine.

'Well, if you're sure?'

'I am.'

Grace finished her tea but kept hold of the empty mug because the warmth of it was nice in her hands. She leaned into Harry's shoulder, and he placed an arm around her.

'Night,' she said, closing her eyes for a moment.

'We'd be better off heading back upstairs.'

Grace's answer was to bring her legs up onto the sofa and hook herself into Harry with her knees.

'In a bit,' she said, then stared at the fire still flickering in the stove and allowed herself to sink into Harry's embrace.

To her surprise, Harry fell asleep first, and Grace was left in the gloom, still wondering about the letter and why the man she loved had burned it.

TWENTY-FIVE

'He's awake.'

That news was enough to make Harry forget the awkwardness of being caught red-handed by Grace the night before. The story he'd come up with had been believable, and he'd been very chuffed to have come up with it so quickly. He was also fairly sure that, despite seeming initially suspicious, Grace had eventually accepted what he'd told her, that the letter was about a reunion he had no interest in attending. That bit at least was true, because if there was a reunion of his old army pals, there was no way in hell he'd be making the journey. That was a lifetime ago now. He was a different person in so many ways. He had no interest in being reminded who he had once been; he knew that, had accepted it, and had moved on.

As to the actual reason he'd thrown the envelope and its contents on the fire, well, he'd be keeping that to himself for a good while yet, that was for sure. It was his business and his alone for now and she'd find out when the time was right.

Harry had received the call from Matt on the way to the

office that morning, and despite his usually reserved nature, given a fist pump at the news.

'When can we visit?'

'All I've been told is that he's awake,' said Matt. 'He's okay, and he's talking. They just want to keep the crowds away from him for now so as not to overwhelm him.'

'He's not out of the woods, then.'

'Not quite, but he's not far off, like. Shouldn't be too long. I got the impression we should be able to pop in later this morning, if that suits.'

'It does,' said Harry. 'More than. Nice to start the day with good news. You at the office?'

'I am.'

'Good. Have a tea ready for when I arrive in five.'

Harry killed the call, stuffed his phone into his pocket, and smiled. He then looked down to give Smudge a celebratory pat, only to realise that once again he'd left her with Grace. He was sorely tempted to turn around and go and fetch her, but he forced himself to keep walking, once again astonished by how much the dog meant to him, and how much he missed her when she wasn't by his side. He wondered what she would think about the subject of the letter he'd thrown on the fire, whether she'd approve, or give him that disappointed look she seemed to save for when he didn't give her any bacon from a sandwich.

Hawes was already busy. The place always managed to surprise Harry with just how vibrant it could be. Really, there was nothing much in the area beyond the stunning scenery, some scattered villages and hamlets, and the sheep and cattle farms. Yet still, Hawes was the heartbeat of upper Wensleydale, and it drew people in from all over, not just for supplies, but for family, for friends, and this morning, judging by the number of people who were enjoying the spectacle, to watch flocks of sheep shepherded through the town.

Having found himself outside the market hall, Harry stopped for a moment to watch the sheep trot past. They were being herded by two border collies and a young man on a quad bike, who waved at Harry as he rumbled past.

'Jim!' Harry called out, realising too late who it was.

Jim raised his hand again, but his focus was on the sheep in his care.

The smell of the animals settled over the town as Harry walked on, kicking up the scent of fleece and engine fumes as he went.

Arriving in the office, Harry was presented with his requested mug of tea.

'Perfect,' he said, taking a sip. 'Just seen Jim.'

'Really?' said Matt. 'What's he up to? He's not on duty today.'

'That's a relief,' Harry laughed. 'Because if he was, then he's currently trying to bring a couple of hundred sheep to work.'

Harry then explained how he'd seen Jim driving a flock through Hawes.

'He's at his happiest when he's on with farm work,' said Matt. 'We'll lose him to it, eventually.'

'It's not a loss if he's doing something he loves,' said Harry.

Hearing that, Matt gave Harry an odd look, then reached out and gave him a gentle prod with his finger.

'What was that for?' Harry asked.

'Just checking it's you,' Matt replied. 'When did you get all wise, then?'

Harry smiled.

'I've always been wise, Matt. It's just that it's taken you 'til now to realise and start listening.'

Over the next half hour, the rest of the team arrived. Jadyn, however, like Jim, wasn't on duty.

'He's looking after Steve today,' Jen said, smiling, when Harry asked if she knew what he was up to.

'How did you manage to persuade him to do that?'

'He actually volunteered,' said Jen. 'He's taking Steve to the vets for me. Needs a check-up. Said he might take him out for the day after, show him the sights.'

Harry's mind presented him with the image of Jadyn wrestling with Jen's huge lizard.

'He's joking, right?'

'I'm not too sure. I think a part of him rather likes the idea of walking through Leyburn with an enormous lizard on a lead at his side.'

Harry saw that Dave was in a considerably better state than when he'd turned up the previous day, and he slipped over for a quiet word.

'How's things, then?'

'Good, like,' said Dave. 'Yes, they're good.'

'You'll be on with the nest box stuff today, right?'

'That's the plan, yes. I'm meeting up with the wildlife group again, see if there's been any further trouble. Then I'm going to catch up with Maddie.'

'And how are you going to do that?'

'It's already arranged,' said Dave. 'I'm meeting her for lunch. She works at Campbell's in Leyburn, so it's a good excuse for me to get a few supplies in for myself at the same time.'

'You'll not be shopping on police time, Dave.'

'What? Oh, right, yes, I...'

Harry smiled, and punched Dave softly on the arm.

'I'm joking. So long as you're not doing your weekly shop, I'm sure it's fine.'

Before gathering the team together, Harry took Ethan to one side.

'You're the DI,' he said. 'How's about you taking the team meeting and divvying things up?'

Ethan agreed that it made sense.

'Anything I should know about?' he asked.

Harry thought for a moment, then ran through everything.

'No Jadyn, he's out walking a lizard—don't ask. We've Mike who's awake now, so get Matt to talk about that, and I'll be heading over to speak to him later, I should think. It's worth checking in on the farmer who was involved in the accident as well. Dave needs to be cracking on with the bird eggs theft and should have someone with him. There's also Barnaby Shaw.'

'Not sure I know about that?'

Harry explained how he and Matt had bumped into Barnaby's parents in the hospital.

'Does seem odd that someone like that, in the business he's in, would be that careless.'

'Accidents happen,' said Harry, 'but I said we'd check up on things, and I think we should. I want you on that.'

He then gathered the team.

'Ethan's going to run through everything today,' he said. 'Let's make this a quick one so we can all get cracking, especially as there's plenty to do.'

While Ethan sorted everything out for the day, Harry sat back and observed. So far, he hadn't quite figured out the new DI yet. It was impossible not to compare him to Gordy, whose forthright personality was something Harry really missed. Ethan was quieter, a little too obsessed with detail, and his dress sense was still very much urban rather than rural Dales wear, if that was such a thing. Not that Harry expected him to start turning up at work in a flat cap and wellies, but how he was managing to keep his shoes so clean and shiny was baffling. He knew how to run a meeting, though, and it was soon done and dusted.

'Efficient,' Harry said, as everyone left the office to go out on their various tasks.

'I'll take that as a compliment.'

'Good, because it was one.'

Dave came over.

'Away, then, lad,' he said, resting a hefty hand on Ethan's shoulder, 'best we get shifting and see if we can do something about this egg theft, like.'

Ethan smiled awkwardly. Harry could tell he wasn't used to working with someone like Dave.

'I'll fill you in on the details as we go,' Dave continued. Then he looked at Harry and added, 'And I'll keep you updated on it as well. It's all in hand.'

Harry watched them leave. Soon the office was empty, bar him and Matt.

'I'm going to check up on Barnaby,' said Matt. 'What about yourself? Ethan didn't mention you in the duty roster.'

Something pinged into Harry's mind about Barnaby, something his mum, Penny, had said, but then his phone buzzed, he saw it was Ben calling, and whatever the thought was, it just disappeared.

Harry excused himself and answered the call.

'Everything alright there?' he asked.

'Just had a message from Mike,' Ben said. 'He's doing okay and taking visitors.'

'What? The hospital was supposed to let us know when we could visit.'

'Seems Mike's doing that on his own.'

'Where are you? I'll swing by and pick you up.'

'I'm already on my way. Set off about fifteen minutes ago, then thought I should give you a call to let you know. I've just spoken with Liz as well. She's not coming, obviously.'

'I am,' said Harry. 'I'll see you there,' and a few minutes later, he was in his old Rav and heading down the dale.

TWENTY-SIX

Jane Patterson's morning had been everything she could have wanted. Having decided she needed the day off, she'd marched straight up to the boss and told her so. The boss, for once, had been astonishingly understanding and signed off on the request without hesitation. But then that was the advantage of working for yourself; telling your reflection in the hallway mirror that you needed a break never got old. Jane even wore different glasses when such conversations took place, so she could switch between characters, even have arguments. Not that her husband, Darren, or indeed anyone, knew. They'd think she was mad. Perhaps she was. She was making good money now, though, and no one had ever thought that she would.

Proving them wrong had been a relief more than anything, and she'd understood everyone's hesitation at the idea. Opening a retail space was always risky, true. Then there was opening a shop called Nostalgia, where walking through the door was to step back in time, bringing back memories of simpler times. She'd believed in the idea, though, because she felt deep down that people were growing tired of everything being, download this and app that. The disposable nature of society was something folk were turning against just a little, and she wanted to encourage it.

Two years ago, when she'd opened Nostalgia down a little lane in Richmond, that first day, everyone who'd come along had been a little confused: was it a shop or a museum? Sort of both had been Jane's answer, because everything she had for sale was a little piece of history. She had curated it all with the simple mission to invite people inside and hopefully persuade them to leave with something that brought back the best of memories, that they would use and cherish, and perhaps come back for more.

Nostalgia was a wide subject area, but Jane somehow managed to cover most bases. In the fashion section, you could get your hands on bellbottom jeans, miniskirts, denim jackets, vintage suits, and cocktail dresses. If you wanted music and entertainment, you could browse vinyl, cassette tapes, VHS, CDs, even laser discs. Then there was the section filled with the comics everyone remembered popping down to the newsagent to get every Saturday morning, along with a ten-pence bag of penny sweets. There was a homeware section and an appliance section, and she'd been amazed at just how popular fondue sets really were. The most popular part of the shop had been the same from day one, that being the toy section, and Darren had joined in with that, so much so that he was now fully in control of stocking it. He was a big kid at heart, so sourcing vintage toys was little more than an excuse for him to be that even more.

Over breakfast, Jane had mentioned she fancied the day

off. The kids had already left for school, both of them old enough to get themselves there on their bikes.

Darren had leaned over the table and given her a kiss, then said, 'You're the boss, so you can do whatever you want, right?'

That was why Jane had the conversation with herself in the mirror, though only after Darren had headed off for work himself to deal with a large sycamore, which needed to come down, piece by piece. Not an easy job either, due to the proximity of a house, so rope work was involved to make sure nothing came close to damaging the property.

So, while Darren's morning was no doubt spent dangling off the end of a rope and wielding chainsaws, getting all sweaty and dirty, which she really liked, Jane had taken herself off for a bit of pampering over in Richmond. A facial, a massage, a haircut, some really good coffee ... it had been wonderful.

Now, arriving back home, she floated through the front door as though walking on air. She felt wonderful, she felt relaxed, and she felt that when Darren got himself home, there was a high chance of her dragging him upstairs with the offer of helping him to get out of his work clothes and into the shower for a very personal wash. Then, at the bottom of the stairs, she saw Darren's bag, which contained his lunch, a flask of sweet tea, and plenty of treats. Jane knew he'd be starving by now, and with his job, keeping the calories up was vital; tiredness and fatigue didn't mix with using a chainsaw.

Picking up the bag, Jane giggled, the sound surprising her because it sounded so young and free. Not that she was old, but having just nipped past forty, she was starting to realise just how long ago being eighteen was. The giggle, though, had come from another thought; why wait till Darren got home for a little bit of slap and tickle? A tree was something sturdy to lean against, wasn't it?

Leaving the house, Jane jumped in her car. She knew where Darren was, because that was all part of the little safety protocol they had. With the nature of what he did, they both agreed it was important that she knew where he was and when he would be back. Sometimes his jobs were in remote places, which added an extra risk.

Arriving in the village of East Hauxwell, Jane navigated her way to the house where she was sure to find Darren metres above the ground lopping off branches, lowering the larger ones to the ground, and probably singing along to himself some god-awful tunes from the nineties. Not that either of them would be able to hear it because of the chainsaws, which was a blessed relief because Darren couldn't sing for toffee. The owner was away, which was why they'd booked Darren in for the job. They didn't fancy being around and getting in the way. It also made Darren's life a lot easier if he were left alone to just get on with it.

Pulling up the driveway to the house, Jane let out a faint whistle. It was a large, detached Victorian, the kind she dreamed of living in, but knew she never would. Her parents did, but they'd been able to buy it back in the seventies when houses were actually affordable, even for those on a modest salary.

The tree was around the back, and as Jane turned off the engine, it was replaced by the familiar buzz of one of Darren's chainsaws. A flutter of excitement tickled her stomach as she grabbed his bag, shut the door, and followed the driveway along the side of the house, spying her husband's truck just ahead.

To still feel like this after so many years was something special, she knew that, but her morning had certainly made her a little giddy. Right now, all she wanted to do was grab him, pin him against the tree he was busy felling, and rip off his clothes. And there was nothing wrong with that!

A scream cut through Jane's lusty thoughts like a cheese wire. She froze to the spot, the sound of the voice as unfamiliar as it was familiar. That was Darren, she knew that, but it couldn't be, because why? The yell had been a twisted thing, horrifying, the sound of someone experiencing something so awful that it wasn't just the body reacting, but the soul. That's what the scream had sounded like; the soul being ripped out of a body.

Jane ran. She knew that she shouldn't, that when Darren was working, she should approach carefully, stay well back, wait, but now was not the time for caution. Then one of the heels she was wearing snapped, and she tumbled, hammering down onto the ground as a sharp pain raced up her leg from her ankle and she, too, now screamed.

Grazed and bruised and bleeding, Jane was soon back up on her feet. Not running now, hobbling, but doing so as fast as she could, because what was worse now than that godawful wrench of a scream, was the silence. It was almost louder, as though what she had heard had in its violence removed all other sounds, sucking them into oblivion.

The tree came into view as Jane stumbled around the corner of the house to view the large rear garden. It towered above the house, and she could see why the owners needed it felled, and carefully. Then she saw Darren. He was hanging upside down from the tree, metres from the ground, a brace of chainsaws hanging from ropes attached to his belt.

'Darren! Darren!'

Jane forced herself to keep moving, to close the distance between her and her husband despite the pain.

She shouted Darren's name again, but still got no response.

Finally, standing beneath Darren's body, she saw that he was, at least, breathing. That was something. And right now, she needed anything. Because all she could see was the horrific gash which had gouged its way from Darren's head, across his face, and opened up his chest. Then she saw the worst thing of all, the thing that made no sense whatsoever, because she knew Darren better than anyone, and he wouldn't, would he? He just wouldn't ...

Sitting on a small garden table, the cast iron kind that Jane thought really suited a garden like this, and if she owned such a place, she'd have one, too, she saw her husband's helmet.

With shaking hands, she took out her phone and called emergency services.

TWENTY-SEVEN

Matt arrived at the house of John and Penny Shaw around mid-morning. They'd lived on the edge of Muker for as long as he could remember. John was in his mid-sixties, or thereabouts, Penny a couple of years younger. Everyone knew them. Hard not to, really, when you go through the ranks at the local secondary school and eventually become head teacher. John had retired at sixty, pulled out of the mountain rescue at the same time, and Penny had decided she couldn't be doing with waiting to join in, so had done the same.

Since then, when they weren't exploring the myriad footpaths of Swaledale, they were travelling around Europe in their very plush motorhome. The vehicle was almost as large as their actual house and was in the drive when Matt pulled up outside. He just about managed to bite back a smidge of envy as he strode past it and knocked on the front door.

Taking his family away for a few days in something like that would be fantastic, but imagine just being able to go off whenever you wanted to? The freedom of it! That they lived in Muker as well? He was happy in Bainbridge, always had been, but he thought Swaledale held something magical, and he often found himself wondering what it would be like to move.

The front door opened.

'Matt!'

Penny threw her arms around him like he was a long-lost son.

'Now then, Penny,' he said, feeling a touch awkward. 'Good to see you. Is John in as well?'

'He is,' Penny said, releasing Matt from her grip. 'You popping in for a few minutes, then?'

'If it's no trouble.'

'Of course it isn't.' Penny stepped back to allow Matt inside. 'How's that lovely wife of yours? And that daughter? She must be growing some now.'

'Joan's still the light of my life,' Matt said.

Penny gave an approving nod.

'Glad to hear it, otherwise we'd be having words.'

'Mary-Anne is a right little bugger! Has me wrapped around her little finger.'

'Of course she has,' cooed Penny, then poked Matt playfully in the ribs. 'You wouldn't want it any other way, believe me.'

'Oh, I do; believe you, I mean. She's a joy.'

The hallway to the house was lined with photographs. Matt leaned in to stare at one, then lifted a finger and pointed at it.

'There I am,' he said. 'Bloody hell, look at my hair! And there's John! He was the head of music back then, wasn't he? Does he still play the trombone?'

'No, thank God,' Penny replied. 'Awful thing.'

Matt laughed.

'You can't mean that.'

'I can and I do. It was the only thing Harris and I agreed on; brass instruments are the work of the devil, especially when practised alone!'

'Harris?' Matt repeated.

'Mr Fothergill.'

Then Matt remembered. 'The school caretaker! Goodness, I'd forgotten about him. He still wear that huge flat cap? Never could work out how it stayed on his head. We all used to think he slept in it.'

'He still works there, would you believe? Not for long, though, as he's finally being forced to retire. I think his last day is Friday. Won't be happy about that, but there we are.'

Matt did his best to remember the caretaker.

'He was quiet, I remember that,' he said. 'Stared a lot. We tried to talk to him, everyone did, but he never really responded. Probably because we were kids and us talking to him was actually us being cheeky little sods.'

Penny leaned in somewhat conspiratorially.

'Between you and me and that porcelain dog on the mantlepiece in the lounge, he always struck me as a bit strange. Not in a creepy way. Well, not too much. More that he was just really, really distant, like he was there, but not. How he managed to get married and have a child, I'll never know. But there's someone for everyone, isn't there, as my grandmother used to say?'

'I remember that massive bunch of keys he carried with him,' smiled Matt. 'We used to wonder what half of them were for, even tried to work out a way to nick them and go around the school trying them out!'

'You didn't! You rascally little buggers!'

'Kids will be kids, Penny! We never managed to, either.

We made up stories about him, said he had a room under the school where he'd put kids who'd been especially bad, never let them leave, keep them in cages, that kind of thing.'

Penny gasped.

'What overactive imaginations you had!'

'And a few too many horror movies as well. What about his wife? I can't remember anything about her. They had a child as well, didn't they? Used to run around the garden sometimes. Their house was at the back of the school.'

'Harris was quiet, and Helen was always a bit distant,' said Penny. 'Hardly ever left the house, and when she did, it was at the weirdest times. Used to see her walking or driving about either early morning or late at night, and that was about it. Now, what will you be having, tea or coffee?'

'Tea,' Matt replied. 'It's always tea. How old is Fothergill now?'

'A few years older than John, touching seventy, I think. He was there when John started at the school, you know.'

Penny pointed into a room off the hallway.

'Set yourself down in the lounge. I'll give John a call. He'll be pleased to see you. You're here about Barnaby, yes? Of course you are. That's good. It'll be a relief to have the police looking into things. Anyway, I'll go sort us a brew.'

Penny wandered off down the hall. Matt had another look at the photo of himself, amazed by how much he could remember from his time at school. He then stepped back and had a look at some of the others. He spotted plenty of people he knew, not just friends, either, but relatives, people he knew from his job. Some he knew were no longer around, others life had taken elsewhere and from whom little, if anything, was heard of now. It was quite the display, he thought, photos of every final year of students for every year that John had taught at the school.

'It's a bit odd, I know,' said John, coming to stand beside Matt. 'It all started off as a bit of fun, you know? Putting the photos up, then it just became a thing. There's thirty-one, would you believe? That's a lot of years to be at one school, isn't it?'

'Must've been happy there.'

'Was never anything else.' John gestured into the same room Penny had pointed to. 'Best we get sat down before the trolley arrives.'

'Trolley?'

'Oh, there'll be a trolley.' John smiled.

'Excellent,' said Matt, and he rubbed his hands in anticipation as he followed John into the room.

John gestured to a comfy armchair for Matt to slump down into, and he gratefully obliged.

'You don't miss the school, then?'

'Yes and no. The kids I do miss, but I see plenty of them still, don't I? No matter where I go in the Dales, someone will recognise me. The job, though, it was stressful. Did my best to implement change I thought was needed.'

'Doing your best is all you can ever do.'

Matt heard the sound of crockery chinking, then Penny arrived in the lounge, pushing a well-laden trolley, just as John had promised. Matt's eyes went wide at the sight of it. The teapot was huge, and beside it were scones, jam, cream, fruitcake, and Wensleydale cheese.

'Milk and sugar?' John asked, standing up to serve, as Penny handed Matt a small plate.

'Help yourself,' she said, before Matt had a chance to answer John. 'It needs eating, so don't go being all polite.'

'Just milk, please, John,' Matt said, and reached for a scone, then scooped up some jam and cream. 'Can't say I was expecting this.'

'Well, you enjoy it,' said Penny.

Soon, they were all sitting down and munching their way through the delights Penny had provided.

'All made by Barnaby,' she said. 'Gifted lad, he is.'

'And how's he doing now? Is he still in hospital?'

Both John and Penny shook their heads.

'No,' said John. 'Came out last night. Went round to see him. He's exhausted. Lost a lot of weight, too.'

'Did he say anything about what happened?'

'Don't think he wants to talk about it,' said Penny. 'I still can't believe he'd poison himself, though. It makes no sense.'

'And neither do we think he tried to take his own life, either, no matter what anyone says,' said John.

Matt was a bit taken aback by that statement.

'How do you mean?' he asked. 'Has someone suggested that?'

'We were asked about it at the hospital,' said Penny. 'As if things weren't upsetting enough ...'

Matt remembered something from the hospital at that point, but it was what Harry had said to him. And they'd certainly never mentioned suicide.

'I think you mentioned that he had someone professional in to do stuff like that.'

'He does,' said John. 'They come round every few months to check any bait traps. There's not a rat problem at all, but Barnaby likes to be doubly sure. Anything like that could shut him down, damage his reputation for good. That's why it's so spotless. And bless him, Craig does a good job with that, can't knock him for that.'

Matt asked for Barnaby's contact details, which Penny provided.

'Who's Craig?'

Penny looked confused.

'You know, Barnaby's best friend? I told you about him at the hospital, out in the car park.'

'That must've been Harry,' corrected Matt.

Penny frowned.

'Really? Oh, well, there you go, me and my wandering mind! Anyway, yes, Craig is Barnaby's best friend. They met at primary school, back when we lived over in Leyburn. Inseparable ever since. He has other staff who work in the café and at the bakery counter. But he does all the baking himself.'

'I used to think Craig was a problem,' said John. 'Didn't think he was a good influence. Looking back, though, I can see I was a little bit blind to things, and that it was probably the other way round.'

'How do you mean?'

John laughed.

'Craig used to mess around at school, like so many, I suppose, and so did Barnaby, but I never really saw it, or should I say, I probably chose not to.'

'Fair enough, you're his dad. We're none of us perfect. As I said to Penny a few minutes ago, kids will be kids. I was certainly no angel.'

'Well, looking at what Barnaby's done with his life, I think he's done alright, hasn't he?' John said. 'Still, I think he probably got away with murder at school. Craig got it in the ear a bit more, that's for sure. Water under the bridge, though, as they say. He pops in to see us a fair bit now, runs errands for us as well. Funny how folk change, isn't it?'

Matt asked, 'Craig works for Barnaby now, right?'

'As well as helping his dad out at the school,' said Penny. 'But once his dad's left, I believe he'll be working full-time for Barnaby. School's employing the services of some company or other that provides cleaning on a contract basis. Cheaper than having someone on staff permanently.'

It took a moment for that piece of information to sink in, then Matt said, 'Wait, you mean, Craig's the caretaker's son? He's the little kid we used to see running around that garden?'

'You didn't know?'

'Craig's a lot younger than me.'

'They're very different, him and his dad, well, him and his mum as well, actually,' said John. 'Couldn't be more different if he tried. Harris was a student at the school back in the day, but it was tougher then. Did you know that when I took over the headship, there were still canes in one of the cupboards? Can you believe that? Not that they were used, seeing as corporal punishment was banned in eighty-six, but the fact that they were still there says a lot, I think.'

'Thankfully, I missed all of that,' said Matt. 'What did you do with them then, the canes, I mean?'

'Harris was having a bonfire after school one day. I popped out and threw them on as well, because that's where they belonged.'

'Sensible.'

'Didn't stop a few of the teachers lobbing board rubbers at students, though. Old habits, I suppose. Couldn't get away with it nowadays, for sure, but back then, I think some of the parents actively encouraged it.'

Matt laughed at that, remembering the whoosh of air from one narrowly missing his head.

'Would Craig know anything about the bait traps?' he asked. 'Maybe he helped with them, moved them, something like that?'

'Best you ask him for yourself,' said Penny, and gave Craig's contact details to Matt. 'He lives in Leyburn with his parents still. Not sure that's healthy, but then it's not easy to buy a house, now, is it? The house comes with the job. Not sure what they're doing about finding somewhere else to live.'

'Moving house is never easy,' said Matt. 'It'll be a wrench, especially if they've been there for so long.'

'When he left home, Barnaby lived in Leyburn for a while as well,' continued Penny, 'what with there being more going on there than over here. But with his café here in Muker, and the bakery in Reeth, he moved back this way for convenience more than anything. Rented in Reeth at first, and now he's got himself a little place down the lane just round the back from here. Lovely it is, too.'

'Expensive, though,' added John. 'He's done well to be able to afford it.'

Matt finished his scone, looked wistfully at the fruitcake and cheese, but decided it was for the best, and for his belly, not to have any more.

'Top up?' John asked.

'And what about a bit of cake?' added Penny.

Matt laughed.

'I've just this moment persuaded myself to have nothing else to eat, but I'll not say no to more tea.'

John topped up Matt's mug.

'I'll wrap you some up to take with you,' said Penny. 'How would that suit? I'll put extra in as well so you can take it home; I'm sure that daughter of yours has an appetite.'

Matt took a mouthful of tea.

'It's all a bit confusing, isn't it?' he said. 'You're both sounding fairly adamant that there's no way Barnaby would be messing about with rat poison, and hearing what you've told me, I'm inclined to agree. And yet here we are, with him only just out of hospital. Doesn't make much sense, does it?'

'Makes no sense at all,' said John. 'Could be another baker has it in for him?'

Matt knew the bakers in Leyburn and Hawes and everywhere in between, better than most. There was nothing going on at all with that line of enquiry.

'I can't see that being it,' he said. 'It's hard to know where to go with this, though, isn't it? He keeps his business spotless, has a professional come in to deal with any potential rat issue, never touches the stuff because of what he does for a living, and yet ended up in hospital because of contact with rat poison. Doesn't add up. But then again, accidents happen, and it sounds to me like he works too hard. Tiredness, exhaustion, it can do funny things to the mind.'

For the next few minutes, the conversation went round the houses about everything they'd talked about, but when Matt finished his second mug of tea, they were no clearer as to a reason behind what had happened.

He placed his mug back on the trolley and stood up.

'Right,' he said. 'Thanks to you both for that. I reckon the best thing for me to do now is to go and have a chat with Barnaby. Do you think he'll be well enough for that today?'

'Don't see why not,' said Penny. 'Probably still tired.' A look of concern passed over her eyes. 'I don't want him thinking we're interfering, though. I mean, we are, I suppose, but we're not, if that makes sense.'

'We're just worried, that's all,' said John. 'We're his parents, so it's impossible not to, isn't it?'

'I understand that completely,' Matt said.

'It's just hard to see how or why something like this happened. We're just looking for answers. Then maybe, if we get some, we can have a chat with Barnaby and see if we can't get him to consider hiring in someone to help with the baking. That's really the outcome we want, isn't it, Love?'

'It is,' agreed Penny.

'Are you saying you'd prefer me to keep you out of this for now?' Matt asked. 'That's easy enough, as I can say the hospital mentioned the poison and asked us to check up on things. How's that?'

'Perfect,' said John. 'Thank you.'

Matt left John and Penny's house carrying a large foil-wrapped parcel containing both fruit cake and half a dozen scones. There was even a little pot of jam, and another of cream. Tempted as he was to have a nibble as he went, he instead dropped the parcel in his car, then walked around to Barnaby's house. Arriving at the cottage, he knocked at the door, but there was no answer. He knocked again, waited a while, checked his watch, then heard a voice calling. Turning, he saw a man approaching, mid-thirties, dressed in clean overalls.

'You looking for Barnaby?'

Matt gave a nod. 'Is he not about?'

'I was just popping by myself to check in on him,' the man replied. 'I'm guessing not if you've not had an answer. I'll go see if his car's round the back, just a minute ...'

Matt had no idea who the man was and waited for him to return.

'Well, it's not there. Must be out. My guess, seeing as I've just been past the café, is that he's over at the bakery. He's had a lot of time off with what happened, so he'll be looking to catch up. Keep telling him to get some staff in to help with all the baking, but will he listen? Will be buggery, like. I'd help, but I'm no baker. He'll have lost a bit of trade, won't he, being shut? But I'm sure he'll bounce back.'

Matt showed his ID.

'Police? Really? Why's that? It's not to do with what happened at the bakery, is it? That was awful.'

'You're a friend, are you?' Matt asked.

'I'm Craig,' the man said. 'I do the cleaning, the deliveries. We had some stock to keep folk happy for a few days, but we've had to disappoint people as well. Still, this is the Dales, so I'm sure everyone will be more concerned about what happened than where their bread rolls have been for the last few days.'

'Don't suppose you've a few minutes to spare for a chat, have you?' Matt asked.

'Of course,' said Craig. 'I'll call Barnaby as well if you want. See when he's back?'

'That would be very helpful,' said Matt, and on spotting a couple of benches up against a wall, said, 'How's about over there? Looks comfy enough.'

Then he led Craig over, sat down, and started asking questions.

TWENTY-EIGHT

Harry arrived at the hospital to find Ben sitting beside Mike's bed. Ben was talking. Excitedly, too, judging by all the arm and hand movements, never mind the sheer volume of words falling out of him. On the bed between him and Mike was a large diary, open to display pages covered in notes. Mike, on the other hand, was sitting, listening. He looked exhausted.

It took a moment or two for both Mike and Ben to notice that Harry was in the room. When they did, Harry could see that Ben was happy to see him, but the look he received from Mike was confusing. He smiled, yes, but there was a nervousness to it, in the corner of his mouth, and especially so in his eyes. It was as though he knew he should look happy, knew that involved his mouth, but couldn't persuade the rest of his face to join in. Harry was used to that. It was all part of his line of work, people not being that pleased to see him. But he knew Mike, so really there should be no nervousness at all. Unless something was wrong.

'Now then,' said Harry, raising a hand as he walked over to the bed, grabbing another chair to sit down beside his brother. 'Stupid question, Mike, I know, but how are you doing?'

'Hard to say,' replied Mike. 'I've felt better, for sure.'

'Looked it, too.' Harry winked.

He understood the importance of joking at times like this; laughing in the worst conditions, while also having a brew, were the two things which had got him and so many through their life in the Paras.

'I'm lucky,' said Mike. 'Could be a lot worse.'

'Having seen the state of your vehicle, yes, you could say that. How many bits of you are broken, then?'

'Three ribs, my left leg, this arm—' He waved the fingers of his left hand, which were sticking out the end of a cast that stretched all the way to his elbow. 'Plus lots of bruising, as you can see from my face.'

'Look nearly as bad as me.'

'No chance of that,' said Ben, chipping in.

'My insides got fairly rattled, including my brain, but it looks like my healthy diet of too much coffee, pastries, and very little exercise have served me well.'

'You're not exactly unfit, though, are you?' said Ben. 'Some days, I can't keep up with you.'

'Don't confuse physical fitness with sheer bloody-mindedness,' Mike replied.

Harry reached out and tapped the diary.

'What's this, then, Ben? Or do I need to be having words with both of you, because it looks to me very much the diary you use to plan jobs, correct?' Harry didn't give either of them time to answer. 'Not something you should be worrying about right now, Mike. Your job is to repair and recover. The quicker you do, the quicker you can get back to your workshop, have your head under a bonnet, and start juggling wrenches again.'

Ben went to answer, but Mike got in first.

'Don't blame Ben,' he said. 'He's only doing what I asked him to do. I'm going to be out of action for a while, what with so many bits of me not working properly, but I need to know what's going on to some degree, don't I? Plus, with a man down, there's a lot of reorganising that needs to be done. Ben can't manage it all on his own.'

Ben looked at Harry, and his eyes went wide with just enough irritation for Harry to get what he was saying without uttering a word.

'I'm sure Ben will be fine, Mike,' he said, backing up his brother's unspoken request for support. 'He'll have managed the place without you before, surely, when you're on holiday, that kind of thing.'

'Yes, but—'

Harry took the diary, closed it, and handed it to Ben.

'I'm no doctor, but I've been where you are right now plenty of times to know that the only way to recover is to let it happen. Putting things in the way, pretending you're fine, all that does is slow things down. It's not fair to yourself, and it's not fair to those around you, either.'

Harry noticed that Ben's stare had morphed now into one of concern.

'Honestly, it's alright, really,' Ben said. 'Mike's just—'

'Mike's just woken up after an induced coma because he was in a vehicle collision that could've killed him, but somehow, luck mainly, he survived. That's the only "Mike's just" anyone here should be worrying about right now.'

Harry let his words settle.

'Well, now that's all decided,' he said, 'how's about we all have some tea? Ben, you mind grabbing some?'

'What? Tea? Oh, right, yes. I'll go get some then, shall I?'

'You fancy a tea, Mike, don't you?' Harry asked, but didn't wait for an answer. 'Something to nibble on would be good as well.' He handed Ben his bank card. 'I'm paying.'

'In that case, I'll be bringing cake, not just biscuits,' said Ben, stood up, and left Harry with Mike.

Once Ben was gone, Mike said, 'He mentioned much to you, about him and Liz?'

Harry wasn't expecting the sudden change of subject and was immediately concerned.

'What? Why? Something wrong?'

Mike smiled, though doing so clearly caused him pain.

'He's keen to get planning the wedding, but it sounds like Liz is wondering what the rush is all about.'

'You think she's having second thoughts?'

Mike shook his head.

'No, I don't think it's that, but there's definitely something going on. I don't think it's serious, anything to worry about, like. Maybe just have a chat with him about it, though? I get the impression Ben can't believe his luck. Maybe his enthusiasm is a little overwhelming.'

'He's excited, that's all. No bad thing.'

'Like I've said, just have a chat with him, brother to brother.'

'I don't know anything about weddings.'

Mike said nothing in reply to that, just held Harry's gaze for a moment, then rested his head back against his pillows.

'What happened, then?' Harry asked. 'Actually, more to the point, why were you over there in the first place? Ben said there was nothing in the diary.'

'There wouldn't be,' said Mike, opening his eyes to stare at the ceiling. 'I'd been tinkering with the old Land Rover, needed to take her out for a run, make sure everything was tickety-boo, that was all. Next thing I know ...'

Harry gave his chin a scratch, trying to work out how best to question Mike about the collision, the phone, the missing wheel nuts ...

'Do you remember what happened?'

'I've had flashbacks, but it's all broken, doesn't make much sense.'

'Why?'

'What?'

'Why doesn't it make sense? You know your vehicle, you know the roads. I've seen where the collision happened, and it's hard to see how it did.'

Mike leaned his head forward.

'Accidents happen, Harry.'

'Yes, they do, Mike, but not everything is adding up right now. I need you to help me try to do that.'

'What are you suggesting?'

'I'm not suggesting anything. I'm asking, Mike, that's all. And believe you me, I know how hard it is to look back on a traumatic experience, to force yourself to understand what happened, to examine it. Needs to be done, though.'

Mike turned his attention to where Ben had left. Harry could see he was hoping for him to turn up sooner rather than later, so he wouldn't have to talk about what had happened.

'Not sure what you want me to say,' he said.

'I don't want you to say anything, if by that you mean make stuff up. Just need you to go through what happened so that we can understand. Someone else was involved. They were lucky to come out of it relatively unscathed. Had a few choice words about your driving, though.'

'How do you mean?'

'What speed were you doing?'

Mike's jaw clenched, then he said, 'How the hell should I know? I can't remember, Harry!'

'The driver of the tractor said you were going at a hell of a rate.'

'In a Land Rover? You're having a laugh.'

'Doesn't take much speed to be too much, considering the road.'

'Well, I don't remember,' Mike repeated. 'Maybe I will in a day or two, but right now? Nothing.'

Harry wasn't so sure.

'We found your phone.'

'You mean it was in one piece? How's that possible?'

'My guess is that the duct tape helped cushion things a bit for it.'

'Probably it.'

'Even more amazingly, it was still on. Screen was open on a messaging app.'

'Really?'

'Collision investigator told me that it was on a video call when the accident happened. No way to know who with, mind, as it's all encrypted or whatever, but even so, Mike; a video call? While you were driving? Anything you can tell me about that?'

Mike had looked pale when Harry had arrived, now he looked positively ashen.

'No.'

'No? What, nothing at all?'

'I don't remember.'

'You sure about that?'

'Yes!' Mike snapped back. 'Why are you asking me all these questions?'

Harry stopped himself from saying, *Detective, remember?* and instead said, 'One more thing, then ...'

'What, Harry? What one more thing?'

'During the collision, when you hit the corner, by the looks of things, the front offside wheel came off. It hammered into the tractor's windscreen, then bounced off on a little jaunt all of its own.'

'Seen that happen before,' said Mike. 'Used to do grass track racing; if a wheel comes off, they can travel for miles. You don't want to get in the way of one either; kill you.'

'It was found yesterday,' Harry said. 'Collision investigator came over as well to have a look. She said a few things that were a bit strange.'

Mike said nothing.

'Can you tell me why the wheel was held on, not by the five bolts you'd expect, but only two? And also, why those two bolts were so loose that when you hit the corner, they sheared off?'

'That's impossible,' said Mike.

'I'd think that, too, if I'd not seen what happened, seen the wheel for myself, spoken to the collision investigator. Just doesn't add up, does it, Mike, like not in the slightest?'

'I can't explain the bolts.'

'Can't, or won't?'

Mike fell quiet again, which told Harry plenty.

'Mike,' he said, leaning forward, lowering his voice, 'I think you know way more than you're willing to tell me right now. I think there's a reason why your phone was on a video chat. I think there's a reason why the bolts were missing from that wheel. There's probably also a reason why you were going fast enough for it to come off. I'm not asking you to tell me now. But I will be asking again. Something's going on, Mike, I know it. I just don't know what. I'm police, so I have to investigate. I'm also a friend. Not only that, I respect you hugely, and I've a great deal to thank you for; you've played a huge part in Ben's recovery after coming out of prison. Let me help you, Mike. That's all I'm saying, okay? Just let me help.'

Harry sat back, waited. Mike didn't move, didn't speak, then, at last, he sat forward.

'Harry,' he said. 'I—'

At just that moment, Ben came back carrying a tray.

'Not sure I'm allowed to bring all this in here,' he said, 'but no one's stopped me yet, so here we are.' He rested the tray on a table, looked over at Mike and Harry. 'Everything okay? You both look very serious.'

'Just concerned about Mike here, that's all,' said Harry, and stood up, then looked at his watch. 'Actually, I'd best get going.'

Ben handed Harry his bank card back.

'What? But you asked for tea. That's why I went to get it, because you literally requested it.'

'Didn't realise the time,' said Harry, already moving away from the side of Mike's bed. 'Extra cake for you two, though, right? And I'm sure that tea won't go to waste.'

'Oh, I don't know about that,' said Mike. 'Hospital tea has a certain tang to it.'

To avoid any further awkwardness, or discussion about why he was leaving, Harry said farewell and marched out of the room, down numerous snaking corridors, then outside and over to his Rav.

Dropping himself in behind the steering wheel, he paused, key in the ignition. Mike's answers, the way he'd acted as Harry had asked him all those questions, none of it seemed right. He knew that Mike was hiding something, but what? And how was he going to find out?

Then Ethan called, and all of that was put on hold, as Harry left the hospital car park to make his way to a village he'd never heard of and the scene of another accident. And not because he didn't have anything better to do, either, but because, inexplicably, something about it was ringing alarm bells.

TWENTY-NINE

Harry pulled up to face a familiar scene: a rapid response vehicle, no doubt first on the scene, carrying paramedics to deal with the casualty before anyone else arrived; a fire engine to help get the casualty safely down from where he'd been found hanging; police vehicles bringing his own team in to make the scene safe, deal with the general public, and to record details of what had happened and how; and finally, an ambulance, to rush the casualty to hospital.

A person on a stretcher was being lifted gently into the ambulance as Harry parked up. He climbed out of his vehicle to be met by Liz.

Harry thought about what Mike had said about Ben and the wedding, but thought it best to keep that to himself for now.

'What've we got?'

'Chainsaw accident,' Liz said. 'Darren Patterson. Local tree surgeon. Felling a monster of an ash tree round the back of the house. It'll keep the owners in firewood for years. His wife didn't see it happen, but she arrived just as it did. Good job, really, as it meant emergency services could get here quickly. But that's not why you were called.'

'No, I get that,' Harry replied. 'Where is it, then?'

Liz pointed over to the house.

'You need to head round the back. The tree Darren was working on is round there. As is everything else.'

'Rest of the team?'

'Jim and Jadyn aren't on duty,' Liz said. 'Dave is round the back with Ethan. Jen is over with the ambulance.'

'Matt?'

'On his way over from Muker.'

Harry left Liz and made his way towards the house as directed. On the way, he passed the ambulance. As Liz had said, Jen was with them.

'How is he?'

'Lucky, by the sounds of things,' Jen said.

One of the paramedics came over, a man with piercing eyes, and a nose and ears that told Harry he'd done a bit of boxing in his time.

'He's stable. Could've been a lot worse.'

'Do we know what happened exactly? Or are details still fuzzy?'

'I'm not sure,' said the paramedic, 'but one thing bothering all of us, is why the hell he didn't have his helmet on?'

'Did it not come off when he fell from the tree?'

'What, and somehow make its way over to a table all on its own?'

Harry let the comment and its tone slide; crime scenes were stressful places for all involved. He waited for the paramedic to continue.

'Makes no sense, does it? We're not talking about some weekend gardener who decided to buy a chainsaw off some dodgy website to go hack at a couple of old trees. He's a professional. Fully qualified. This is his job.'

Harry looked at the man on the stretcher, saw bandages and blood.

'I'll leave you to it,' he said. 'You stay here for now, Jen, okay? Come round to the tree when you can.'

The next vehicle Harry had to navigate past was the fire engine. He approached the crew as they were busy tidying away their gear.

Holding up his ID, he introduced himself and asked what they'd found when they'd arrived on the scene.

'We got here a few minutes before the paramedics,' one of the firefighters said. It was another man, this one tall, slim, wiry. 'To her credit, Jane, that's the casualty's wife if you didn't know, was relatively calm. Not much she could do, though, what with her husband dangling like he was from a tree, and out of reach. Still, she'd been talking to him, reassuring him, as he was falling in and out of consciousness.'

'How did you get him down?'

'As gently as we could. There was nowt wrong with any of his ropes, so it wasn't actually too difficult. Just needed a head for heights. Couple of our team are climbers, so we have that covered, but then you can't exactly join the fire service if you get dizzy a few metres up, right? Once he was down, the paramedics arrived. We let them focus on stabilising him while we all waited for the ambulance. Had a couple of my team sit with Jane. She was in shock. Fair enough, too. It looked like something out of a horror film when we arrived, body hanging from a tree, blood everywhere. He's lucky.'

Exactly what the paramedic had said, thought Harry.

'Any idea what happened?'

The firefighter shook his head.

'Jane doesn't know herself. All she heard was a scream when she arrived at the house. She ran round the side of the building and found her husband hanging from the tree. You know he wasn't wearing his helmet, right? Must've forgotten to put it on. Easy to do. And it's always when you do something like that, when the accident happens, isn't it? Sod's law.'

Harry thanked the firefighter for his time and walked up the drive, past two further vehicles, then came round to the back of the house. The garden was considerable, he noticed, and the tree, though partly felled, still dominated. He spotted Dave standing over by a small garden table and chairs.

Ethan approached from beneath the tree, where Harry spotted ropes dangling.

'DCI Grimm,' the DI said.

'It's Harry,' said Harry. 'You'll get used to the familiarity eventually, Ethan, I promise.'

'Doesn't feel right.'

'Doesn't mean that it isn't. Just the way things are round here. Took me a while, too. You'll get the hang of it. Anyway, best you show me what you've found. I didn't rush over here just to have garden envy.'

Ethan led Harry over to where Dave was standing.

'Now then, Harry,' he said. 'Thought we'd be seeing you soon enough. Bit of a do, this, isn't it?'

'It is,' Harry agreed. 'How did everything go this morning?'

'Mixed bag,' said Dave. 'But I think we're getting somewhere.'

'That's good. We'll talk about it later.' Harry took a closer look at the table and chairs. They were made of cast-iron and painted white. He could imagine it would be a lovely place to sit on a sunny evening, bottle of wine and some cheese, bit of music. Now, though, the table wasn't holding anything of the kind.

'That's Darren's helmet,' Ethan said, pointing. 'And that right there, well, you can see what it is, can't you?'

The helmet was the kind Harry had seen plenty of tree surgeons wear; bright orange, with face protection and ear defenders. Not cheap. The kind of equipment owned by someone who took safety very seriously and spent good money on it, too. Grace had her own and a couple of chainsaws for when she was working in woodland and sorting out pens for birds, as well as sorting out firewood with her dad. But it wasn't the helmet that drew Harry's eye, because leaning against the side of it was a phone. Harry could see that the screen was pointing directly at the tree.

'It's still on, then?' he observed.

'It is,' said Ethan.

'Would I be right in thinking that's an app that's open on the screen?'

Ethan confirmed that assumption with a nod.

'Same one that was open on Mike's phone,' he said. 'Bit of a coincidence, isn't it?'

'And we both know what I think about coincidences, don't we?' said Harry. 'Someone was watching the accident when it happened, then?'

'As mad as it sounds, it certainly looks that way. It wasn't his wife, either; she's been out all morning, and we've confirmed that already. The only reason she came over here at all was because he'd left his lunch at home. She found it when she got home and came straight over with it. Good job that she did, otherwise ...'

Harry allowed his eyes to travel from the phone to the

tree, then back again, thinking back to Mike's collision. As far as what had happened there, he felt that he could, in time, put the things they'd found out about the accident down to just an odd collection of circumstances. Mike was giving the Land Rover a run after doing some work on it. He had his phone attached inside because he probably didn't know every lane in the Dales and just attached it without thinking about it. That the app was on, well, that could be simply that he'd opened it by accident and hadn't realised. There was nothing suspicious in itself about having the app on his phone; it was one used all over the world. The wheel coming off was another matter entirely, but then again, what if that was nothing more than tiredness, a mistake? It wasn't entirely inconceivable, even for someone like Mike. Errors happened, even potentially catastrophic ones.

This, though? No, thought Harry, there was no way he could sensibly shrug it off. The similarities were striking; the phone, the app still open, the supposed accident happening to someone who was a professional in their field.

'Ethan?' Harry asked. 'Do we know what actually happened? I can see that Darren fell out of the tree, but by all accounts, his gear stopped him hitting the deck. Yet, there's a lot of blood. I've seen his face, the injuries, and they're not from a fall.'

'Oh, I thought you knew,' said Ethan.

'I can guess, but if you know, then don't keep it a secret.'

'The chain snapped,' explained Ethan. 'Chainsaw's over there, if you want to have a look.'

'Show me.'

Harry walked beside Ethan as they went over to the chainsaw.

'Firefighters cut it from Darren in the process of getting

him down from the tree. It was attached to his belt by a length of rope and a carabiner. There's another one as well, smaller, but the blade's fine on that one. Intact.'

Seeing the chainsaw firsthand, Harry thought back to the paramedic who'd said how the scene looked like a horror movie. The chainsaws only added to that picture. The one that had injured Darren looked like something a prop designer would be proud of. The chainsaw itself was splattered in blood, already turning dark as it dried. The chain hung from it like a snapped necklace. Harry was able to make out, not just blood on its teeth, either, but small chunks of flesh.

He stared a moment longer at the chainsaws, then allowed his eyes to drift across the garden, first to the tree, where Darren's ropes still dangled, then to the phone leaning against the helmet.

He checked his pockets, found them empty.

'Ethan, can I borrow your phone? Left mine in my vehicle. Need to make a call.'

'Of course. Who, the detective superintendent?'

Harry shook his head, dialled a number.

The call was answered on the third ring.

'Hello, Rebecca,' he said. 'Don't suppose you're free, are you?'

THIRTY

Of the two people Harry was waiting for, Matt arrived first. While he was waiting, he helped the team cordon the area off with an enthusiastic amount of tape.

'Missed all the fun, then?'

'No,' said Harry. 'I think it's just about to start. Or will do, as soon as Rebecca arrives.'

That got Matt's attention. He stepped in closer.

'Sowerby? I thought it was an—'

'Accident? No chance,' said Harry, rightly guessing what Matt had been about to say.

'What makes you say that? Tree surgery's a dangerous job. Lethal, actually. There's a lad in one of the rescue teams we work with, lives over in the Lake District now, I think. Anyway, he's got some stories that'll make your toes curl.'

'I'm sure.'

'Are we dealing with a fatality now as well, then?'

'Thankfully, no, but if you ask me, the victim, Darren, is seriously lucky. Chain snapped on the chainsaw he was using.' Harry drew a jagged line across his face, down his chest. 'Caught him all across here. I know a lot about scars, and he'll be carrying one for the rest of his life in a very obvious place, that's for sure. Dealing with that will probably be even more traumatic than what he's going through right now.'

Harry led Matt around to the back of the house, then went through everything that had happened.

'Trouble is, there's only two people who really know what happened,' he said, once they were done looking at everything. 'The victim ...'

'And whoever was on the other end of that call,' finished Matt. 'We've a connection, then.'

'We do. I could've let the phone thing slide with Mike, but with this? That's not happening, I'm afraid.'

'I don't get it, though,' said Matt, scratching his chin as though doing so would somehow give him clarity. 'Why would someone be watching Mike crash a vehicle, and our chap here have a chainsaw accident?'

'There's also the how,' added Harry.

'How? In what sense?'

Harry took Matt back to the front of the house to wait for the arrival of Rebecca.

'The why is important. That's the motive for whatever's going on, right? That's a given. And we've no idea what that could be, not yet. But the how ... that's just as important. If someone watched what happened to both Mike and now to Darren, then the only conclusion we can draw is that they were doing so to witness the apparent accidents, yes?'

'Makes sense, as weird and messed up as it is.'

'Can you see, then, why I'm saying the how is important? How did they know there was going to be an accident in the first place? How did they know Mike was going to have that accident, or that the chain on the chainsaw Darren was using was going to snap? Throw in a few other things, and it's all a bit ...'

'Twisted and horrific?'

'Good words, well chosen.'

'Thank you. What other things?'

'Take Mike's Land Rover,' said Harry. 'We've that wheel, haven't we? Three missing bolts, and the two that were still in were loose. Speed played a part in him having the accident, as did the tractor, but take those away, and I think we're left with the fact that the stuff with the wheel, that's what was the cause. The tractor was chance, really, I think. My gut tells me that what happened to Mike was all about what the speed and that corner, or indeed any corner, would do to that wheel.'

'It's deliberate? Is that what you're saying? Hell, Harry ...'

'And now we've got Darren, right? He's a professional tree surgeon. He has a wife, two kids, takes safety seriously; his gear is expensive, which is proof enough of that. Yet, what did we have on that little table in the garden?'

'Darren's helmet.'

'Exactly, his helmet,' said Harry. 'And leaning against it, a phone with the same app open on the screen. And there's Darren, up in the tree, his chain snaps, he falls. So again, we're back to the how, aren't we?'

Matt frowned.

'You think someone tampered with both Mike's Land Rover and Darren's chainsaw?'

'What I think,' said Harry, 'is that Mike is very much not the kind of person to not only forget to put all the wheel bolts in, but also to leave the other two loose. That's just madness, and Mike's not mad, is he? He's respected. His business is strong. People trust him.'

'And Darren?'

'I had a look at the website he has for his business. Reviews are superb. All of them say how professional he is, how safe, how he's done some really technical jobs with perfect outcomes. They don't read like reviews of someone who doesn't wear a helmet and uses shoddy tools.'

'I'm not liking the sound of this,' said Matt.

Harry couldn't agree more.

'We've two serious accidents; All things considered, we're damned lucky we've not had a body to deal with.'

'Not accidents, though, are they?'

'I don't think so, no. Which leads to my next worry.'

Matt was quiet, and he and Harry watched as two large white vans pulled up at the front of the house.

'You think we could be dealing with more, is that it?'

'No idea,' said Harry. 'There's a reason both Mike and Darren had these accidents, and that reason belongs to whoever was watching things as they unfolded. Both events were planned, and maybe that's it now. Maybe, whatever this is about, it's done. But what if it's not? What if whoever is behind this has other things planned, whatever the reason for doing so might be?'

The doors of the vans opened and white-overalled figures began to ooze out of them and unload equipment. One broke off from the others and started to walk towards them.

'Anyway,' said Harry, 'how were things with Barnaby's parents?'

'I'm no clearer about what happened,' said Matt. 'I think they're just concerned parents. More concerned than ever, thanks to someone suggesting that Barnaby might have taken the poison deliberately.'

'Crossed my mind, too,' said Harry. 'Could be a call for help.'

'How so?'

'If someone's going to take their own life, and they're determined to do it, then there's really very little anyone can do about it; they'll find a way, regardless. That's the brutal truth of it. The thing is, with Barnaby, he's not only still alive, he called emergency services himself, as well as his parents. Those aren't the actions of someone bowing out.'

'That makes some sense,' agreed Matt. 'Certainly sounds like Barnaby is a bit of a workaholic. He doesn't want any help in the bakery, does all of it himself, so my guess is he's exhausted. That builds, doesn't it, over time?'

'Have you spoken to Barnaby himself yet?'

Matt shook his head.

'Wasn't in. Waited around a while for him to turn up but then got the call to come here. Had a chat with Craig, though.'

Harry remembered the name from his conversation with Penny in the hospital car park.

'What did he have to say?'

'He's just as confused by it all as everyone else. Said it was completely out of character. Barnaby called him as well, after emergency services and his parents.'

'Why?'

'Craig said it was Barnaby's obsession with his business kicking in, despite the circumstances. Said that when he answered, Barnaby told him he needed an emergency cleanup at the bakery, then hung up. He arrived just before

John and Penny and stayed on to do exactly as Barnaby requested.'

'He cleaned up, no questions asked?'

'Having met Craig, I think he's just the kind of person who'd do anything to help anyone,' said Matt. 'Kind heart in him. So yeah, he cleaned up. Said the place was a mess, that Barnaby had been baking a small batch of something, not that he knew what. There was vomit on the floor as well. He did a full sweep of the place, and he deep cleaned everything, put away what Barnaby had out on the work surface that he'd been using, the bowls, bun cases, laptop, ingredients, then he went home.'

Sowerby came to stand with Harry and Matt.

'I've been told there's no body for me to be worrying about,' she said. 'Makes a change.'

Harry ignored that comment.

'Good to see you,' he said. 'How's Margaret?'

'Mum's the same as ever,' Sowerby replied. 'Loud, abrasive, brilliant, unstoppable, and still terrorising all road users by insisting on not getting rid of that ridiculous Range Rover of hers.'

Harry smiled at that.

'Didn't mean to interrupt,' said Sowerby. 'I can just crack on if you show me what's what.'

Harry turned to Matt.

'I think we're done, aren't we?'

'Yes,' nodded Matt. Then, as Harry went to take the pathologist through everything that had happened, he said, 'Oh, I meant to say, I called the hospital as well.'

'About Mike?' said Harry.

'No, about Barnaby,' said Matt. 'Thought it would be worth getting some details on the poison he'd ingested.'

Harry saw Sowerby's eyes light up on hearing that.

'What, you've had a poisoning as well?' she said. 'Well, today's just getting more and more interesting, isn't it? What did the hospital tell you?'

Harry narrowed his eyes at Sowerby, not least because her enthusiasm was laced with a touch of glee. It wasn't macabre, though, more that she was just in a good mood.

'You do know I'm in charge, right?'

Matt said, 'The hospital confirmed it was rat poison and that it was ingested rather than through exposure, you know, absorbed through the skin, or whatever. There was an analysis of the stomach contents as well.'

'Hadn't he vomited everything up all over the floor of his bakery?' said Harry.

'Still enough left inside to analyse. They gave me a chemical breakdown, which wasn't very useful really, so they helped out by giving me what's basically a list of things you'd expect in a bakery anyway; butter, sugar, flour, eggs.'

'Not very useful.'

'What poison was it?' Sowerby asked.

'Thal—something or other,' answered Matt. 'I wrote it down, but my notebook's in my car. I'll go fetch it.'

'Thallium?' said Sowerby, before Matt could head off.

'You've heard of it?'

Harry noticed an odd look fall upon Sowerby's face.

'Something wrong?' he asked.

'Well, it's just that thallium as a pesticide was phased out and then banned in the seventies.'

'It was? Why?'

'Because of exactly the kind of thing you've just described,' Sowerby answered. 'Accidental poisoning was all too easy when using it. It's actually known as the poisoner's poison, because it turned up in a few too many murder cases over the years. Not now, though, because it's considerably more difficult to get hold of.'

'And yet here we are,' said Harry. 'And you're saying it was banned in the seventies? So, how did Barnaby get hold of it?' He looked at Matt for an answer to that question.

Matt said nothing.

'Old rat poison still turns up,' Sowerby said. 'You've got to realise that it was readily available for a very, very long time. People buy stuff like that, store it in garden sheds, garages, and they forget about it, don't they? There's probably loads of it lying around still.'

'Worrying thought.'

'Somewhat. This Barnaby fellow, he's okay, though, yes?'

'He was in hospital for over a week, I believe,' said Harry. 'Home now, though.'

'Sounds about right. He'd have been given potassium ferric hexacyanoferrate to absorb it. Probably had his stomach pumped early on. Activated charcoal is good as well.'

'Anyway,' said Harry, keen to hurry along now with the case they were actually dealing with, 'that's something else entirely, isn't it? Probably best if we park it for now and get on with what happened round the back.'

'Sounds mysterious,' whispered Sowerby, leaning in close to Matt.

'It's bizarre, is what it is,' said Harry. 'And I'll need you to have a chat with the collision investigator as well.'

'Caitlin? Why? This isn't a collision, unless there's a vehicle hiding somewhere that I'm not aware of.'

'Had one earlier in the week. We think it's connected to what happened here.'

'How?'

'Probably best I show you,' said Harry, and with that, led Sowerby down the side of the house and to the rear garden.

THIRTY-ONE

The rest of Harry's day was spent working alongside Rebecca and the rest of the SOC team while at the same time feeling somewhat surplus to requirements. So much so, that in the end, he let the rest of the team go.

Ethan had to catch up with Detective Superintendent Walker. Harry had a quick chat with him before that, to make sure things were okay, and to ensure she was getting an honest account of what was going on, good and bad, though really, he was sure there wasn't that much bad to report.

Matt left to try and see Barnaby again; Harry wanted that all done and dusted so that they could then focus on what was going on with Mike and Darren and whoever was behind their 'accidents.' Distractions were never welcome. Dave wanted to see if he could hurry things along with regards to the nest box thefts, so Jen went off with him to do that. And he sent Liz off to Mike's garage in Hawes under the notion of checking up on things, seeing if there was anything she could learn from the place, from Ben, that might give them some idea of who was responsible.

In reality, he just wanted someone to keep an eye on Ben, and he could think of no one better to do that than Liz. Also, after what Mike had said about the pair of them, and what was going on, or not, with their wedding plans, he thought a bit of extra time together would be good. Which left him alone with the spectral figures of the SOC team as they busied themselves around the site, investigating this, examining that, and taking numerous samples of all kinds of things back to their vans.

Harry was, for possibly the tenth time that afternoon, checking the cordon tape, when Sowerby came over to see him.

'I'm glad you're doing that,' she said, pointing at the tape. 'There's not nearly enough of it.'

'Really? You think so?'

'Of course. I mean, right now, I can actually see where everything happened, and my guess is that we want to hide it from prying eyes completely, don't we?'

Harry found himself nearly agreeing with her and saying yes, then stopped, having seen the glint in the pathologist's eye.

'Ha ha.'

'Not funny?'

'No.'

'You need to lighten up.'

'This is me lightened up.'

'Ouch.'

Harry twanged one of the strips of cordon tape, then said, 'Beyond your critique of the tape situation, I assume you came over here for another reason as well?'

'You looked lonely.'

'I am not lonely.'

'Then I suppose we should just talk shop, then, shouldn't we?'

Harry wasn't used to having his leg pulled, certainly not so playfully, and he immediately grew suspicious. Not in a bad way, though; Rebecca did seem to be on good form, and he wondered why, but could probably guess.

'Who is he, then?'

'Who is who?'

'The reason behind your chirpiness.'

'I'm always chirpy.'

Harry's look was enough to let Sowerby know that was very much not the case.

'Sharp, yes, and sometimes funny with it, but this is different.'

Sowerby cocked her head to one side.

'Well, whoever he is, and I'm not saying there is, but if there was, I still wouldn't tell you.'

'So, there is, then.'

'That's not what I said.'

'Well, it's what I heard. Now, moving on from me being lonely and you clearly not being ...'

Sowerby led Harry over to the two garden chairs. The table between them had been cleared of the helmet and phone, both taken as evidence by the SOC team, along with the rope Darren had been found dangling from the tree on, and all his gear, including the chainsaw which had caused him such appalling injuries. She sat down. Harry followed suit.

'What do you want me to begin with? Caitlin, or this?'

With that, she gestured at the huge tree in front of them with a wide sweep of her arms.

'Start with Caitlin,' said Harry. 'That was the first thing

we were called out to, and it's because of what we found there that I grew suspicious about this.'

'And rightly so, too,' agreed Sowerby. 'The links are clear.'

'The phone?'

'And the fact that in both supposed accidents, something's been tampered with.'

'What did Caitlin have to say, then?' Harry asked.

'She ran through the collision, her findings, told me about the wheel, the phone that was found at the scene of the collision. Everything, really.'

'And where has that led?'

'To me arranging to have some of my team go and have a look at everything tomorrow.'

'You're not going yourself?'

Sowerby shook her head.

'Not my area of expertise, examining twisted bits of metal. I'm more a blood and guts type of gal.'

'It's why we like you.'

Sowerby laughed at that.

'But you agree there's a link, then?'

'I mean, there has to be, doesn't there?' Sowerby replied. 'Neither incident was an accident, that's for sure. No way anyone would ever believe it, either.'

'Why do you say that?'

Sowerby lifted a finger. 'One, because the incidents themselves are seemingly very far removed from how the people involved, Mike and Darren, work in a professional capacity. What happened to them, how it happened to them, just doesn't sit right with how they work, their reputations.'

'And two?'

Sowerby lifted another finger.

'Two, because they would never have been seen as accidents, would they? Because of what I've just said, and because of how each incident happened. Mike would never drive a vehicle in that condition, and Darren would never shimmy up a tree without his helmet and use a chainsaw whose chain has been tampered with.'

That detail got Harry's attention.

'You think that's what's happened, then?'

'I know so,' said Sowerby. 'Not because of where the chain came apart, because at first glance, all you're seeing with that is a broken chain, aren't you?'

'Then what?'

'Someone's been at it with a file or something in various other places as well.'

'What? Why?'

'That's what I was going to ask you.'

Harry thought about that for a second, then said, 'They were making sure, weren't they?'

'In what sense?'

'Well, if you tamper with a chain on a chainsaw, the only reason you'd do that is because you want something bad to happen. Throw in the fact that they were watching it happen on that app, then my guess is that they wanted to be sure of the outcome, that there was no room for error.'

'Sort of a guarantee,' said Sowerby.

'Exactly that.'

Sowerby then said, 'I did have one thought, though ...'

Harry noticed a change in Sowerby's tone of voice.

'And what was that?'

'Have you heard about these suicide websites?'

'Do I want to?'

'Probably not, but anyway ... You see, there are websites

out there providing instructions on how to take your own life. Hard to believe, because you and I can't fathom that kind of thing, can we? But there are people who can, and they act on that. There are even websites where you can try to meet others to take your own life with. I've always maintained that if you can think it, then someone, somewhere, has probably done it.'

Harry sighed heavily at the darkness behind Sowerby's words.

'What is wrong with this world?'

'A lot. And if you search hard enough, you'll soon enough find someone happy to watch you go through with it, either in person, or on webcam. There have been an awful lot of documented cases where individuals have taken their own lives online; they wanted an audience for their final act.'

Harry looked over at the tree and thought back to Mike's crash. Then, as he was about to say something depressing about what Sowerby had told him, he remembered what he'd been talking about with Matt earlier, just before she had arrived. He stood up.

'Something I said?' said Sowerby.

'Yes,' Harry replied. 'What you've just said, horrific as it is, it's got me thinking.'

'Really? What about?'

'A laptop and a phone,' Harry replied. 'And just what the hell the first of those was doing in a bakery in the middle of the night ...'

THIRTY-TWO

With Barnaby's address from Matt, Harry left Sowerby to finish up at the house. He then called Grace to let her know he would be home later than expected, but also to check up on Smudge.

'You don't need to keep asking how she is,' said Grace, and Harry heard the faint note of irritation in her voice.

'Yes, I do,' Harry insisted. 'I've not had a pregnant dog before.'

'What difference does that make?'

'I've no idea, I'm just saying.'

Grace laughed at that.

'Well, she's fine, and I'm sure she will be fine tomorrow, and the day after that, and so on, until she pops the little fur balls out. And even then, she'll be fine, because motherhood will be all instinct, and my guess is that she'll be a fantastic mum.'

'Do we need to get anything in for that?'

'Like what? And if you say towels and plenty of hot water ...'

Harry decided it was best to say nothing at all.

'Ignoring your worry about Smudge, how's the day been?'

'Busy. That's why I'm going to be late. Something's come up from a scene we attended today, and I think there's a link to something else, so I need to check on that to be sure.'

'It's like you're a proper detective and everything.' Grace laughed.

'But I am a proper detective and everything. I've even got a badge to prove it.'

'So sexy.'

Conversation over, Harry focused on the road ahead. The afternoon was slouching its way into evening, with the sun already sleepy in the sky, soon to bed down for the night beneath the blanket of the horizon. Harry loved this time of day, the fading light giving way to night, shadows chasing each other across the fells. The air changed too, he noticed, and he dropped his window to take advantage of it, slowing down a little as he did so.

The day had been both warm and cool and was now overburdened with all the smells of the day. Harry caught all kinds of notes on the air rushing into the cabin, a cocktail of cut grass and dry heather, of fern and stone and farm. It swept in front of him as the songs of the landscape chased him, with sheep calling to each other in the fields, a distant plane cutting the sky in two, and the roads buzzing with humanity in a rush.

There was nothing, Harry thought then, that he would change about the Dales. It was, in every possible way, as perfect a place as he could think of. He had travelled well in his life, especially during his time as a soldier. He had seen awe-inspiring landscapes, dug holes in them to sleep, fought in them, been scarred by them, yet here was something untouchable. The history of every nook and cranny was written by the becks that etched into the landscape, tales only the fells themselves understood and remembered.

He could not imagine living anywhere else, and neither would he, either. The Dales had him now, and there was no escape. He had family here, friends here, someone he wanted to share the rest of his life with, and a dog. It made no sense that all of this was his, especially if he thought about it too deeply, so he didn't. Instead, he accepted it, embraced it, and as the sun dipped lower still, realised he was smiling. But then, how could he not?

Especially as his journey took him down into Swaledale. Harry, not one for words at the best of times, found that he wished he had the ways of a poet about him, because this ancient place deserved it. He'd followed the River Swale many times since moving north, and he loved Reeth, its village green, the cobbles, and the pure darkness of the place when night fell, with the only sounds that of far-off sheep and the chatter of people chasing conversation from one pub to the next. Yet the view further along, where he would slip through Gunnerside, then on to Muker, was one so startling that, as he had done so many times before, he stopped just to take it in.

Pulling over into a small layby on the left, Harry eased his vehicle to a stop, turned off the engine, and climbed out. Walking around to the front of the Rav, he leaned against the bonnet and just stared. Here, the valley bottom was pond flat, but the surface was not that of still water. Instead, it was a patchwork of fields stitched together with drystone walls so perfectly, Harry felt as though he could, at any moment, simply reach out, take hold of a corner, and give it a pull.

At the far end of this view lay Gunnerside, the gateway to Gunnerside Gill, and home to the King's Head pub. Harry thought about giving Grace a call, see if she fancied meeting him there for a pint, but with the thin fingers of evening now snatching at him, he decided it was better to just get on with the reason he was there in the first place, and then head home after.

A few minutes later, and having arrived in Muker, Harry parked up and made his way to the address Matt had given him. He'd phoned ahead and Barnaby had answered, said he was fine to receive a visitor, but that he'd be heading to bed soon as he was still weary from what he'd gone through.

At Barnaby's house, Harry gave the front door a knock. It was answered quickly.

'Barnaby Shaw?'

'You must be the detective,' Barnaby replied, and stepped back, allowing Harry to enter the house.

Inside, Barnaby guided him through to the kitchen, where they both sat down at a nice old pine dining table, well worn, well loved, and covered in the scars of a life lived well. Barnaby made a pot of tea, because that's what everyone in the Dales did if someone turned up at the door. Harry was used to it now, hardly drank coffee at all, wasn't sure he even really missed it. What he certainly didn't miss was paying for the stuff, the queues to get it, and the interminable wait for the takeaway bucket of the scalding hot liquid to be eventually handed over.

Handing Harry a mug of tea, Barnaby presented a small tin which had, at some point in its life, contained Christmas chocolates. The artwork on the sides and lid was faded and battered, but the contents were now perhaps even more delicious.

'Shortbread, that's all,' said Barnaby. 'Fresh, though. Had to bake something as soon as I got home. Missed it.'

Harry took a biscuit, had a bite. There was no doubting, even from just that first nibble, that Barnaby knew what he was doing in the kitchen.

'Well, how can I help?' Barnaby asked, taking a biscuit for himself to dunk in his tea before taking a bite.

'Every time I do that, I lose half my biscuit,' said Harry.

Barnaby smiled.

'You leave it in the liquid too long, then, that's all.'

Harry considered going in for a dunk, then decided not to.

'How are you doing, then?' he asked. 'Been through it a bit, haven't you?'

'It's been rough, I can't lie,' Barnaby replied, and Harry heard weariness in his voice. 'I'm okay, though. On the mend now, thankfully.'

'You were lucky, by all accounts. Rat poison isn't something to be trifled with.'

Harry did his best to ignore that he'd just used the word *trifled* and took a sip of tea.

'Don't know how it happened,' said Barnaby. 'I am lucky, you're right about that.'

'You've no idea at all, then, how you ended up with rat poison in you?'

Barnaby shook his head, dipped a bit more of his biscuit, took another bite.

'What were you doing at the time?'

'Baking.'

'You were taken to the hospital in the middle of the night.'

'We bakers have strange working hours.'

'I know, but the middle of the night is a bit more strange than usual, isn't it?'

'Is it?'

'I'm asking you.'

Harry wondered if he was pushing too hard too soon, but then an image of Smudge and Jess and Grace came into his mind, and he stopped wondering; he wanted to know what was going on, and then he wanted to get home.

Barnaby remained quiet.

'What time do you usually get to work to start baking?'

'Maybe four or five in the morning. Depends on what needs to be done, I suppose.'

'What had you in the bakery so early, then?'

'I was trying something out.'

'What?'

'A new recipe.'

'That's exciting,' Harry smiled. 'What is it?'

Barnaby paused, then said, 'Trade secret.'

'I'm a police officer,' answered Harry. 'I'm good at keeping secrets. Even better at finding them out,' he added. 'The poison you ingested, it's really quite rare.'

'Is it? I didn't know.'

'You use a professional to do bait traps for you, correct?'

Barnaby confirmed that with a nod.

'Well, everything checks out; they don't use it, the poison found in your system, because they can't, seeing as it was banned for use as a pesticide back in the seventies.'

This was a lie; Harry only knew what Sowerby had told him. But he wondered what reaction that statement would get. The answer was one that told him nothing. Not yet, anyway.

'They're good at what they do,' said Barnaby. 'That's why

I use them. A business like the one I run, you have to be so careful, otherwise your reputation, it's ruined, just like that.'

He clicked his fingers above the table.

Harry changed tack.

'I've been told you called your parents.'

'Yes. After I contacted emergency services.'

'Why?'

'Why what?'

'Why did you call them?'

'I was scared. I was suddenly really ill, vomiting, coughing up blood. That's not normal, is it?'

'No, it certainly isn't. You also called your friend, Craig, yes?'

'So I've been told. Can't say that I remember, but then I hardly remember calling my parents either seeing as I was in such a mess. Everything that's happened seems to have scrambled my brain. It's all a bit of a blur, really. When I do remember bits of what happened, I try to forget it as soon as I can, believe me.'

'Craig works for you.'

'Part-time. He does odd jobs all over the Dales. You'll have seen his van about, I'm sure.'

'I will?'

'He got it when he turned twenty-one; birthday present from his parents. It was old then, because it had been theirs first, and they'd really looked after it, or his dad had, anyway. Must be thirty years old now, at least, probably older.'

'Vans don't generally stand out.'

'I know, but Craig's does.'

'Why?'

'Because he's kept it in such good condition, and not just

because his mum's kept on at him about it, either. He loves it, almost to the point where he treats it like a pet.'

'Bit odd.'

'Odd or not, most Transits that age, they're either falling apart or no longer on the road, aren't they? Not Craig's though, his is mint.'

Harry really didn't care about Craig's van.

'If you'd called your parents after suddenly falling ill, why did you call Craig as well? Can't see why you'd need to.'

'He cleaned up the mess for me. Knew I wouldn't want to be coming back to the bakery and finding the place stinking.'

Harry took another biscuit.

'Barnaby, can I ask you a really personal question?'

'You're going to anyway, aren't you?'

Harry dipped the biscuit into his tea, lifted it out, rolled his eyes. 'Bugger ...' Half the biscuit was gone. He looked over it to Barnaby. 'Tell me, have you ever thought about taking your own life?'

Barnaby's eyes went as wide as dinner plates.

'What? Why the hell would you ask me that? What's wrong with you? I mean, I just don't get where you—'

'That's a no, then, right?'

'Of course it bloody well is! Why would I want to take my own life?'

'What was in the bun cases?'

The change of subject clearly caught Barnaby off guard again.

'What?'

'Craig said he cleared up bun cases. I assume they were used for whatever you were baking.'

'Butterfly cakes,' said Barnaby. 'They're a bit of a

customer favourite. I use butter for the icing, not margarine or whatever, that's what makes them so good.'

'Between you and me, that doesn't sound like much of a new recipe, now, does it?'

Barnaby didn't reply.

'Why did you need your laptop?'

Another change of direction with the questioning.

'Pardon?'

Harry finished his tea.

'Your laptop. Craig cleared that away, too. Same as the bun cases, and everything else you had out that night. Mopped up your vomit. That's a big ask, even from a friend, especially considering the hour, and the state you were in.'

'Is it? And yes, he did, but ...'

Harry could tell that Barnaby was starting to get confused. *Good.* So, he kept pushing.

'What you're saying then is that you have absolutely no idea how you managed to get a rat poison that is now nigh on impossible to get a hold of, into your bakery and into the food you were preparing, and which you then ate?'

'No, I don't.'

Harry took a third biscuit.

'And yet here I am, happily eating these. As are you.'

'So?'

'So, what happened to the butterfly cakes?'

No answer.

'Craig didn't say anything about there being butterfly cakes. He mentioned bun cases, that's all. If you were baking them, surely there would be some in the kitchen, right? So, what happened to them? Where are they? And how many were there?'

'I ... I can't remember.'

'You ate some of them, didn't you, Barnaby? Well, I know you did, because the contents of your stomach were analysed.'

'I tasted them, because it was a new recipe, like I said.'

'There's tasting and sampling, and then there's eating all of the cakes. That's two different things. Is that what you did, ate the lot? Which again makes me wonder why. Did you do that knowing there was poison in them?'

Harry saw Barnaby's eyes go wide enough to pop out of his skull.

'What? Why would I eat something if I knew there was poison in it? That makes no sense!'

'You're right. It doesn't make any sense, Barnaby. None at all. Anyway, back to that laptop of yours, seeing as you didn't answer my question about it.'

'My laptop? Why do you care? What's it got to do with me ending up in hospital because of poison?'

'That's an interesting question you're asking there, Barnaby.'

Barnaby shook his head as though the question didn't matter in the slightest.

'Like you said, Craig must've cleared it away, like he did everything else.'

'But why was it there at all?' Harry pressed. 'That's what I want to know.'

'Because I use it as a recipe book, for research, that's why.'

'Where is it?'

'In my office, upstairs.'

'And you aren't concerned, then, that it has traces of rat poison on it?'

'No, why would I be?'

'That's another very interesting question, Barnaby, don't you think?' said Harry. 'Why would you be, indeed? Or, perhaps, more accurately, why wouldn't you be? I mean, it was with you when you somehow accidentally mixed a very rare rat poison in with what you were baking, and it was with you when you ended up so ill you had to call the emergency services, so ...'

'I'm not following you.'

Harry ate the third biscuit in one go.

'Someone else was, though, weren't they?' he said. 'Following you, I mean. Though perhaps a better word would be watching. From your laptop. In fact, I'm fairly damned sure, Barnaby, that if I got a hold of your laptop right now, I'd find out that there's either an app on there, or some internet history of it, that would allow someone to watch you eat whatever it was you baked for yourself in that bakery of yours with poison in it. But what I want to know is not just who the hell that person was, but also why the hell they wanted to watch you in the first place. Well, Barnaby? Are you going to tell me, or ...'

Barnaby's answer was to spring from his chair and bolt for the door.

Harry caught him as he hit the stairs, dragged him back, spun him round, and stared at him with eyes hard as steel.

'It's not you I want!' he said, his voice flint hard and sharpened to a spear point. 'It's them, Barnaby, it's them! Just tell me what happened, please, so that I can help!'

For a moment, Barnaby didn't move, held as he was by the heat of the anger in Harry's eyes, his frustration that Barnaby wasn't telling him what he needed to know. Then, like a puppet with its strings cut, he collapsed into Harry's arms, and released a wail so broken, all Harry could do was hold him tight enough to try and keep him together.

THIRTY-THREE

By the time Barnaby had calmed down enough to tell Harry all that he knew about what had happened to him, and why, whatever fight he'd had in him when Harry had arrived had disappeared completely. Which was why, once he felt sure there was nothing else to learn from the now physically, emotionally, and psychologically exhausted Barnaby, Harry called his parents. They were round to Barnaby's house in minutes.

'He's okay,' Harry said, meeting them at the door, a hand raised just enough to hold them off for a moment. 'He's been through a lot as it is, so my advice is we all just take it gentle, like.'

Harry noticed the way he finished that sentence, another bit of the Dales slipping into his life, changing his DNA.

John Shaw pushed against Harry's hand, but Harry held fast.

'We came like you told us to. Now, let us see our son.'

'I'm not stopping you,' Harry replied. 'I just want to go through a few things, that's all. Understood?'

Penny Shaw was standing at her husband's side, her hands wrapped around his arm. Her eyes were red with tears.

With no answer from either parent, Harry led them both through to the kitchen and gestured to the dining table and chairs.

'Barnaby's upstairs,' he said, sitting down. 'Resting for now. He'll be alright, but it's going to take some time and a lot of love and understanding. He knows I've asked you to come round. He just wants a bit of time to prepare himself to see you.'

John and Penny sat down.

'He doesn't need to prepare himself; we're his parents, we love him!' said John.

'That I don't doubt, and neither does he.'

'What's the problem, then?' Penny asked. 'What's changed since he got home from the hospital?'

Harry rested his elbows on the table, his hands together, fingers interlocked.

'Your son was blackmailed into poisoning himself.'

John and Penny stared back at Harry with horror and disbelief in their eyes.

'Barnaby poisoned himself? What are you talking about?' said John, his indignation sending him to his feet. 'You mean he tried to kill himself, is that what you mean? But Barnaby would never do that! He just wouldn't!'

Penny said nothing, just stared at Harry, face white with shock.

'I didn't say he tried to kill himself,' said Harry, his voice calm and patient. He understood how difficult it was for John and Penny to hear any of this. 'There was a risk that he could've died because of what he did, but he didn't, and I think that's the point of what happened to him.'

John sat back down, pulled into his chair by Penny.

'What do you mean by that?' Penny asked. 'Are you saying someone wanted him to try and kill himself, but also that they didn't? That makes no sense.'

'None of this makes sense, Love,' said John, and Harry watched the couple find each other's hands on the table and interlock fingers.

'I think that someone wanted to punish your son,' said Harry. 'He saw no way out other than to do as the blackmailer requested. That's how blackmail works, after all. If it didn't, then it wouldn't exist.'

Harry noticed how John was clenching his jaws and was not surprised when he exploded across the table.

'Punish Barnaby? What the hell about? He's a good lad! This is ridiculous! I mean, it's bollocks, all of it! He's not done anything wrong. Who is this blackmailer? Where are they? I want the bastard!'

Harry was impressed by the fight in John, but knew he had to keep him calm. Penny, on the other hand, as far as he could tell, was rather shocked at the sudden outburst of rage by her husband.

'Right now, we have no idea who the blackmailer is,' he explained. 'Barnaby doesn't know either. However, I can assure you that my team and I will be working flat out on finding them.'

'How?'

'I can only tell you so much, John, which is very little, if I'm honest. What I can tell you, though, is that there are links between what's happened to Barnaby and a few other things we're looking at.'

Penny gasped.

'You mean, Barnaby's not the only one? This blackmailer, they've done the same to others?'

'Looks that way, yes,' Harry confirmed. 'As to what Barnaby was being blackmailed about, I think that's down to him to tell you.'

John went to speak again, but a sound at the kitchen door had everyone turn to see that Barnaby was standing there.

'Hi,' he said.

Harry stood up and helped Barnaby over to a chair.

'I'll leave you to it,' he said.

'No, it's fine, I'm okay,' said Barnaby, then he looked at his parents. 'I'm sorry,' he said. 'I should've told you, back when it happened. But I couldn't ... I didn't know how ...'

Harry waited at the door.

'It was a few years ago now. Business was hard, I was running out of money big time.'

'What? When? Why didn't you tell us?' said John.

'I was also ... I was ...' Barnaby's voice cracked. He took a moment or two to gather himself. 'I started using cocaine. It kept me awake, helped me focus, distracted me from what was really going on.'

Harry expected John and Penny to respond, but they said nothing. Instead, he watched them both reach across the table for their son's hands.

'The cocaine only added to my money problems. I ended up taking out a loan. Not a bank loan, something private. Someone over in Darlington. It was a contact through the person I was buying the cocaine from. I wasn't thinking straight. I'm sorry, I know this is hard to hear ...'

'What happened?' asked Penny, and Harry noticed that her voice was firm and caring all at once.

'I got into more debt, couldn't keep up the payments. I went round to see if I could talk it out, come to some kind of arrangement. I took something I'd baked, to try and sweet talk them, I guess, I don't know. It made sense at the time.'

'You tried to bribe a loan shark with cake?'

John's question was all disbelief.

'Yes, but ... Well, you see, I added something to the ... to the cakes I took round.'

John exchanged a look with Penny, then Harry, before turning back to Barnaby.

'What did you add?'

'Anything I could get hold of,' said Barnaby. 'Laxatives, pain killers, anything, really, can't remember exactly. I wasn't trying to kill them, I just wanted them to be really ill, to teach them a lesson. I know it sounds ridiculous now. It does to me as I say it. I didn't know what I was doing. I was exhausted, using cocaine, trying to run my business ...'

'And it's this person who made you poison yourself, is that what this is?' John asked, sending another quick look Harry's way. 'You poisoned them, so they forced you to poison yourself, my guess is to stop them telling us, your friends, whoever, about what you'd done, the cocaine, the loan.'

'That's where this takes an unexpected turn,' said Harry, stepping in. 'According to Barnaby, the person who loaned him the money. He's dead.'

Both John and Penny gasped, then they both stared at Barnaby.

'You ... you didn't ...' said Penny. 'You didn't poison them? Barnaby, please tell me you didn't ...'

'What? No, of course I didn't!' said Barnaby.

'How can you be sure?' asked John.

'Because when I went back to see him a couple of days later, he was ...'

'He was what?'

'Someone had shot him,' said Barnaby. 'The door was open. I walked in, called for him, noticed a smell. He was in his lounge. There was blood everywhere. I left, never heard anything more. Weeks went by, then months, then years. I thought I was in the clear for the money. Then ... then this person, I don't know who, contacted me. Left a message for me on my business phone. I should've ignored it, but I couldn't; I was terrified. They knew about it all, the cocaine, the loan, everything. They said they'd tell everyone, tell the police, if I didn't do as they said. Told me I needed to be taught a lesson. The poison, it was left outside my house the night before I added it to what I was cooking. I had no choice!'

As those last words left Barnaby's lips, so did a cry, and he collapsed onto the table. Penny and John jumped out of their chairs and were around to him in a heartbeat.

Harry turned to leave, and as he did so, he reached for the laptop on the kitchen worktop. It was Barnaby's. He'd handed it to him before he'd headed upstairs.

'You'll find them, won't you?' John asked. 'I'm not condoning what Barnaby's done, not by a long shot, but to use it against him like this? Who does that? And why?'

'I'll be in touch,' Harry said, and with that, left the Shaws alone, and headed home.

THIRTY-FOUR

Harry had a restless night, his mind whirring with what he and the team were now dealing with. Finding a connection between the collision involving Mike and the chainsaw accident was one thing. To realise that what had happened to Barnaby was also linked, was enough to ensure his mind wasn't interested in sleep, despite what the rest of his body thought. He and Matt had stumbled on it by chance alone, and yet what he'd found out from speaking with Barnaby had given him more than he'd learned from either of the other two incidents.

Come morning, Harry was bleary-eyed and grumpy. He apologised to Grace and the dogs for his mood, then to cheer himself up, decided he should follow up on what had been in that expensive envelope he'd thrown into the fire in a panic. So, with Grace and Jess gone for the day, and Smudge happy to stay at home and rest, he began to type an email on his phone. When it was done, and he was happy that he'd been specific enough in what he'd decided on from the options provided, he hit send, then let out a very long breath of relief.

There was no turning back now, really, especially considering what that email was going to cost him in the end.

That done, it was time to head to work, so he headed back upstairs, showered, and made sure he was on the right side of looking almost presentable.

A car was parked in front of the house, when Harry stepped outside. He recognised it immediately. He walked straight over to the driver's door, yanked the door open, reached in for the driver, and dragged him out, pinning him to the side of the vehicle, his forearm jammed in hard under the man's chin. With his other hand, he did a quick search around what the man was wearing and removed what he found.

'I can arrest you for carrying this,' he said, holding up a folding knife he'd pulled from the man's belt. The only other thing he'd found was a phone, which he handed back. He opened the blade, which locked in place. 'Damascus steel as well. Not cheap. Pity I'm keeping it to have it destroyed.'

'It was a gift. From your uncle,' the man said, his voice coming out in a wheeze thanks to the pressure of Harry's arm on his throat.

'He's not my uncle, and you're not my cousin. You're just people I've been unfortunate enough to meet, that's it. Nothing more.'

'Blood ... doesn't ... lie.'

'Blood is all it is, blood. It certainly doesn't make people into a family, of that I can assure you.'

Harry leaned in harder, stared into the man's eyes, then stepped back, releasing him.

'Best you leave,' he said.

The man adjusted what he was wearing, doing his best to brush off the shock of Harry's attack.

'This is your last chance,' he said.

'You wouldn't be threatening me, now, would you?' Harry asked.

'I'm simply stating a fact. Nothing more. Nothing less.'

Harry slipped the knife into his pocket, took out his phone, made a call.

'Turning up in Hawes, where I work, that's one thing,' he said, as he waited for his call to connect. 'But coming to my house?' He shook his head.

The man, his cousin, opened his mouth to speak, but Harry shut him up with a lifted finger as his call was answered.

'It's me,' he said. 'I've someone here I want you to speak to.'

Harry then flipped the screen around and had it on video. The man's eyes flickered between Harry's face and the face staring at him from Harry's phone screen.

'Dad ...'

'Where are you?'

'Away on business.'

'He's here, with me,' said Harry. 'He's paid me a few visits these last few days. Seems keen to have the family back together. Not so keen to give me his name, though. His enthusiasm for this reunion must've got the better of him, though, because right now, we're standing outside my house.'

'What?'

'Look, Dad, it's fine, honestly, there's nothing—'

'Enough. That you're where you are says it all. I've told you what I'm doing. There's nothing you can do to change my mind.'

'Dad, please, just listen!'

'No, you just listen. Whether you can accept it or not,

what I'm doing is giving you another chance at things, can't you see that? I ruined my life by choice, and the lives of so many others. It's too late for me, but by doing this, I can maybe make a difference.'

Harry's arm was beginning to ache from holding his phone up. His cousin laughed, the sound cold and mean.

'You can't buy your way into Heaven, Dad, you can't! I've said it a thousand times, and you're still trying to do it! It's pathetic!'

'I'm not trying to do that at all. What I'm actually doing is everything I can to stop you ending up in Hell.'

Harry gave a cough.

'This is all very dramatic, but I do have a job to do.'

Harry's cousin pushed himself away from his car and walked over to Harry until the phone was only inches away from his face. Harry also noticed that his cousin's phone was in his hand.

'There's nothing I can say, then, Dad? Nothing I can do to change your mind?'

'Nothing.'

'Then you leave me no choice. Sorry.'

He raised the hand carrying the phone and tapped the screen with his thumb.

'Sorry? What do you mean, sorry? For wh—'

The voice cut off. Harry, confused by the sudden silence, checked his phone, saw the screen had gone blank. His cousin slipped his phone back into his pocket.

'Signal's never good round here, is it?' he said, and turned to walk back to his car.

Harry stayed where he was, tried to call the number again, but there was no reply. Something wasn't right.

'What did you do?'

His cousin slipped behind the steering wheel, then glanced over at Harry. He winked, pulled his door shut, started the engine, then slowly, carefully, reversed out from where he was parked, and turned away from the house. At the bottom of the lane, he lifted a hand out of his window and waved.

Harry did not return the wave, just watched the car disappear, tried the number once again, then gave up. He had enough to be dealing with today as it was, without also having to worry about his criminal relatives and their spats. So, deciding that the best thing to do was to forget about it for all now, or at least until his cousin made another surprise appearance, he headed off in the Rav to Hawes and the office.

THIRTY-FIVE

The team meeting was fast and furious as Harry went through everything he had learned from speaking with Barnaby the night before. The arrival of his cousin that morning, a man clearly intent on redefining the word 'unwelcome' in every possible way, was quickly erased from his mind, as everyone worked together to decide what they were to do next. When that was done, and the loyal whiteboard filled with numerous notes by Jadyn, Harry went through everything one more time, just to make sure everyone knew what they were doing.

'There's a connection,' he said. 'That's clear. What happened to Barnaby also happened to Mike and Darren. The motive seems to be punishment instead of money. The worry is, as with all blackmail, that it will either escalate, grow to include more victims, or both.'

'There's also a possibility there have been victims prior to the three we're now dealing with,' added Ethan, then added, 'Sorry, just thought I'd bring it up. We didn't mention it before.'

'No need to apologise,' said Harry. 'That's a good point. Glad you raised it. So, each of you, tell me what you're doing. Ethan, you start, then we'll just go round the room.'

Ethan started to stand up, but Harry stopped that with a small gesture of his hand, and he sank back into his seat.

'I'm going to follow up on the loan shark, see if Barnaby's story checks out,' he said. 'It was well before my time in Darlington obviously, but someone on my old team might know something. Maybe there's a connection between the loan shark, Barnaby and the others. Could be they all went to the same person for financial help. Part of that will be me speaking with Barnaby and his parents, and staff at the café and bakery. Maybe they spotted someone acting suspicious; always a longshot, but sometimes something stands out.'

Jadyn was next.

'I'm going to see if there's any evidence of other similar accidents. Might be that this is all happening now, or it could be that whoever's behind the three incidents has done it before.'

The next person to speak was Liz. Harry remembered he'd yet to speak to Ben about what Mike had said. Unsurprisingly, that had been driven from his head by what they were doing now.

'Although there's no CCTV where Barnaby poisoned himself, there's a chance there might be security cameras on other properties. We know when the poison was left for Barnaby, so there's a chance we might be able to pick up a vehicle or a person that we can then cross-reference to both Mike's place and Darren's. I'll also be maintaining a presence here at the office. Oh, and I'll give Nevis a call as well. I think he's calmed down since the collision with Mike and, by all accounts, he's injury free, by which I mean, that's what he's said, and he's standing by that assessment.'

'Typical Dales' farmer, then.' Harry smiled. 'Knows better than a qualified doctor.'

Now that Liz had finished speaking, Jen jumped in.

'I'm going to check up on Darren, see how he's doing. I've already been in touch with the hospital, and he's fine to have visitors. Obviously, he's been through a traumatic experience, so I'll go easy. Hopefully, there's something in what he can tell us that will give us a clue as to who is behind what's going on. No doubt I'll be speaking with his wife as well.'

'On that,' said Harry, 'we can't assume that money is the only issue here. That was Barnaby's secret, and it was used against him. His supposed punishment matched what he'd done to the loan shark so specifically that my gut tells me there will be a similar correlation between what Darren and Mike each went through, and whatever it is in their pasts that the blackmailer used against them.'

Dave sat beside Matt, and he twisted his wrist to point a thumb at the sergeant.

'I'll be joining him,' he said.

'LOOKS like it's my turn, then,' said Matt. 'I'll be in touch with Sowerby, see if we've anything useful from the SOC team's work yesterday at Darren's job site. I'll also have a word with Caitlin, see if there's anything else from Mike's collision. Once that's done, I'm going to do what I can to dig into the lives of our victims, which will involve some coordination across the board, really. Ethan, I'll want anything and everything from Barnaby; clubs, pubs, interests, and take that all the way back to when he took that loan, and earlier, too.

Jen, same goes for you and chatting with Darren.' He then turned to the remaining member of the team. 'Harry, I'll wait to hear what you can get from Mike.'

'I'll get everything I can,' Harry said. 'He's no longer in hospital, correct, Liz?'

'Home last night. Ben went round straight away.'

'Then that's me. I'll be round at Mike's, seeing what's what.' Harry paused, then added, 'We need to all be aware that there's a chance whatever was used against both Mike and Darren is illegal. If that's the case, then we will deal with that accordingly. Revealing it will be problematic for those involved, which is what the blackmailer is counting on. That something they did, which was against the law, would be made public. Hope that makes sense? Now, any questions?'

The room was quiet, with not one single hand raised to query any of the points discussed or tasks given.

'Then let's crack on, shall we?' said Harry, clapping his hands together. 'I won't be expecting answers by the end of the day, either. This could take a while.'

Meeting closed, the team broke off, and soon everyone, bar Liz and Harry, had left the office. Harry went to leave but paused at the door, before turning back to say something to Liz.

'How's Ben been, with Mike being away?' he asked.

'Busy,' Liz replied. 'I think he's enjoyed it, though. The responsibility seems to be something he's relishing. He's been in charge at the garage before, but not for as long, and it'll be a while yet before Mike's back, won't it?'

Harry avoided answering that last question, simply because there were too many variables.

'And you'll let me know when I need to start looking for a suit, won't you?' he said. 'Grace has mentioned it a few times, because she's more than a little excited about an excuse to get properly dressed up.'

'You're not excited yourself?'

'I didn't say that.'

Liz laughed.

'Well, I'm sure we will,' she said. 'There's no rush, though, is there? We're engaged, and that's enough for now, I think. Plus, it's not cheap, is it, getting married? No idea how we'll afford it.'

'A wedding doesn't need to be expensive,' said Harry.

Liz raised an eyebrow at that.

'Is that your extensive experience of weddings speaking there, Harry?'

Harry shook his head.

'No, I'm just saying that you don't need to spend a lot to make a day special, do you? I'm not suggesting you cut corners, either. You know so many people, you just need to get folk organised a bit, have them involved, instead of trying to do and pay for everything yourselves.'

'I'm not good at asking for favours. I've not even started thinking about what I'm going to wear.'

Harry smiled.

'The focus of the day is not the dress and how much it costs. It's not the catering. It's not the gifts or the venue or the band or any of that. In fact, none of that matters at all. The focus, what really matters, is you and Ben, and the celebration of who and what you are, and the life you have decided to share. Keep your mind on that, and you'll be fine, I'm sure.'

Harry noticed then that Liz was staring at him in an odd way.

'Something I said?'

'Yes, actually,' she replied. 'You're actually quite wise, aren't you?'

Harry laughed.

'Funnily enough, someone else said something like that this week as well. I'm not, though, not by a long shot. Just saying what I think, that's all.'

Liz stood up, walked across the office, and to Harry's surprise, hugged him, then planted a kiss on his cheek.

'What was that for?'

'Off you go, Harry,' Liz said. 'And thank you.'

Harry smiled to himself, then left the office. Mike lived up in Gayle. Harry knew that he could drive there, but the walk across the footpath from the back of St Margaret's Church to the bottom of the village seemed like a better way to spend his time. So, that's exactly what he did, pushing through the doors of the Community Centre, and out into the morning air.

THIRTY-SIX

Ben answered the door.

'Harry? You'll be here to see Mike, then.'

'Well, I'm not here to see you, am I?'

Ben slipped his jacket on.

'I'm going anyway. Busy day at the garage. Mike was absolutely intent on coming into work, but I've managed to persuade him to take a few more days off to recover.'

'Strikes me that you're rather enjoying running things yourself a bit.'

'I suppose so.'

'I know so,' said Harry. 'So does Liz. Told me as much this morning.'

Ben pushed past Harry and out into the morning.

'Don't suppose she told you she wants to just stay engaged for a few years, did she?'

'Not that I recall,' Harry replied. 'She mentioned the wedding, though. Seems to be worried about the cost of it more than anything.'

Ben hesitated on Mike's doorstep.

'Something the matter?' Harry asked.

'I'm worried about it, too,' said Ben.

'You don't need to be.'

'I do, because it's important, Harry. It's the most important day of our lives!'

That response took Harry aback. He heard panic in it, and a little note of desperation. He could see the worry in his brother's eyes.

'It isn't,' he said.

Ben huffed.

'You wouldn't understand.'

Harry let that pass, for now.

'It's an important day, for sure, but not the most important. If you look at it like that, it's downhill from there, isn't it? And that's no way to live, certainly no way to start a life with someone.'

'That's not what I meant.'

'But it's what you said, and the more you say it, the more you'll believe it. So, don't, you hear me? It's the start of something, that's all. A celebration. But what it is not, is more important than every day that follows, because those days, well, that's when it really starts to matter, isn't it? What you and Liz do together, how you love each other, the choices you'll make, the way you'll support each other through the rough stuff as well as the smooth.'

Ben narrowed his eyes at Harry.

'You alright there?' he asked.

'I think so, why?'

'Not sure, just sounds like you've been thinking this through a lot to come out with something like that.'

Harry laughed, remembering then what both Matt and Liz had said.

'Getting wise in my old age, aren't I?'

'You're not old. Ugly, yes, but not old.'

Harry laughed at that.

'Bugger off, then,' he said. 'Mike inside?'

'Kitchen,' said Ben, and with that, jogged over to his vehicle.

Harry stepped into Mike's house and called for the owner.

'Through here,' came Mike's reply. 'Tea?'

'Always,' said Harry, and chased his own voice down the small hallway.

In the kitchen, Mike was dressed in a faded blue dressing gown, which Harry noticed, was carrying a disturbing number of oil stains. He was just in the process of placing a pot of tea on the table. Beside it was some buttered toast and a magazine about classic tractors. Harry did a double-take on seeing that, amazed that there were enough readers in the world to justify its existence.

'Work on vehicles in that dressing gown, do you?' he asked, sitting down at the dining table.

Mike slumped down into a chair and laughed. 'Don't think I own a single piece of clothing that isn't carrying an oil stain or two.' He handed Harry a mug. 'Ben's doing really well without me around, you know. It's a bit worrying.'

Harry noticed that Mike's mood was somewhat brighter than when they'd last spoken in the hospital.

'It's good to see,' he said. 'And yourself?'

'I'm home,' Mike replied, pouring out two mugs of tea. 'Just going to put what happened behind me and crack on, I think. Toast?'

Harry really hated to ruin that thought, but sometimes, those were the breaks. He wasn't here to mess around and waste time, either, so it was time to ignore the toast and get straight to the point.

'Who's blackmailing you, Mike?'

The smile fell so immediately from Mike's face that Harry half wondered if he'd had a heart attack.

'What?'

'Blackmailing you,' Harry repeated. 'That's why you had only two loose wheel nuts on that Land Rover of yours, why you threw it into a corner at a ridiculous speed, why you crashed; they were watching it all happen from that app that was still open on your phone.'

Harry watched Mike attempt to force a smile.

'Why would anyone blackmail me?'

'Why would you do what you did to your Land Rover, then crash it?'

'I explained that in the hospital.'

'You talked bollocks in the hospital, Mike, that's what you did, and we both know it!'

Harry's sharp tone had Mike push his chair back with a screech.

'Harry, if you've just come round here to throw insults, then—'

'Stop it, Mike, just stop, okay? No more. I want the truth.'

'I've told you the truth.'

Harry didn't bother giving that answer enough time in the open before he shot it to pieces with a reply.

'You're the third case we're investigating,' he said. 'Someone is blackmailing people and forcing them to do something that could, quite easily, kill them. Their motive seems to be about teaching you and the others a lesson.'

'Others? What others?'

'Not your concern, though by asking me that, you've just confirmed I'm right about the blackmail, haven't you, Mike?'

Mike's mouth dropped open, but he had no response to give.

'How about I just talk for a bit? Might make it easier for you,' Harry continued. 'And just so you know, I'm here to help, though my guess is that it doesn't feel like that right now, does it? That'll be the panic you're feeling, the twist of your gut making you want to throw up, the shake in your hands at the worry about the blackmailer, what they'll do if you tell me what you know, if you help me.'

'But I don't know anything, Harry. I don't.'

'I'll be the judge of that.'

Harry leaned back, sipped his tea. Mike reached for the toast, took it to his mouth, then placed it back on the plate, not even a nibble taken, his appetite gone.

'Tell me about the accident.'

'You know about the accident. You've seen it!'

Harry shook his head.

'No, not that one, the one you were responsible for. The one you kept secret. The one someone else found out about.'

'There wasn't another acci—'

'Mike ...'

Mike hung his head, then leaned forward to rest it in his hands, his elbows on the table.

'I don't understand,' he said. 'How do you know?'

This time, Harry said it, because he just couldn't help himself.

'Detective, remember?'

'It was decades ago. I was a kid, Harry, a kid!'

'Not here to judge, Mike. I'm here to catch a blackmailer,

someone who managed to have you, and at least two others, nearly kill themselves.'

Mike took a few moments to suck in some deep, lung-filling breaths.

'You've heard of Mischief Night, Harry?'

THIRTY-SEVEN

Memories of his own childhood, distant and dark as it was, flickered faintly for a moment in Harry's mind. Sepia photographs of a time long gone, and for the most, best forgotten.

'Actually, I have,' he said. 'Not just because I've experienced it up here, either; down in Somerset, we have it on the same date, the night before Bonfire Night.'

Mike tried again with the toast, but to no avail.

'It's not as popular now as it used to be,' he said. 'But back when I was a kid, some of us used to be a nightmare. We'd run rings round the police, round anyone who tried to catch us. Up here, you can just jump over a wall, and you're gone, no one's catching you.'

'Usual stuff, I suppose,' said Harry. 'Throwing eggs and flour at front doors and parked cars, that kind of thing?'

'More fun if the cars were moving, to be honest,' admitted Mike. 'We'd throw garden gates in the beck, drop bangers through letterboxes, let down car tyres ...'

Harry couldn't help but laugh.

'It's not really funny, is it, but still ...'

Mike managed a smile.

'It was exciting, and we didn't really see the trouble we could cause.'

'But you caused it anyway.'

'Wouldn't you?'

'I did.'

Mike's smile broke into a laugh.

'Like I said,' said Harry, 'we have Mischief Night in Somerset as well. I grew up with it.'

'You ever put anyone in hospital because of what you did, though?' Mike asked. 'I did.'

And here it is, thought Harry, the thing the blackmailer had used against Mike, the dark secret the man had probably hidden so deep that he'd forgotten about it. Then someone had come along, someone who somehow had access to that secret as well and then used it against him.

'I was over at a mate's place in Leyburn, Sam it was. Stayed over at his for the night. Parents were pleased for a break from me, I think; I was a git of a teenager, I can tell you. Anyway, we were out, doing the usual, like, making a nuisance of ourselves, when Sam, he got caught.'

'Doing what?'

'The whole bangers through the letterbox thing I mentioned,' Mike said. 'In went the banger, just as the door opened. A hand grabbed Sam round the neck, the banger went off, and the owner of that hand, some old bloke I, to this day, don't know the name of, threw Sam halfway across his garden. I've never seen anything like it. Then he just walked over and gave Sam the biggest hiding I've ever seen. Beat the crap out of him, slapped him around that garden like he was nothing. Sam was screaming, but he just kept getting hit, and every time he tried to break free, that old bastard, he'd grab him and slap him and shake him.'

Harry was genuinely shocked.

'That's assault, Mike, you know that.'

'No one cared,' Mike replied. 'We told Sam's parents, and all they said was that he shouldn't've gone doing what he did, that he deserved it. Then they slapped him around a bit themselves before throwing him in his room and locking me out of the house.'

'Not the night you planned, then.'

Mike shook his head.

'I was too scared to tell my parents, too angry as well. I stayed in Leyburn the whole night, just wandering the streets, raging about what had happened.'

Harry sensed a big reveal was drawing near.

'You did something, didn't you, Mike?'

'Too bloody right I did,' Mike replied. 'I went round to that old bastard's house, and I smashed every window in the place. He came out looking, and I ran. Then I went back.'

'Your response to assault was criminal damage. Clever.'

'What are you going to do, arrest me?'

Harry said nothing. Just waited for Mike to continue.

'The windows weren't enough, not by a long shot. After what he did to Sam, the black eyes, the bruises, the blood ... I couldn't let him get away with it.'

Harry sighed, then rubbed his eyes, already weary, and the day wasn't even halfway through yet.

'Not sure I really want to ask this, Mike, but what did you do?'

'I loosened the wheel nuts on his car. Every single one. Then I thought I'd go a step further and take some of them out completely. So, I did, and I threw them down a drain.

Then I spent the rest of the night sleeping in one of the sheds at school. It was easy to break into, was some shelter against the night, and I managed to get some protection from the cold by burying myself in a pile of stinking cricket pads. Not comfortable, and not exactly a duvet, but they stopped me freezing to death.'

'That's not the end of the story, is it?'

Mike shook his head.

By the time I got home the next day, I'd forgotten about what I'd done. I was more worried about Sam. Then, a few days later, I heard ...'

'Heard what?'

'About the accident. The bloke who'd kicked Sam around like a football. He was on the road from West Witton to Wensley, that straight bit where everyone speeds a bit. I'd done the bolts so that the wheels would be fine for a while, and then not. Turns out, that "not" moment was when he was doing around sixty. Front wheel came off, passenger side, he ended up barrel rolling. Was in hospital for I don't know how long, then in a wheelchair back home while he recovered. Everyone assumed it was an accident. Poor maintenance. I knew different. I knew what I'd done.'

Harry let the weight of what Mike had said sit at the table with them for a while before he said anything himself.

'Bloody hell, Mike.'

'Yeah, I know,' Mike replied. 'You're the only person I've ever told. Sam never knew it was me, no one did. The shock of what I'd done, it changed me. I never went out on Mischief Night again. I knuckled down a bit at school, tried to camouflage the guilt I felt with bettering myself. I sometimes wonder if the only reason I ended up a mechanic is that in some weird way, I'm trying to pay the world back for what I did to that man's car.'

'And maybe that's what you've done,' said Harry. 'That's not for me to judge. Someone else, though, they clearly think that for them, it absolutely is, and they have.'

'An email came through to me at work. I ignored it. Then another email, then another, all with little details about what I'd done. Then there were photos, from the accident, newspaper clippings, that kind of thing. What really did it for me, though, was the photograph of the shed I'd slept in. That's when I knew I was in trouble.'

'What was the threat?' Harry asked. 'What did the blackmailer say they would do if you didn't do as you were instructed?'

'Everyone up and down the dale would know,' Mike replied, his voice breaking just enough to let Harry know that what he was hearing, and had been told, was the truth of it all. 'It would be plastered everywhere, and I don't just mean sheets of paper pinned to telegraph poles, either. This is Wensleydale, Harry. Next time you're on your way to the shops down in Leyburn, tell a handful of people in Hawes something secret about yourself or someone else, it doesn't really matter, and I promise you, that news will get to Leyburn quicker than you will. You'll probably have someone telling you it when you're at the till in Campbell's.'

'Who is it, then, Mike? Who's behind this?'

'No idea. They had me nigh on kill myself, and I still don't know who they are. But they knew all about what I'd done, every damned part of it.'

Harry finished his tea.

'That's quite the tale, Mike,' he said. 'You're sure this is the first time anyone's mentioned what you did? You're positive you never told anyone?'

'It's decades ago, Harry. No one knew.'

'Why wait till now, then, to use it against you?' Harry asked.

Mike stared across the table.

'You tell me, Harry, you tell me.'

At that moment, though, Harry couldn't tell Mike a damned thing.

THIRTY-EIGHT

Leaving Mike to his cold toast, Harry left the house and made his way back to the office to see if anything had come in from the rest of the team. Autumn was a golden thing that morning, with the sun high as midday approached, and a cool breeze gamboling down the street. It was the perfect day for a stroll with Grace and the dogs across the fields to the Green Dragon at Hardraw, but that would have to wait for now. It was a favourite walk of theirs, particularly as it brought back the memory of the sneaky little dip they had back in the early days in the pool beneath Hardraw Force.

Taking the same path that he'd wandered along earlier, Harry tramped across flagstones worn smooth by numerous feet, taking the same route over so many years. There was water in the beck, and he could imagine the fun kids had splashing around in it, the wild abandon of childhood, something he wasn't entirely sure he'd ever experienced fully.

His phone rang.

'Grimm,' he said, not bothering to check if the number was from a contact or not.

'Harry,' came the reply. 'It's Jameson.'

Harry smiled at hearing the voice of his old friend.

'Wasn't expecting a call.'

'I wasn't expecting to make one.'

'Why do I get the feeling that doesn't bode well?'

Jameson was quiet for a moment.

'I've been keeping an eye on things,' he said. 'After your meeting in the café in Kendal, thought it would make sense for me to keep the radio dialled to the right channels, so to speak.'

'Well, since then, I've met another new family member,' Harry said. 'A cousin. Don't know his name, nor do I want to. He's been turning up unannounced, talking about his father, my uncle.'

'And how did that go?'

'We had words.'

'Ah.'

'I made it clear he wasn't welcome.'

'He still in one piece?'

'To my own credit, yes.'

'That's good, Harry,' said Jameson. 'The thing is, though ...'

Another pause.

'What?'

'Your uncle.'

'What about him?'

'He's ... well ... I'm afraid that he's not still in one piece, if you know what I mean?'

Harry stopped dead.

'What's happened?'

'Earlier this morning, explosion at a large house. Cause as yet unknown. Whole place was destroyed. Emergency services still attending the scene. They've had confirmation that the owner of the property was inside at the time everything went boom.'

'Boom?'

'I don't think bang does justice to the extent of the damage.'

Harry remembered the way the conversation between his uncle and cousin had been so suddenly cut off. He also remembered his cousin toying with his own phone.

'Well, thanks for letting me know.'

'I'd say I'm sorry for your loss, but I'm not. It's a worry, though, isn't it? If he's gone, then who's going to take his place?'

'I know exactly who,' said Harry. 'I'm not condoning the life he led, but he wanted to make amends.'

'You never did tell me how.'

'I flatly refused to have anything to do with any of the money he'd made through his criminal activities, but that wasn't what it was about. He wanted to shut everything down, turn informer, plus he'd set up a number of legitimate businesses none of his close associates knew about, charities, that kind of thing. Asked if I could keep an eye on them, make sure nothing untoward happened to them once he was gone.'

'Well, that happened sooner than he probably expected, didn't it?'

'He wanted me to bring him in,' Harry continued. 'Said I was the only one he trusted to do it properly and keep him safe. I failed at that.'

'No, you didn't, Harry,' Jameson replied. 'Your uncle failed at life and thought a last-minute good deed might be bright enough to blind the world to all the bad deeds he'd done. No chance, I'm afraid. That stuff, it comes back to haunt you.'

Harry thought about Mike, Darren, and Barnaby, and how their own bad deeds had returned to bare their teeth.

'You're not wrong,' he said. 'I appreciate you letting me know. How's Gordy?'

'Settling in. Seems to like Somerset. Don't think she's decided on where to actually live yet, but that'll come with time. She misses Anna, but is doing what I think Anna would've wanted, and trying to live as fully as she can.'

'That's good to hear.'

'Even a little bit of a fledgling romance blossoming. Early days, but I think it's given her a bit of a lift. Lovely lass, too. Very different to Anna, but also similar in unexpected ways. Some would argue it's a little too early for her to be getting involved with someone, but that's the way life is, sometimes, isn't it? Presents you with surprises, and sometimes, they're actually pleasant.'

'Well, at least this conversation wasn't all bad news.'

'I'll leave you to it, then, Harry,' said Jameson. 'Speak soon.'

Harry said farewell and continued on his way. The rest of his stroll to the office was taken up with everything Jameson had told him.

When he arrived, Liz was sitting at a computer and looked busy. Harry thought it best to leave her be for a moment, especially as his mind was rather full, and tried to creep past and over to the kitchen area to sort another tea. He didn't want one, but he felt like he needed one.

'Best you take a seat,' said Liz.

Harry looked over to see she was now facing away from the computer.

'Why?'

'A few reasons.'

Harry sat down.

'Go on, then.'

'Everyone's calling in,' Liz explained. 'Phone hasn't stopped ringing. My guess is, with Mike involved, it's touched a little too close to home.'

'Everything round here touches close to home,' said Harry, 'but that does make sense. What have you heard, then?'

Liz brought a document up on the computer screen.

'Been recording it all as it comes in,' she said. 'Jadyn's over at the station in Richmond but hasn't found anything yet regarding other cases, but that's probably going to be a longer search. Ethan's come back to say that so far there's nothing on the loan shark, mainly because that case was years ago, and anyone who would've worked on it has long since left, so he's had to put a request in for the files. And, unsurprisingly, it hasn't been digitised, so he can't access it on HOLMES. There's some data on it, but not much.'

Harry found the acronym for the Home Office Large Major Enquiry System a ludicrous one, not least because the words Large and Major seemed to him to mean the same thing. He also knew that, while the database was used by police forces nationwide, it wasn't infallible.

'I wasn't expecting much on that,' said Harry.

'He's been chatting to staff at the bakery and the café as well, and nothing has come up that is in any way suspicious. They say they'd notice as well, which is fair enough.'

'Why?'

'Small place. They know everyone, what they drive, even what hat they wear, believe me, so if something was out of place, they'd spot it. Plenty of vehicles are out and about at odd times as well, with farmers keeping strange hours, just like Barnaby, who's at work the same time every day in his Golf, and Craig out and about doing deliveries in his van.'

'So, nothing there, then. Can't say I'm feeling the need for sitting down quite yet.'

'Patience,' said Liz. 'Matt's heard from Sowerby and has also had a brief chat with Caitlin. There's nothing to add from Mike's collision that we don't already know. As for what happened to Darren, they've established that the damage to his chainsaw was done with his own tools; they matched markings on the chain to a file in his toolbox. This has also been confirmed by Darren.'

'Who Jen was speaking to.'

'He's recovering well, all things considered, though will need further surgery and a fair amount of physio, as well as counselling.'

'Has he said anything about the blackmail?'

Liz gave a nod.

'He has. Someone contacted him via email about an accident on a job that happened about ten years ago. A co-worker fell out of a tree. He and Darren were working as part of a large team. They'd all been working long days, and things had got a bit lax over time. Tiredness. Probably exhaustion. Anyway, one of the team fell and faults were found with the ropes and knots. However, it was impossible to identify any one member of the team as responsible for the knots and ropes not being sufficiently secure.'

'Don't they check their own gear as a matter of course?'

'Like I said, tiredness and exhaustion,' said Liz. 'The one who fell from the tree broke both legs, an arm, fractured his skull. The company was taken to court over it and a settlement was agreed to outside of proceedings.'

'What's this got to do with Darren?'

'He knew it was his fault that the knots and ropes failed. He just never admitted to it.'

'And that's what was used against him?'

'It would seem so, yes. With the addition of the tampered-with chainsaw. My guess is that falling out of a tree wasn't lesson enough and might be something he'd walk away from. Throw in the dodgy chainsaw ...'

'The opposite is also true,' said Harry. 'There's a very good chance if you fall out of a tree, you'll end up dead. I don't think the blackmailer wants that. They want the victims to live with what they've done, and the punishment meted out.'

'Couple more things,' said Liz.

'What's left?' Harry asked. 'Your bit and that's it, isn't it?'

'There's a wee bit more from Matt as well. I've spoken with Nevis. He's fine. The damage to his tractor is all being sorted out via Mike's insurance. On the day the collision happened, I think he wanted to go a lot further and press charges, not anymore though.'

'Any reason why?'

'Chalking it up to being a case of "accidents happen." He wasn't hurt, Mike was. He doesn't see the point in going further with it all.'

'A lot of people wouldn't see that as entirely sensible.'

'Nevis isn't a lot of people. Yes, he's the size of a lot of people all squeezed together, but he doesn't see the point in trying to get money out of the situation or anything like that.'

Harry was, for Mike's sake, hugely relieved.

'Which leaves?'

'CCTV, which I've been looking into, and Matt seeing if he could find anything from the wider lives of the victims.'

'Did he?'

'They all went to Leyburn school,' said Liz.

Harry frowned.

'What, that's it?'

'Not much, really, is it? That's a connection an awful lot of people have in common around here.'

'There must be something else, surely.'

'They've all supported the Wensleydale Rugby team. They've used some of the same pubs. Darren and Jane were married at the church in Leyburn, and Barnaby provided the cake.'

'That's something.'

'Not really; he's done dozens of wedding cakes over the years.'

Harry dropped his head in despair.

'Sometimes, Liz, this job …'

'Just my bit, now,' Liz said. 'You might want to take a look at this.'

Harry lifted his eyes to see that Liz was pointing at the computer screen.

'And what's that when it's at home? All I'm seeing is a collection of black and white fuzzy images of vehicles in different locations.'

'That's because that's exactly what's on the screen. This one is the road in Muker by the café, from a security camera over the gallery there. This one is from the camera outside the doctor's surgery just down the road in Hawes. And this one is from the house opposite where Darren was felling that tree.'

Harry narrowed his eyes to help them focus.

'I'm still none the wiser.'

'That, right there, is a van,' said Liz.

'There are a lot of vans in the Dales, Liz. Vans, four-by-fours, tractors, that's what the roads are mostly full of, if you ignore all the caravans and campervans when the tourists roll in. And just because that one has been seen at each location doesn't mean we have a suspect.'

Liz zoomed in.

'See the driver? They're wearing a flat cap.'

'Again, like the van itself, there are a lot of those in the Dales as well. You've been to the auction mart, right? It's a sea of flat caps some days.'

Liz then added, 'The times for all of these are a bit odd, really early morning, or late at night.'

'What about dates?'

'All from last week.'

Harry cocked his head to one side, as though to do so would make the image clearer.

'Numberplate?'

At that question, Liz smiled.

'And this is why I've got you sitting down. I couldn't get all of it, but I got enough.'

'You've the owner, then?'

'Owner, driver, both,' said Liz. 'It's Craig Fothergill's.'

Harry stared at the images for a while longer, then looked at Liz.

'That's a connection, isn't it, Liz?'

'Isn't it, just?'

Harry stood up, as Liz said, 'One more thing ...'

Harry sighed.

'What?'

Liz pushed herself out of her seat and looked Harry dead in the eye.

'Ben and I, we've had a chat, about everything you said, to both of us.'

Harry smiled, gave a shrug.

'Just trying to help, that's all.'

'And you have,' said Liz. 'We've not set a date quite yet, so don't go rushing out to buy that suit you mentioned. But we have agreed on something.'

'And what's that?'

'It'll be next year, if that's good enough?'

Before Harry knew what he was doing, his arms were wrapped around Liz. She returned the gesture and for a moment, neither of them said a word.

'You've made my day,' Harry said, releasing Liz.

Liz sat back down.

'Shame that Craig Fothergill's ruined it,' she said.

THIRTY-NINE

While Liz printed off copies of what was on the screen, Harry, his eyes now back on the image of the van on the computer screen, called Barnaby.

'Craig? He's not working for me today,' said Barnaby. 'He's part-time, like I said. Not sure where he is.'

'No idea at all?'

'Sorry, no. Do you have his number?'

Harry realised that he didn't and took it from Barnaby.

'Everything okay?' Barnaby asked.

'Just need to check a few things with him, that's all.'

'Just a minute, I'll give him a call myself. I'll ring you back.'

A minute went by, then two. Harry was having trouble seeing how Craig could be involved in any of what was going on. He'd not met him yet himself, but from what Matt had said, he seemed right enough. Plus, Barnaby and he had been friends since childhood, and now he worked for him. There was no reason for there to be anything nefarious going on at all. Still, coincidences and all that ...

His phone rang.

'Yes?'

'Found him,' said Barnaby. 'He's over in Preston-under-Scar. Doing a bit of gardening for someone. One of his regulars. Which is going to be a problem if he ever wants to go full-time for me, which I could do with, if I'm honest.'

'Why a problem?'

'A lot of folk depend on Craig. There are many people out there who do odd jobs as a thing. He's trusted, built up a really nice list of clients. Does really well out of it.'

'Well, thanks for your help,' said Harry. 'Craig knows I'm on my way, then, does he?'

'He does. I'll text you the address.'

'That's great.'

Harry hung up, and a few moments later, a text came through from Barnaby.

'Need anyone to meet you there?' Liz asked.

Harry shook his head.

'I think I can deal with this on my own. Don't want to turn up with a whole gaggle of us and terrify him. For all we know, there's an innocent explanation for what we've found.'

Liz said nothing, just gave a nod and turned back to the computer. Harry left as the phone rang. He didn't stick around to hear who it was or what it was about. Outside, he jogged down the lane, past the pet shop and its disturbing mannequin, sent a wave to Mandy from the Fountain, who was just coming out of Elijah Allen & Son with a couple of heavy-looking carrier bags, and jumped into his Rav. Then he was out of the marketplace, left at the surgery, over the river, and right onto the road between Hardraw and Askrigg.

Yes, he thought, *a walk to the Green Dragon really would be nice,* remembering his thoughts from earlier in the day.

He'd be chatting with Grace about a stroll over soon, that was for sure, maybe even tie it in with what he'd paid for, courtesy of that letter Grace had found so mysterious, mainly because he'd not helped matters by lobbing it into the fire. *Nothing wrong with a bit of mystery, though,* Harry thought, smiling to himself.

The drive to Preston-under-Scar went by smoothly. Had Harry not been otherwise engaged, he might have enjoyed it more, but as the glory of the Dales swept by, his mind was elsewhere. He barely registered Carperby, where. he and Grace had got together, hanging out in her little cottage, taking a walk to the Wheatsheaf Inn for a meal and a drink or two. There were good footpaths leading out of the village, as well, thin tracks that sent you up into the hills, where the world seemed to pause and breathe, and nature drew you ever onward, away from everyday life. Today, Harry was oblivious to them all.

In Preston-under-Scar, Harry found his way to the address Barnaby had given him and there, parked outside the house, was Craig's van. Barnaby's description of it had been accurate. The vehicle was old but in superb condition. Pulling himself out of the Rav and going over for a look, he was struck by the shine of the paint, that there were no rust spots anywhere, the wheels were clean, even the interior looked new. Probably refurbished considering the age, but even so, who looks after such an average van with such care?

'Didn't take you too long.'

Harry looked up and saw a man coming towards him.

'Craig Fothergill?' he said. 'I'm—'

'Grimm,' said Craig. 'We've not met, but I've heard plenty about you. Bit of celebrity up and down the dale, you know.'

'Hard not to be noticed when you look like I do,' Harry replied.

Craig was standing by the bonnet of his van. He reached out with the cuff of his jacket and gave a small section of it a buff.

'Nowt wrong with the way you look. And it's your reputation people talk about, isn't it?'

'In a good way, I hope.'

Craig winked.

'Now, that would be telling, wouldn't it? Anyway, Barnaby said you wanted to have a chat. I've a few minutes spare. Need a break anyway. Could do with a brew. My flask's in the van.'

Craig walked around to the back of the van and opened the door. Looking inside, Harry saw that, like the rest of the van, it was in superb condition. Craig removed a small rucksack, closed the door, locked it.

'Your van's in good nick,' said Harry, following Craig as he made his way over to a garden wall and perched himself upon it.

'Parents gave it to me years ago. Mum made me promise that I'd look after it. That's what I've done. It's got a full service history, any chips with the paint work are dealt with as soon as they happen, I've even reupholstered the cabin. I've done right by it, and it's seen me good, too. If you look after something, it pays you back tenfold, doesn't it?'

'Not always,' said Harry, 'but I think that's a good way to approach most things.'

Craig held out a cup.

'Tea?'

'I'm good, thanks.'

'Didn't ask that, did I? Go on, have one. You know you

want to. Biscuits too, by the way, courtesy of Barnaby. Chocolate chip. Delicious.'

Harry accepted the tea and a biscuit. He was having a hard time thinking that Craig could have anything to do with what was going on. Just didn't make any sense at all. Here he was, out on a job, doing some gardening, eating Barnaby's biscuits, not giving any signs at all that it was a mask, and behind it was a blackmailer. Still, though, Harry had met people with far darker and better hidden secrets.

'You get out and about a fair bit in that van of yours, then?' he said, starting with something nice and innocent so as not to set the hares racing.

'That's why I look after it,' Craig replied. 'I've my own odd-jobs work, which has me travelling all over the place. I've a lot of regular work now with a good number of people, like the couple who live here, for example.'

'And what are you doing here, exactly?'

'They're in their eighties. Sorting the garden is a bit difficult for them, but they're still really independent, and like to enjoy it as best they can. So, I come round and do all the big stuff, like mow the lawn, sort the borders out, the hanging baskets, and then help them out with a few raised beds and pots that I've sorted for them. Put them at a height they can both reach, so they're still involved. I also do a big shop for them every couple of weeks or so.'

'You're like a veritable Good Samaritan.'

'They pay me, though,' said Craig. 'I don't do it for free.'

'Even so, it makes a difference.'

'I hope so.'

'And you work for Barnaby.'

'I do. We've known each other since we were kids. He's done so well. He was having trouble finding someone who could work the hours he needed as a delivery driver. We realised while chatting over a few pints that I could probably fit it in, so we gave it a go, and here we are, still going strong. Hardest job I do, though, really. Driving around with a van smelling so delicious isn't easy.'

Harry wondered how well Matt would fare with such a job.

'What are the hours like?'

'It's not a nine-to-five, if that's what you mean,' said Craig, sipping his tea. 'I prefer that, though, keeps things interesting.'

'Late nights, early mornings, then?'

'Very much so.'

'You get out to East Hauxwell much?'

Craig frowned.

'Probably. Don't think I've any of my regulars there, but I've no doubt been out that way to clear a gutter or two, that kind of thing.'

'What about Hawes?'

'Not been that way in ages. Barnaby doesn't deliver anything over that way, what with Cockett's being King of the Hill at the top of the dale. Odd jobs-wise, I did a bit of fencing for someone up in Gayle, but that was at least a year ago. Little place, up near where the wash is. Right squeeze, getting the van through those narrow lanes. Pretty place, though.'

Harry finished his biscuit, drained his tea.

'You weren't over there last week, then?'

'I'd remember,' said Craig. 'Why do you ask?'

'Don't suppose you know Mike, do you, at the garage?'

'Not personally, no. If I lived closer, I'd take my van to

him, that's for sure. He's got such a good reputation. Used to do grasstrack racing, you know.'

'You're positive you weren't in Hawes?'

Craig took his cup back from Harry.

'Why would I lie about something like that?'

Harry pulled out of a pocket what Liz had printed for him, unfolding the sheets of paper.

'This your van, Craig?' he asked, showing Craig each image.

Craig leaned in for a closer look.

'Looks that way.'

'Then you must've been in Hawes,' said Harry. 'This one here is your van going past the surgery.'

At that, Craig laughed.

'That's not me,' he said.

'But it's your van, right? We've checked the numberplate.'

'Oh, it's my van alright, but I'm not driving.'

'Then who is?'

'That flat cap gives it away.'

'It does?'

'Yeah,' said Craig. 'That's my Dad.'

FORTY

Harry was on his feet.

'You're sure?'

'That cap never leaves his head,' said Craig. 'Kids at school used to make fun of him for it. My granddad was the same. I think that might even have been Granddad's cap. It's huge. Dad says it'll be mine once he's gone. Not much of an inheritance, really, is it, a manky old thing like that?'

Harry asked, 'Where will your dad be right now?'

'School, working, as always. He's only got a few days left, but that doesn't mean he'll slack off. Proud of what he does, is Dad. He keeps that place spotless.'

Harry turned away from Craig and jogged past the van and over to his own vehicle.

'What's wrong?' Craig called out after him. 'What's Dad driving my van got to do with anything?'

Harry opened the driver's door of the Rav.

'Why would your dad be driving your van to any of those places, Craig? Can you think of a reason?'

Craig was quiet, thoughtful, then said, 'Can't say that I

know, really. Always thought it was Mum who kept odd hours, but maybe it's both of them. I'm not their keeper, am I?'

Odd statement, thought Harry, as Craig went on.

'I don't have a problem with it, like. My parents don't really charge me much in the way of rent for living with them, so I've always shared the van with them. Didn't know he was nipping out for late night drives, though, but sometimes, I think he just needs to get out, clear his head, what with Mum ...'

Craig's voice faded at that point.

'What about your mum?' Harry asked, and saw sadness drag at the corner of Craig's eyes.

'She's not easy to live with,' he said. 'Don't get me wrong, we both love her, because of course we do, but she does like everything to be a certain way.'

Harry had his phone out now, readying to call Liz.

'How do you mean?'

'There's a lot of rules, put it that way. If we abide by them, everything's fine, and we're all happy. But if something's out of line, she can't half go off on one. Gets a bit stressful. Wish Dad had told me he was taking the van out. Didn't realise things had got that bad. Probably stressed about the job coming to an end, that'll be it.'

Harry gave Craig a farewell nod, told him he'd be in touch, then dropped into the driver's seat. Liz answered his call.

'I'm heading to the school in Leyburn,' Harry said. 'The one Craig's dad's the caretaker at. I could do with some backup, just in case.'

'The school? Why? What about Craig?'

'It's his dad, in those images, not him,' said Harry. 'I still don't have a clue what's going on, but I think we're close to finding out. Which is why I want a few extra bodies with me.'

'I'll call the team,' said Liz. 'Where do you want them to meet you?'

'The school car park will be fine. I'll be there in ten minutes, so send whoever's closest.'

'Will do.'

Harry hung up, waved to Craig, then pulled away from the side of the road. The journey to the school took no time at all. When Harry arrived at his destination, he still couldn't work out why there would be any connection between Craig's dad and the blackmailing of Barnaby, Mike, and Darren. The whole thing seemed just too bizarre. Was he about to confuse the hell out of Craig's dad, or was he really this close to arresting the person responsible?

Harry slowed down and drove through the school entrance, then down to the car park. Pulling into a space, his phone rang.

'Liz?'

'Everyone, bar Jadyn, are on their way,' she said. 'Should be with you within the next ten minutes or so.'

'Tell them I'll be in the school and to wait for a call from me.'

'You sure it's sensible to go in on your own?'

'I'm not dealing with an armed killer,' replied Harry.

'You don't know what you're dealing with.'

Harry ignored the rebuke.

'Call the head teacher, tell them I'm on site,' he said, and hung up.

Heaving himself out of the Rav, Harry eased the door shut and looked at the school. With it being a weekend, the place was quiet. Bright sunlight caught the glass of dozens of windows, scattering the view with flecks of gold. He could hear the sound of Leyburn in the distance, traffic rolling in and out of the marketplace, tractors in fields, lawnmowers making the most of the dry weather. If Craig's dad was on site, then the only way to find him was to go looking for him. Unsure where to start, Harry made his way to the main entrance, tried the door, and to his relief, found that it was open.

Stepping into the building, he was struck by the eerie quietness of the place. There was an air to it of a church, a building that was used to people filling it with their noise, their lives, which, when empty, felt oddly without purpose.

Harry considered calling out for Craig's dad, but instead thought it might make more sense to make his way through the various buildings, listening out for any sign of activity. A shout might send him running. Assuming, of course, he had something to run from. He explored the main building, climbing stairs to wander through empty corridors. Harry hadn't been in a school since his own days as a teenager. Those days had not been happy ones.

Main building thoroughly explored, Harry left through another door into an open area, onto which stared various other blocks of classrooms. A lawn with trees lay in front of him, and he crossed it to try another door. He gave it a yank, but the door was locked. He continued around the building, looking for another way in. He saw the school's large sports fields below. Built into what had once been sloping land, they stepped down from the main site in a series of high grass banks to the largest field at the bottom. Here, Harry saw someone trundling around on a sit-on lawnmower. Craig's dad ...

Harry made his way between the school buildings and down towards where the lawnmower was doing a very neat job of trimming the grass into careful lines. The smell of cut grass was in the air. As he drew closer, Harry waited for the driver of the lawnmower to make his way back from the far side of the field before lifting a hand in a wave, then moving himself onto the field to intercept him. Soon after, the lawnmower pulled up in front of him, and the driver killed the engine. The world fell silent. He then removed the ear defenders he was wearing.

'This is private property,' the man said, his face grubby with dirt from the task he'd been on with. 'And I can't see that you're lost, either, so do you mind telling me what you're doing on school grounds?'

Harry took out his ID.

'Detective Chief Inspector Grimm,' he said. 'Mr Fothergill?'

'That's me.'

'Mind if we have a chat?'

'I do, yes. I'm busy. Need to get the grass done before the weather changes, and it's doing that later today, by all accounts.'

'I'm sure it can wait.'

'Expert on mowing, are you?'

'Please?' said Harry, and gestured to the ground beside him in the hope that Fothergill would join him. Fothergill didn't budge.

'If you don't mind, I'll stay where I am.'

Harry moved closer until he was standing next to Fothergill. He was acutely aware of the blades of the mower, but at least the machine wasn't running. He presented Fothergill with the printouts from Liz.

'Could you take a look at these for me, please?'

Fothergill took the printouts, stared at the images.

'What am I looking at here, then?'

'Do you recognise the vehicle in each of those stills?' Harry asked.

Fothergill brought the images closer to his face.

'Am I supposed to? Bit fuzzy, aren't they? It's a van, that much I can tell you.'

'It's Craig's van,' said Harry, and no sooner had he said it, than the printouts were handed back.

'Then why are you talking to me? He'll be out working today. I think he's over in Preston-under-Scar. I need to get on.'

'I've already spoken to him. Drove straight here.'

Fothergill slipped his ear defenders back on.

'Well, you'd be best driving straight back there,' he said, reaching for the ignition key before pushing the starter button.

Harry leaned over and removed the key.

'You can't do that, police or no.'

Harry held up one of the printouts.

'Do you recognise the person driving the van?' he asked. 'Look closely.'

Fothergill shook his head.

'You're sure about that?'

'Key,' said Fothergill, holding out his hand. 'Now.'

Harry slipped the key into his pocket, then stepped away from the lawnmower, holding up another of the printouts.

'Look again. Please.'

Fothergill's lips went thin, then with a frustrated groan, he pulled himself out of his seat and stepped down onto the grass.

'What Craig does with his van is none of my business.'

'Look closely,' said Harry. 'The driver, they're wearing a flat cap. Recognise it?'

'So what if Craig's wearing my cap? It was my dad's before it came to me, so maybe he's just trying it on for size. Now hand me back my keys and stop wasting my time.'

'These images are from last week,' said Harry.

Fothergill laughed then, but there was little, if any, humour in the sound.

'You think it's me, don't you? That's what this is about. Well, I can tell you, it's not.'

'You use Craig's van, though, correct?'

'Not driven it in months.'

'But Craig said ...'

Fothergill rolled his eyes.

'Just because he's not managed to move out yet doesn't mean he knows everything about me. And why would I tell him, anyway? Don't want to go worrying the lad, do I? Not yet, anyway, not until I know for sure.'

Harry immediately understood that there was something hidden in what Craig's dad had just said.

'How do you mean? What would worry Craig if you told him?'

'I'm diabetic,' said Fothergill. 'He knows that, because you can't really hide it, can you, and I've no need to, either, seeing as I've been that way for decades now. But these last few months there's been a complication.'

'What?'

'Retinopathy. Fancy name for vision loss due to the diabetes. Not saying I'll go blind, but I've been advised not to drive. Decided to take the sensible precaution and stop altogether. It's not like I need to, really.'

'You're fine on that lawnmower, though,' said Harry.

'Nowt much in a field to go running into, is there?' Replied Fothergill. 'Saved me a bit of money as well, as I've cancelled my insurance. So, there we are, Mr Grimm. Like I've said, that's not me driving the van, and with three of us in the house, there's always someone else who can if needs be. Now, how's about you hand me back that key?'

Harry stared at Fothergill, then at the image on the printout.

'If that's not you or Craig, then who the hell is it?' he asked. 'Because someone's driving that van, aren't they? And they're wearing your cap!'

He handed over the key. Fothergill climbed back onto the lawnmower.

'Only other person is the wife,' he said, slipping the key into the ignition and giving it a twist. He then rested his thumb over the starter button, before jabbing a finger at a house on the edge of the playing fields. 'She'll be at home if you want to ask her. Can't see why she'd be wearing my cap, though.'

Fothergill pushed the starter button, and the lawnmower coughed itself to life. Harry was already running across the field, phone to his ear.

FORTY-ONE

'Liz? Harry. Change of plan. Have everyone round at the house ASAP.'

'House? What house?'

'Sorry, Fothergill's,' Harry replied. 'It backs onto the playing fields behind the school.'

'You mean the caretaker's place? I know where it is, everyone does,' said Liz. 'I went to school there, remember? I'll let everyone know. Did you not find Craig's dad, then? Why are you out of breath?'

'Running,' said Harry. 'I'll keep you posted.'

Call over, Harry stowed the phone and upped his speed. He wasn't quite sure why he was in such a hurry, but the speed he was going seemed to fit with what his mind was doing with all that it was trying to unravel and understand. If he slowed down, he was worried the thoughts might just fall out of his head and he'd not be able to collect them all up to make sense of them again.

Behind him, he could hear Craig's dad mowing the playing field, the sound clattering through the day and growing no fainter, either. In front of him, his destination grew ever larger. It wasn't a big house by any means, just an average-looking semi-detached with a garden that glowered over a fence at the school. It was home to the Fothergills, had been for a very long time, and here he was pelting towards it like the place was about to explode, and he needed to get there in time to rescue someone trapped inside.

Halfway across the playing field, Harry realised that the fence surrounding it was a little higher than he was expecting. He was tempted to build up speed and try to leap over, then remembered he wasn't twenty-one years old and made entirely of springs. So, he forced himself to slow down, then once at the fence, took a breather, and clambered over. There was no gate from the field into the garden, so it wasn't like he had a choice.

As his right foot came into contact with the ground on the other side, Harry lifted his left leg over the fence. His trousers caught on the wire, knocking his balance. He did his best to stay on his feet, hopped a few times on his right foot to keep himself stable, then his trousers came free, and the momentum of yanking them sent him tumbling onto his back. Harry didn't exactly bounce back up onto his feet. The fall had winded him a little, and a sharp pain stabbed his back as he rolled over onto his knees, then pushed himself back up.

Now in the garden, Harry realised that arriving from this direction probably wasn't for the best, spied a side gate, and made his way across the neat lawn. A vegetable patch sat on the left, behind which stood a greenhouse. At the gate, he flicked the latch and stepped through to then make his way down the side of the house to the front door. He rang the doorbell, rapped his knuckles against the door, was ready to do so again, and harder, when the door opened.

'Oh ...'

A pair of hands reached out for him, grabbed him by the scruff of the neck, then yanked him inside the house. Caught off balance once again, Harry fell forward, landing in a heap on the floor, as behind him he heard the door slam shut. Then something was pulled over his head and cinched at the neck, as a fist slammed into his stomach hard enough to make him retch, and hands started to heave at his arms to pull them behind his back.

Harry coughed, the gut-punch having sent vomit into his mouth, but he swallowed that back down.

'Hold him! Hold him down! Don't let him—'

Harry felt breath on the back of his neck, launched his head sharply backwards, felt it connect.

Someone roared in pain.

'Bastard!'

Another punch came to Harry's stomach, but this time he was ready for it, his abs tight as the fist came in hard. The impact still hurt, but it didn't wind him.

'Get his wrists! Get them!'

Harry felt fingers tearing at his hands, so he yanked them away, then twisted his body. He couldn't see, but he could hear, and he lashed out in the direction of the voices. Then he was on his feet, arms free, ripping at the hood around his neck.

'Don't let him do that! Don't!'

The hood came free.

'Shit ...'

Harry's vision was momentarily blurred by sweat from

his brow and dust and dirt from what had been forced over his head. It was a small, hessian sack, which had no doubt at some point carried potatoes, he thought, remembering the vegetable plot in the back garden. He wiped his eyes clean with the back of his hand. What he saw in front of him, though clearer now, didn't make any more sense because of it.

'Don't look so surprised.'

'Hard to look anything else right now, if I'm honest,' said Harry. 'How did you get here before me?'

Harris Fothergill smiled.

'That lawnmower doesn't hang about. And you're not exactly fast, are you?'

Harry ignored the dig. At least he wasn't out of breath, whereas Harris was blowing hard after the struggle he'd had to try and contain him.

'But you said that it wasn't you in those stills I showed you.'

'It wasn't,' Harris replied. 'I wasn't lying to you about that or the diabetes.'

'Why would he need to?'

Harry rested his mean stare on the other face in the hallway, now glaring at him.

'So, you're in this together, is that it? Though what this actually is, I'm struggling to understand. Can't see that any of it makes much sense.'

'Doing your job for you, I reckon,' said Harris. 'Wouldn't you agree, Helen, my love?'

'I would.'

Harry heard a vehicle pull up outside, guessed that his team had started to arrive. All he needed to do was stall until they were at the door.

'You've put three men in hospital in the last week. How is that anything like my job?'

'Being a caretaker gives you a unique insight into how people are, what they'll become,' said Harris. 'I've watched thousands of kids go through that school. Most are good, I'll give them that, but then I think most people generally are, aren't they? Some, though? Well, they need a bit of a slap now and again, just to keep them in line. Not like that happens anymore, not since it was banned.'

Harry had heard some bollocks in his time, and this was right up there with the worst of it.

'A slap? Is that what you call what you've done? And what do you mean, banned?'

'A good thrashing,' said Harris. 'Cane, slipper, paddle—it's what kids need. Keeps them in line. Never did me any harm.'

Harry wasn't so sure.

Harris said, 'I think we help people learn a lesson, wouldn't you agree?'

Harry realised that question wasn't directed at him, but at Helen, as she gave a nod of agreement.

'I would, my love, I would.'

'If it's punishment you're meting out, then why wait so long after the fact?' Harry asked. 'That makes no sense. Though, arguably, none of this does, does it?'

It was obvious from the look on their faces that Harris and Helen didn't agree.

'It's not just revenge that's a dish best served cold,' he said. 'Punishment, too, is more keenly felt, its blade so much the sharper, if it's wielded when least expected.'

'But you've waited years!' Harry snapped back. 'Mike, he was just a kid when he did what he did! A kid! And you think now's a good time to go teaching him a lesson? Seriously?'

'That's no excuse. He knew what he was doing, of course he did. And if I'm honest, we forgot about that one. Time's running out for us, with the job coming to an end, and us having to leave the house. But we've been doing some catching up.'

Harry heard footsteps outside.

'And how did you even know about what Mike, what any of them had done, for that matter?'

'That's another reason the punishment comes around later than expected,' said Helen. 'We have to make sure, check the truth behind the rumour.'

'Like I said,' added Harris, 'being a caretaker puts me in a unique position to keep an eye on things. I know who the bad eggs are. Together, we keep an eye on them, at the same time as keeping ourselves to ourselves. It's amazing how much you can find out if you just go on quietly living, staying out of people's way, being unnoticed.'

A hard thump at the door cut into the moment. Harry moved to the door before either Harris or Helen could do anything to stop him.

'I'll get that,' he said, and gave the doorknob a twist.

The door swung open.

Harry stared at the person on the other side.

'You have to be kidding me.'

Standing on the doorstep, Craig Fothergill grinned back at Harry.

'Surprise!' he said and threw himself through the doorway.

FORTY-TWO

Harry caught Craig in a bear hug, more due to instinct than a sudden flashback to his hand-to-hand combat training in the Paras. Some of that was still only just beneath the surface, though, and it didn't take much for those old skills to rear their ugly head. Which they did, with surprising ferocity.

Using Craig's momentum against him, Harry, with his feet planted firmly on the ground, twisted his torso to the right and launched him into his parents. Craig, arms flailing, stumbled headfirst into them with a yell, his legs kicking out behind him like a child doing their first dive into a swimming pool. Harris took most of the force of his son's trajectory. Helen stepped out of the way but was still caught by a wayward leg. They all hit the deck in a jumble of shocked, angry groans and cries.

'Now stay down!' Harry roared, jabbing a firm finger at them, like he was chastising a group of naughty children. 'Just stay there, don't do anything daft, and we'll ...' He wasn't really sure what to say next. Events were, much like Craig had just done, seemingly chucking themselves at him with wild abandon. Making sense of any of it was impossible.

'Get up! Get him!' shouted Harris, as Craig struggled to untangle himself from his parents. 'Don't let him escape!'

Escape? thought Harry. Bit of a grand term for what he was about to do, which was simply step carefully out of the house into the front garden.

'Get off me!' yelled Helen. 'Get off! What were you thinking? We had him!'

Harry glanced over his shoulder, willing the team to arrive and give him the backup he needed. Not that he was overly concerned that he couldn't handle himself, despite being outnumbered. It was more that he really didn't want to deal with the kind of crazy he was witnessing.

Craig was first on his feet. He walked to the door, stepping over the threshold with care.

'You know, I told Dad it was too many too close together,' he said, brushing himself down. 'But the job thing, moving house, well, that all made everything a little more urgent, I guess. I tried to persuade him to leave Barnaby out of it as well, but he insisted, as did Mum. Can't have people just getting away with things, can we? And there's not much I can do about it all now, anyway, is there?'

'There is,' said Harry, disagreeing. 'You can stay where you are. Otherwise, you'll only make matters worse for yourself, believe me.' He thought back to his chat with Barnaby, remembering something he'd not noticed at the time, but which was now glaringly obvious. 'And Barnaby didn't call you at all, did he, after he'd been poisoned? You were already there. You went in and cleaned up. Didn't matter if Barnaby hadn't called you because it would just be assumed that he had, even by him.'

Harris was now on his feet, and Harry watched him reach down to help his wife up as well.

'That's about the long and the short of it,' said Craig. 'As to making things worse for us, you seem to be forgetting that there's three of us and only one of you.'

Harry shook his head despairingly.

'Not wishing to blow my own trumpet here, Craig, but they're not the best odds, in case you were wondering.'

'I wasn't,' said Craig, and with a roar he went for Harry.

Harry stepped to the side but left his foot there just long enough to send Craig stumbling into a large rose bush. Then Harris and Helen were in the garden as well, both of them yelling at their son about the destruction he'd just caused.

Craig, yelling with pain as he tried to extricate himself from the thorny bush, shouted to his dad something unintelligible. Whatever it was, it was enough to have the old man dash back into the house, leaving Harry to fend off Helen's malicious stare.

Harry pointed down the street. 'The rest of my team are on their way,' he said. 'Whatever it is you all think you can do to make this situation better, I promise you, you're wrong. Stop. Right now. You're in enough trouble as it is.'

Harris came into view behind his wife, filling the doorway to the house. He was holding something, Harry couldn't help but notice.

'I'm going to beat you, lad,' he said. 'Beat you till you bleed. Then, when your team arrives, and you're safely inside the house where no one will find you, of that you can be sure, we'll tell them you've chased off the person responsible for the little bit you know of what we've been doing all these years.'

Harris stepped out of the house. Harry now saw that in each hand he was carrying a cane.

'Can you believe Barnaby's dad threw these onto the bonfire?' asked Harris, lifting the canes into the air to give them each a flick. He glanced at Helen. 'But we saved them, didn't we, my love? Thrashed a few with them over the years, too. Done them a world of good. I reckon it'll do you some good, too!'

Harry was struggling to accept the level of crazy he was dealing with. Something was clearly very wrong with the Fothergills. That he'd gone from suspecting Craig, to Harris, then Helen, had been odd enough as it was. To go from that, to then being faced with Harris and Helen in it together? Well, that had really tested him. But when he'd opened the door and discovered that Craig was as much a part of it all as his parents? That had really taken the biscuit. Harry knew that description was underselling it all, but right then, it was all that his mind could offer.

'Don't do it, Harris,' he said. 'Please. I'm a police officer. I'm not here to hurt you, any of you, actually. Just calm down, and let's deal with this like—'

Harris let out what Harry guessed he thought was a war cry, only it sounded more like he'd accidentally stepped on a garden rake. The sound clearly surprised him as much as it did everyone else. He tripped over his own feet, arms whirring the canes around above his head like helicopter blades, and in the process, gave Harry more than enough time to take himself out of harm's way. Harris stumbled past Harry, and on towards the garden gate, just as a large figure appeared in the very same space and opened it.

'Now then, we'll be having none of that, will we?' said Dave, catching Harris before he ended up in the road, and relieving him of the canes in the same breath. 'You alright over there, Harry?'

Harry gave a thumbs up as the rest of the team swarmed into the garden from behind Dave.

'What took you so long?'

Matt and Ethan walked over to Craig and pulled him out of the rosebush. Jen placed herself beside Helen, her own stare more than enough to have the woman's shoulders slump in defeat.

'If we'd have known you were having so much fun, we'd have been here all the sooner to join in,' said Matt, as Ethan cuffed Craig's hands behind his back. 'Any chance you could let us in on what's been going on?'

Harry, though, wasn't listening. He was thinking back to something Harris had said to him only moments ago and was making his way back into the house.

'Harry?' Matt called over. 'Where are you going?'

Harry didn't reply as he stepped through the front door. Then Matt was beside him.

'Well?' the DS said.

Harry paused in the hallway. Stairs led up to the first floor, doors downstairs opened to a kitchen, a lounge, a dining room, a toilet under the stairs.

'Something Harris said just before you arrived,' he said. 'Told me he'd have me safely inside the house where no one will find me.'

'Odd thing to say.'

'My thoughts exactly.'

Matt frowned.

'If there's a secret dungeon in here, I'm going to be very upset, Harry, very upset indeed.'

Harry started to check the rooms downstairs, found nothing. He looked again, walking in between the lounge, the kitchen and the dining room enough times for Matt to reach out and stop him.

'I don't think there's anything here,' he said. 'What about upstairs? Maybe round the back?'

Harry wasn't so sure, found himself staring at a wall inside the door to the lounge.

'This,' he said, pointing at it.

'It's a wall, Harry,' said Matt. 'Nothing more.'

Harry reached up, rapped his knuckles against it.

'Sounds hollow,' he said, then walked into the dining room, on the other side of the wall and tapped the wall once again.

'It's bound to sound like that,' said Matt. 'It's the same wall, Harry.'

Harry stepped into the hallway. The lounge was to his left, the dining room to his right. Between both doors, the wall was covered in numerous framed photographs of Craig, each of them cataloguing him at a different stage of his life. He popped his head in through both doorways to look at the joining wall, then turned back to Matt.

'You mind going to fetch Harris for me?' he asked.

Matt did as instructed and returned with the caretaker.

'What?' Harris said, his eyes burning into Harry. 'Actually, it doesn't matter. I'm not telling you anything. I've got rights, haven't I?'

Harry pointed to the photographs of Craig.

'What's behind here, Harris?' he asked.

He noticed just enough of a flicker in the man's eyes to let him know he was onto something.

'What?'

'Right here, behind these photos of your son. What?'

'Nowt. Don't know what you're talking about.'

Harry took down one of the photographs, tapped the wall.

'You said something strange, just before the cavalry arrived. Told me that you'd have me safely inside the house where no one would find me. So, I'm going to ask you again, what's behind here?'

Harry removed the rest of the photographs. The wall was now blank. Something was off about it. Where the door frames met the wall, there was a gap. Not much of one, but enough for Harry to wonder ...

'I'm not a patient man, Harris,' he said. 'I'm also not a massive fan of secrets.'

'Shame that,' Harris replied. 'I'm not telling you a thing.'

Harry, jaw set firm, folded his arms, then leaned back against the wall. 'My guess is, there's a very large hammer around here somewhere,' he said. 'I spotted that greenhouse of yours. Must be a shed out there, too.' He looked at Matt. 'Don't suppose you'd mind going to have a look for me, would you?'

Matt made to leave, but as he did so, a soft click sounded from behind where Harry was leaning. He stepped away from the wall and turned around to look at where he had been standing.

'Well, well, well,' said Matt.

Harry reached out to where the crack between the wall and the frame around the dining-room door had opened wide, slipped his fingers in, and pulled.

FORTY-THREE

'At least it's not a dungeon,' said Harry, as he stood in the small room with Matt. Upstairs, the rest of the team were dealing with Harris, Helen, and Craig.

'Not sure that makes this any better, though, do you?' Matt replied.

On pulling at the crack in the wall, a section of it had popped off, having been held in place by magnets. Removing it, Harry had stared into darkness, then spotted a dusty light switch just inside the opening. Flicking it on had revealed a set of steps so narrow, the only way up or down was to navigate them sideways. Instructing Matt to hand Harris back to one of the others, they had both then ventured down into the gloom.

'This must've taken years,' said Matt, as they both stared wide-eyed at the space around them. 'No easy thing to go digging out a cellar underneath your house, especially without anyone knowing. How the neighbours didn't hear is beyond me.'

Harry guessed that the space was roughly three metres

by three metres. They both had to stoop a little once they were down the steps. The floor was concrete, the walls and ceiling lined with scaffold planks. The roof was reinforced with adjustable scaffolding bars designed specifically to stop the whole thing from collapsing.

'Doesn't feel entirely safe, does it?' said Harry, tapping a knuckle against one of the walls, causing a tiny dust mote to spring out of a crack and dance off through the damp air.

The space was anything but empty. The walls were lined with old, metal filing cabinets, the drawers labelled alphabetically. On the wall was displayed a map of the Dales, covered with numerous pins. Resting on top of one of the cabinets was a bottle with the word *poison* written on a scrap of paper stuck to its surface with tape.

Harry pointed at the bottle.

'My guess is that's a little something Harris kept back from his early caretaking days back in the seventies.'

Matt pointed at the map on the wall. 'What do you think those pins are?' he asked. 'They all seem to have little codes on them.'

A small desk was squashed between the cabinets, and shoved beneath it was an old chair, the kind Harry remembered from school. He opened one of the cabinets, shuffled through the files. Some were marked with crosses, others with ticks. He pulled out one with a tick, then sat down at the desk and opened it.

Matt leaned over Harry's shoulder and let out a long whistle.

'You've got to be kidding me.'

'Oh, I don't think the Fothergills have been kidding for a very long time, do you?' replied Harry.

The file contained information about a woman called

Laura Hoyle. The information inside included not only her school reports, but a comprehensive amount of other data, including photographs, covering everything from where she lived to friends, relatives, her career.

Harry turned back to the front of the file again, saw a code, read it to Matt.

'That's here,' said Matt, pointing at a pin on the map.

Harry read further and was soon in familiar territory. He shut the file and put it back where he had found it. The experience had given him the unnerving sense that he was prying into someone else's life, spying on them, because that's exactly what the Fothergills had been doing for years.

'What the hell are we going to do with all this?' he asked, rising from the chair and shoving it back under the desk. 'This family, they've been punishing people in the Dales for decades. No idea how many.'

Matt gestured at the map.

'By the look of that, plenty of them, that's for sure.'

The thought that so many had suffered at the hands of the Fothergills made Harry feel sick. That what they'd done had gone unnoticed for so long? It was a dark secret only a place like the Dales could hold. Yes, everyone knew everyone else, but there was a privacy to the people that was deep-seated. Friends, neighbours, they were close, cared for each other, but it wasn't as though the place was rife with oversharing. The Fothergills had played on that, used it to their advantage to dish out punishments they deemed necessary to teach people a lesson.

'How did we never know about this?' Matt asked, as though he'd been reading Harry's mind. 'What we've dealt with this week, they're serious incidents, people could've died.'

'My guess,' said Harry, 'and my hope, is that not everything they've done has been so extreme, but we'll only know that once all of this has been looked through properly. It's not as though people are going to want to talk about any of it, either, are they? This is a cellar of secrets, Matt. Long forgotten things dragged up out of the mire to be used against the unsuspecting. No wonder they were so keen to speed things up with what they were doing. With the job coming to an end, and them having to move house, they couldn't risk this lot being discovered, could they?'

'How would they hide it?'

Harry hadn't the faintest idea and wasn't going to worry about that right now either. He gave the cellar one last glance before making his way back up the thin stairs. Jen was in the hallway waiting for them and she was on her phone.

'What've you found?' she asked.

'You really don't want to know,' Harry replied. 'Where are they?'

'In the back of the Land Rover, arguing with each other. Bit of a weird one, this, isn't it?'

'Jen?' sighed Harry, 'You've no idea, no idea at all.'

Matt slipped out of the thin gap at the top of the stairs.

'We're going to need the SOC team in again, aren't we?' he said. 'There's a hell of a lot to be dealing with here. No bodies though, so that's a blessing, I guess.'

'Anything from Jadyn?' Harry asked, looking to Jen and having realised he was the one member of the team—except for Jim, who wasn't on duty anyway—not at the house.

Jen held up her phone and gave it a wiggle. 'Want to speak to him?' she asked. 'He's convinced he's let you down by not being able to find anything. He's going to keep on looking, though.'

Harry reached for Jen's phone.

'Jadyn?'

'Yeah, sorry, Boss,' the constable said. 'I've not found anything useful yet. I'll keep looking, though. Must be something, right?'

Harry said, 'Get yourself back here. You and I need to have a chat.'

There was a pause, and Harry was sure he heard Jadyn gulp.

'Look, no, it's fine, I'll keep looking, I'll find someth—'

Harry gave Matt and Jen a wink.

'That's an order, Constable.'

'Right, yes, okay, I'll, well, I'll come now.'

'Good. And while you're on your way, have a think about what you want to tell me about you applying to be a trainee detective constable, which, in case you're wondering, I fully support.'

Another pause.

'What? You think it's a good idea?'

'Just get yourself here sharpish,' said Harry, then handed the phone back to Jen.

'He'll make a good detective,' Matt said.

'Agreed,' said Jen.

Harry jabbed a thumb back over at the narrow gap in the wall between the two doors.

'Seems like we need as many as we can get,' he said, a yawn suddenly breaking through what he was saying, twisting his words a little, stretching them out. 'The Fothergills have worked for years to keep what they've been doing a secret. And they've been damned successful at it, too.'

To Harry's surprise, Jen reached out and rested a hand on his arm.

'Harry, if you don't mind me saying so, you look knackered.'

'Again, that's literally just my face,' Harry replied, forcing a ruined smile.

Jen shook her head.

'No, it's not, is it? I know you, Harry, we all do. You're allowed to be tired. It's not a weakness.'

Harry agreed but knew other things had been playing on his mind as well. The business with his uncle and cousin for one, which for now he was happy to put very much to the back of his mind, and the thing with Grace was another. Smudge's imminent puppy explosion was also something he'd soon have to be dealing with. At least Liz and Ben were moving on a bit with their wedding plans. Then there was Dave disappearing to sort out something or other with his goddaughter and the thieving of eggs.

'Harry?'

As though summoned by simply being thought about, Dave appeared in front of him.

'Funny, I was just thinking about you,' he said. 'And here you are.'

'Like a genie.'

Harry laughed at that.

'What an awful thought.'

'I just thought I'd best come and let you know everything's sorted,' Dave said. 'With Maddie, my goddaughter, I mean. And her daughter. Well, maybe not sorted, exactly, but certainly better than it was. I think.'

Harry narrowed his eyes.

'None of what you've just said fills me with confidence, Dave. Wildlife crime, which egg theft is, is serious.'

'That's probably why he left.'

'What? Who left?'

'Maddie's husband, Gary. Turns out he was forcing their daughter to steal eggs for him to sell. I think he realised we were onto him, and he's bolted.'

'To where?'

Dave shrugged.

'Not a clue. Maddie said he just packed a bag and buggered off. No warning, just gone.'

'Odd,' said Harry. 'I mean, I know I just said that about thieving eggs being serious, but still, why would he run like that?'

Dave, Harry noticed, was suddenly suspiciously quiet.

'Is there something you want to tell me, Dave?'

Dave shook his head.

'No, I'm good.'

Harry leaned in.

'You sure about that?'

'Very much so.'

The look Harry was now receiving from Dave made his face itch, so he gave it a scratch.

'You think we'll be hearing from him again?' he asked.

'I doubt so,' said Dave. 'Probably for the best. He was no good anyway. They're both better off without him.'

Harry knew there was no getting anything else from Dave, so he gave the man a knowing nod, then walked over to where Matt was now standing with Ethan.

'Suppose we'd better get this shower off to Harrogate,' he said, giving a nod over to the Land Rover, where the

Fothergills were all now sitting, and none too happy about it, either, considering the noise they were all making.

'We'll do that,' offered Ethan. 'Won't we, Matt?'

'Oh, will we, now?' Matt replied.

'Yes,' said Ethan.

Matt glanced at Harry.

'My guess is you don't fancy coming along for the ride?'

Harry looked back at the house, thought about what they'd found hidden in its foundations.

'I'm going to have to give the SOC team a call,' he said. 'Best I stay here and oversee that, I think.'

'Fair enough,' agreed Matt, and turned to Ethan and threw him the keys. 'Away, then, lad. You're driving.'

Harry watched as the Land Rover pulled away then had Dave and Jen crack on with putting up a good amount of cordon tape as he punched a call into the SOC team. That done, and with a bit of time to play with before they arrived, Harry thought back to when Grace had found him up in the middle of the night and he'd thrown that envelope and its contents on the fire. That night, he'd managed to quickly come up with the story that it was an invite to a reunion. It had been just enough, he believed, to stop Grace from wondering too much more about it. The truth, however, was that letter had been a very fancy receipt for the not inconsiderable amount of money he'd spent, and confirmation that the ring he'd ordered would be ready for him to pick up in a couple of weeks. *Well*, he thought, *no time like the present*, and he pulled up another number on his phone. The call was answered in three rings.

'Now then, Arthur,' Harry said.

'Harry?' Arthur replied. 'What are you doing calling me? Everything alright, like?'

'Just wondered if you had a couple of minutes, that's all. Need to chat to you about something.'

'Of course I have, lad. Now, what can I do for you?'

Harry paused, took in a deep breath, then exhaled, forcing himself to stay calm.

'It's about Grace,' he said. 'And I was wondering if I could ask for your blessing before I—'

Harry didn't get a chance to finish what he was saying.

'About bloody time!' said Arthur.

Harry couldn't stop smiling.

UNCOVER DARK SECRETS, scan the QR code and grab the next book in the series, where unwitting victims in the Dales are LEFT FOR DEAD!

You'll also be able to access free Harry Grimm short stories and sign up for my VIP Club and newsletter.

ABOUT DAVID J. GATWARD

David had his first book published when he was 18 and still can't believe this is what he does for a living. Author of the long-running DCI Harry Grimm series, and the new DI Haig Crime Thrillers, David was nominated for the Amazon Kindle Storyteller Award in 2023. He lives in Somerset with his two boys.

Visit www.DavidJGatward.com to find out more about the author and his highly-acclaimed series of crime fiction.

facebook.com/davidjgatwardauthor

Printed in Dunstable, United Kingdom